Pumpkin

A CINDERMAMA STORY

Ines Johnson

Edited by Dragonfly Editing
Cover design by Yocla Designs

Manufactured in the United States of America
First Edition March 2015
ISBN: 978-0-9909228-4-1

Dedication

For my son,
whose internal filter stops working at
the most inopportune times.

But this keeps the frogs away from Mommy.

CHAPTER ONE

"OMG, PUMPKIN! YOU EVEN DRIVE LIKE A PRUDE!"

Pumpkin Tavares allowed the condescension in LaTom's voice to roll off her back. She may not have had a date in a little while —okay, a long while. In any case, she certainly wasn't taking driving advice from her cousin who spent most of her time in the back seat of cars. While they were parked. Somewhere off road. Late at night.

"Next time we need to catch a cab," LaTom said from the back seat of Pumpkin's car.

"Hmm, hmm," agreed her sister, LaRon, who sat in the passenger seat.

Pumpkin raised a dubious eyebrow at the empty threat. Cab drivers expected payment. They also sported those handy off-duty signs on top of their cars. Not that her cousins would pay attention to a come-back-later or closed-for-the-day sign on her car. In their minds, Pumpkin existed as their personal chauffeur.

"I could drive better than this." LaRon drummed her fingers on the dashboard. "I should've gotten my license."

"Me, too," LaTom piped in from behind her sister.

Well, there wasn't anything stopping them now. Except the convenience of being a backseat driver and not having to take any responsibility.

"What did you say, Pumpkin-Head?" said LaTom.

Pumpkin opened her mouth. Her lips flapped like a fish out of water, no air going in or out. She hadn't just said that out loud. Had she?

LaTom glared at her in the rearview mirror. Pumpkin's eyes slid away and onto the baby LaTom bounced on her lap. Yes. On her lap and not in the car seat.

"I really wish you'd strap him in back there," Pumpkin said.

Little LaRico stood on his mom's lap. His chubby fingers played with the automatic window button; watching it magically go up and then down. A few miles back he'd gotten the glass down enough to stick his head out of the window like a little dog, with tongue hanging out of the mouth and all. It kept the fussy baby quiet, but then a cop pulled into traffic and, from her driver's seat control panel, Pumpkin put the window on lock down.

"He's in the back seat." LaTom let LaRico loose on the floor. "When we were kids, there were no laws about car seats."

"That's right," LaRon chimed in from the passenger seat. Her eyes skimmed dot matrix perforated forms. "The government is all up in mamas' business nowadays."

With the attention off her, Pumpkin decided not to point out how these suggestions became laws after the deaths of many children. She'd never win the argument. Neither LaTom nor LaRon had gone to law school, but they both knew the system inside and out.

Instead, Pumpkin focused all her will on the car in front of her to move the last few feet forward so she could break free of the gridlock.

The sounds of the late afternoon traffic assaulted her ears: the impatient bursts from the expensive, new model cars; the wheezing grunts of the hooptie mufflers; the squealing of breaks protesting the snail's pace of Friday rush hour in Saint Anne's Parish, Louisiana.

And then, it appeared out of nowhere. Like a horse —a white horse with flaxen mane and tale— leaping over an agitated mass of trolls. Like a villain appearing in a cloud of magic to deliver a devastating blow to the budding happy-ever-after.

Pumpkin couldn't be sure which role the white, Ford Mustang with gold trim played as it charged through traffic. Its front wheels left the road for a split second. Its tail pipe breathed a sigh of exhaust as it seized a hole in the bumper-to-bumper traffic and escaped off the exit ramp, like magic. The next moment, the highway seized up again.

The horn behind Pumpkin blared, demanding she move the few feet forward to get them all closer to nowhere. Pumpkin's little, orange Beetle obliged, knowing it could never achieve such a feat as leaving the asphalt on its four small tires. Or swerving its round frame across the double yellow divide. Pumpkin stayed in her lane and inched forward along with the rest of the rabble.

A quarter of an hour later, the lane opened up and they reached their destination. Pumpkin pulled up to the front entrance of the Saint Anne's Department of Family and Child Services: DFACS.

"Just drop us off here, Pumpkin." LaRon's hand was already on the door. "That food stamp line always takes long with all those old folks and cripples."

Pumpkin stared straight ahead and gave an internal shake of her head. She wouldn't put it past her cousins to fake a disability to gain an advantage.

It took a few seconds for Pumpkin to register the silence. She turned to look over at where LaRon and LaTom stood outside her car. Two pairs of the darkest brown, nearly black, eyes glared at her.

Crap! She'd spoken her mind out loud again.

Early in life, Pumpkin instinctively developed an internal filter to use when dealing with her cousins and their trifling-ness. It worked thusly: mouth stayed shut, head might nod, or noncommittal grunt might sound from the back of her throat in response to any foolishness they said or did. But never did her true feelings travel from her head to her mouth. This morning the filter appeared in good working condition when LaRon called, and guilted Pumpkin into interrupting her schedule and driving them here.

Pumpkin tried to cover her verbal slip by nodding in appeasement. But then her mouth flew open. "Do you two ever worry that you feed into the negative stereotypes of single moms?"

"What do you mean negative?" they said in unison.

"Well, both of you are able-bodied, educated women. Why not get a job?" Pumpkin's hand flew to her mouth, no one more shocked than she was by its masochistic defiance.

"We have a job."

"We're stay-at-home-mothers."

"Are you saying that's not a job, Pumpkin-Head?"

"Because it's a full-time job."

"And we deserve to get paid for our time."

"I thought you were a feminist, Pumpkin?"

"It is... I am..." Pumpkin wasn't sure which question she was answering. Since their youth, the two of them had a way of firing more than one at a time, so that Pumpkin didn't know who was speaking nor to whom she was answering. "It's just that both of you get child support from your babies' daddies." Six children, five daddies. That's another story. "It's enough money for food, too. Don't you worry you're cheating someone else who may need it more?"

"Who says we don't need it?" LaTom threw a baby blanket over her Dolce top before settling LaRico on her shoulder.

"We want the best for our kids." LaRon's Jimmy Choo's tapped the pavement in annoyance.

"Mama?" The voice came from the backseat of the car. Pumpkin turned to the face of her eight-year-old son, Seth. For both the duration of this conversation, as well as the duration of the ride, Seth's face had been buried in a chapter book.

"Mama, I have to use the bathroom," he said from his booster seat in the back.

Now, technically eight-year-olds don't have to sit in boosters, but Sethie didn't quite reach the seat belt's shoulder strap yet, and admittedly, Pumpkin was a card-carrying, licensed to hover, helicopter parent.

She turned to her cousins. "Could you?"

They both rolled their eyes in annoyance. As if Pumpkin hadn't left work early, yanked her son out of his after-school routine, and scrambled across town to help them run an errand during rush hour.

LaRon made an impatient gesture to Seth. "Fine," she said.

"Thank you," Pumpkin said. "I'm just going to park and be right in."

Ten minutes later, Pumpkin found a spot and headed back towards the building. The Saint Anne's DFACS building loomed, imperious and menacing in the cloudy sky. Time and the elements had faded its facade to a pale shade of brown. Its shadows blotched the countenances of the women ushering their children in and out of its doors. Unlike LaRon and LaTom who typically skipped up the steps, these women looked daunted, despondent, and demoralized as they entered the building. No one took pride in turning to the welfare system.

Pumpkin watched one mother exit the glass doors; one child in her arms, another walking beside her. The little boy walking alongside her reached out and took his mother's hand in his own, a smile on his lips, unwavering trust in his eyes. Pumpkin felt the jolt that halted the mother's steps. The love that passed between the two reverberated in the air. The determination that lit up the mother's eyes was palpable to any witnesses.

Coming down the steps, the family passed a table. The red and white banner strung across its front read "Preston Whitely for Mayor." Pumpkin saw the light in the mother's eyes dim under the scrutiny of the two women stationed behind the table. They handed out fliers to passersby, but their manicured hands retracted as the mother and her children neared. One woman looked down, wrinkling her nose at the mother's worn shoes. The other woman flipped her highlighted hair over her shoulder, the gleaming ring-set on her left hand sparkled.

The light from the ring must've caught the mother's eye because the woman winced. She reached out her left hand, all fingers bare, and pulled her son closer to her.

As the family passed by Pumpkin, the mother glanced up, a brave front on her face. Pumpkin offered her a smile. She'd been in that mom's shoes. A young mother, alone in the world. Wondering where she and her child's next meal would come from. Eyes cast down when approaching home, fearful of a notice on the door. Pumpkin had hated walking up the DFACS steps as a child, certain a mark was being stitched into her hand-me-downs. The clothes Pumpkin wore now were purchased off the rack with her own money. Her shoes weren't designer, but they were brand new. Though she was now a self-sufficient woman, Pumpkin often feared people would spot a scuff or scrape left over from those years.

"Excuse me."

Pumpkin turned and stopped in her tracks. Not because of the near collision, but because of the Adonis who stood before her. Tall and lean with dark, thick curls atop his head. But it was his eyes that arrested Pumpkin. They took her back to her teen years, watching Donnie Simpson on Video Soul; or farther back to Smokey Robinson doo-wopping with The Miracles. They were a pale gray. And he smelled... edible. Like fresh baked, butter croissants sprinkled with earthy spices.

"Excuse me," he repeated, with a slight Southern drawl that was more refined than lazy. He prolonged his vowels just enough to let you know he was Southern, but the consonants he pronounced perfectly. "Are you Heather?"

And of course, he was looking for someone else. "No, my name is Malika."

He looked at her and squinted. Then his eyes rolled past her up the steps of the DFACS building. "Oh, sorry. I thought you could have been one of my volunteers." He stepped away, clearing her path to the entrance.

I thought you could have been one of my volunteers.

Pumpkin looked beyond him to see a voter registration table.

I thought you could have been one of my volunteers.

Part of her knew she should simply walk into the DFACS building to find her cousins and her son, because who knew? LaRon and LaTom could've let him go to the bathroom by himself and just forgotten about him —again. But another part of Pumpkin smarted. He'd taken one glance at her, paired it with her Eubonic-consonant-rich name, added it to her current location, and come away with an incorrect assumption.

"You know, I could have been yours," she said.

He turned back. "Mine?"

"I mean, I have done something like this before."

"Something... with me?"

"No! I've never met you before."

He opened his mouth to speak, thought better of it, then started again. "What exactly are we talking about?"

This was not going the way she'd planned. But what exactly had she planned when she opened her mouth? Her filter malfunction needed to be repaired soon.

Pumpkin took a deep breath, clearly aware of his smokey eyes watching her with... was that wariness or amusement? Growing up in her family, she had trouble deciphering the two.

"I mean, I have been a volunteer. I've done a voter registration drive before."

Having cleared up that misjudgment, Pumpkin assumed the conversation was over. Only, he looked doubtful at her proclamation.

Pumpkin gave her internal filter a kick. In response it sputtered, "I organized it, actually." Pumpkin gave it a mental shove to keep quiet. And then, "It was very successful, actually."

"Where?"

"What?"

"Where did the drive you organized —successfully— take place?"

"Oh," she said. "At my school. My college —university, actually. Louisiana State University."

"I know LSU," he grinned.

Good. Grinning meant amused. He had a nice grin, Smokey Eyes. Straight white teeth. Plump lips that stretched wide. Maybe a little too wide. Almost big bad wolf wide.

"Well," she said. "There's a community college with the name Louisiana so..."

"You have a problem with community colleges?"

"No! I just... I just wanted to make sure you knew... which one I meant." Pumpkin wouldn't have thought it possible, but his grin stretched even wider.

"My opinion matters to you that much?"

Definitely a wolf.

Then, in confirmation, his eyes slipped from her face and did a quick assessment of her body: the B-cups she no longer bothered to pad, the stubborn muffin top she'd given up on a year ago, the wide hips that looked voluptuous on her cousins but pear-shaped on her.

"I don't even know you," Pumpkin said. And she had no intention of getting to know him. Wolves blocked the paths of good girls whether in the forest or on the road of life. Pumpkin had no intention of getting jammed up by a man, ever again.

"Yet, within sixty seconds of meeting me," he said, "you offered to be mine."

"No I... That was a misunderstanding, and you know it."

A chuckle escaped through that predatory grin. The sound rumbled through Pumpkin's body like a divining rod sensing danger.

"I'm sorry, Malika."

But then, with the sound of her name on his lips, the humming of the rod ceased. All previous warning signals muted and Pumpkin's feet took root in the concrete.

"It's been a long day," he smiled and a small sigh escaped his lips at the same time.

She'd read the term Cupid's Bow in romance novels, but the visual didn't do the term justice. The top of his upper lip, where you'd handle the bow was in the shape of a perfectly symmetrical M. Stretched in a smile, his full bottom lip made her wonder what it would be like to get caught in the crosshairs of his kiss.

"I couldn't resist having a little fun with you. I hope I haven't kept you."

Pumpkin took her eyes off his lips to gaze into his smokey eyes. A smile started to creep over her face, too. "No, you haven't kept me."

"You'd better hurry. I'm sure they're about to close soon."

"Yeah... wait. What?" Pumpkin followed his gaze to the DFACS entrance. Everything unmuted and red flashed behind her eyes. "I just told you, I went to college."

"Oh?" His gray eyes furrowed this time. "So, people with degrees don't fall on hard times?"

"Well... yes. They do. But I'm fine," she insisted, tapping her new shoes on the pavement for emphasis. "I have a job." A job that she hated, but it paid all her bills. No government checks came for her and Seth. No child support checks either.

"So, you're not here to volunteer to help. And you're not here seeking help. What? Are you here to gloat?"

"No!"

He chuckled again, but Pumpkin was no longer amused.

"I've taken advantage of some social programs, like federal grants for the university I attended while on academic scholarship." Pumpkin conveniently neglected to mention that her childhood kitchen had been stocked from food stamp monies. "But I'm not gloating about my successes because I'm resentful that this society assumes that I can't succeed without its help."

He cocked his head, eyes intent on her. "So, you'd rather the rules be unfair and harder for you so that you can save face?"

Pumpkin blinked. "No, that's not what I mean."

What did she mean? How did she get into this conversation? All her life, Pumpkin typically kept her opinions to herself. It had been the safest way to navigate her adolescent and teenage years in a household where the family motto read: everyone for themselves.

"You know how they say if you give a man a fish, he'll eat for a day," she continued. "But if you teach a man to fish, he'll eat forever?"

Smokey Eyes nodded.

Pumpkin hesitated, realizing he was actually listening to every word she said, and waiting for her to say more.

Why not? Her internal filter had taken the day off. "I think the flaw with social programs is that the poor start to believe they can't do for themselves without it and the rich believe the poor can't act without their help. And it winds up being a vicious cycle with each side resenting the other."

Pumpkin glanced at the DFACS door remembering her son was still inside with two professional "cyclists." She turned back to Smokey Eyes.

He stared up at the clouds in concentration. She could see him turning her words over in his head. It gave her a thrill. She was used to men leering at her body, because, though her curves weren't artful like her cousins', they were round enough to grab attention. Watching Smokey Eyes focus inward and contemplate her words was possibly the most intimate experience of her thirty years.

After a moment, his tongue peeked out, like an arrow, to pull taut his upper lip. Pumpkin's own lips parted as a quiver went through her long dormant core. Any moment now, he would aim words at her.

Any moment now.

Turning his gray eyes back to her, he said, "I do see your point. But I also feel that with great wealth comes great responsibility. And if you've caught a lot of fish, you should share. It's good manners. It's how I was raised."

Pumpkin gave a woeful shake of her head at that. "I was raised by people who wouldn't fish; would take yours; and then demand you go get more."

"But not you."

It wasn't a question. There was something behind those smokey eyes. Not empathy. He was obviously moneyed, in his expensive shirt and tailored pants, where Pumpkin's teen closet had been sponsored by Goodwill, and her adult closet now sported Target.

"Me? No," she said holding his gaze.

"And you wouldn't ask for any food off my table? Even if I'm willing to share?"

It seemed like a trick question. On the one hand, Pumpkin harbored an image of him feeding her bits of food. On the other hand, "Is there something wrong with a woman who is self-sufficient?"

"No. Those are my favorite kind." He grinned again, the wolf rising to its haunches once more. "I just have a problem when independent women feel the need to trash and discard strong men like myself. I'm part of a marginalized group, too." He grinned.

Pumpkin couldn't imagine any woman in her right mind discarding this man.

"I look forward to the day," he continued, "when independent women and strong men can sit down at the same table and share each other's..." he paused for another wolfish grin, "...catch of the day, instead of starving by themselves."

Pumpkin couldn't help herself. She grinned, too. This wasn't the type of man who would stand in her way. This was the type of man who opened doors. The type of man people lined up behind to propel forward. The type of man going places. The type of man people expect big things of. The type of person Pumpkin used to be before she took a detour and crashed headlong into glaring, yellow hazard signs.

"Pumpkin, the food stamp line was way too long!"

"You'll just have to bring us back Monday morning."

LaRon and LaTom had an uncanny knack for timing.

"I can't." Pumpkin turned to face her cousins. "I work on Monday."

"Well, you'll just have to take the day —Oh! Hello, there."

Uh, oh. The Amazons spotted prey in the clearing.

"You look like a Marine or maybe an Air Force pilot," purred LaRon. "Are you in the Armed Forces?"

"You look like you own that white Mustang over there." LaTom switched a fussy, little LaRico to the other hip. Mother and son both salivated.

"Are you a prince?"

That last voice was unexpected in this hunt. It was Seth.

"No." Pumpkin heard the amused grin in Smokey Eyes' voice. "I'm just a regular guy."

"Oh," Seth said, clearly disappointed as he took his mother's hand. "That's too bad. My mom's looking for a Prince Charming to help her heart, cuz my dad broke it."

What the! Pumpkin was used to her cousins embarrassing her in public. But her son? When did he become a traitor to her pride?

"No, no." Pumpkin knelt down, partly to be on par with her son, partly to be out of the scrutiny of Smokey Eyes. "He didn't break my heart. He just confirmed my disbelief in all the fairy tale nonsense I was fed as a little girl."

All the adults stared at her now. Even little LaRico gave Pumpkin his undivided attention. Probably because she was arguing fairy tales with an eight-year-old.

Pumpkin tried to save face. "Besides honey, a heart is a muscle. It can't break. You can have a heart attack, where it stops beating."

Oh, God! In a panic, Pumpkin attached a defibrillator to her internal filter as it continued to flat line.

Seth scrunched his face in concentration. "So, Dad gave you a heart attack and made your heart stop beating? And now you need a prince to make it start again?"

What did she expect? The child had her gift of logic and her newfound diarrhea of the mouth. Pumpkin glanced over at her cousins for help.

Not likely! They were still sizing up the smokey-eyed candy behind her.

Pumpkin chanced a glance over her shoulder. Sure enough, gray eyes were locked on her and Seth, an amused, wolfish grin spread over his handsome face.

Fantastic!

Okay. What were her options here? She could continue the philosophical argument with an eight-year-old who used the undefeatable formula of child-logic. Or she could turn tale and run. Of course, Pumpkin did what any sensible woman would do!

"Okay, guys! Time to go!" Pumpkin ushered them all to the parking lot.

"It was nice meeting you, Malika!"

Pumpkin didn't even bother glancing back over her shoulder. She kept her eyes trained forward until she saw the salvation of her bright, orange getaway.

"He was cute, Pumpkin," said LaTom as she buckled herself in the backseat and bounced LaRico on her lap.

Pumpkin pursed her lips and remained silent.

"He looked rich," mused LaRon.

Probably, Pumpkin thought as she started the ignition.

"He looked familiar," said LaTom.

"Yeah," agreed LaRon. "But I can't place him. What's his name, Pumpkin?"

"Hmph," was Pumpkin's noncommittal answer as she pulled onto the highway. Great, now the filter was back online.

"You spent all that time talking to him and you didn't even get his name, or at least give him your number!"

"God, you're hopeless, girl. One baby by him and you probably could've been set for life."

Pumpkin didn't need his name. She knew enough to know that Mr. Smokey Eyes was out of her league. Devastatingly handsome, likely wealthy, more than an ounce of intelligence, and a firm grip on the ladder to success. Yeah, that type didn't go for girls like her: single moms, with dead-end jobs, and a weak foothold on the fringe of the lower middle class. No. There were no princes in Pumpkin's reality. Only frogs. Frogs who stayed frogs long after repeated sloppy-slimy kisses.

For the rest of the drive, the cousins went on and on about Mr. Smokey Eyes. But that man, whom Pumpkin was never likely to meet again, no longer concerned her. Another did. And later that night, she confronted him.

"Seth?"

"Yeah, mama?"

He settled into his bed, the newest Dragonslayer Academy chapter book lay open and half-read on his small chest. He got that from her: the book-wormishness along with the small chest. He also got her dark eyes and dark, curly 'fro that tinted copper in the sun.

Seth had his father's long face and protruding chin. It looked like he might inherit the uni-brow, too. That concerned Pumpkin. Uni-brows were rumored to be a sign of the devil. It was a rumor she knew to be true.

"Seth, what made you say those things today? About my heart?"

He shrugged and concentrated on his Transformer's bedspread.

Pumpkin prepared herself to ask the question she really didn't want to hear the answer to. "Do you miss your dad?"

"No." Seth said it without hesitating. But he looked her in the eye when he said it, and that's how Pumpkin knew he was telling the truth. "You're better off without him."

Pumpkin's eyes widened in genuine shock. She and Seth never talked about his father. Pumpkin didn't because she struggled to find nice things to say about the man, and she didn't want to be one of those women who dogged the other parent. Even if the other parent was an absentee father who didn't call, write, or support his child in any way.

So, instead, she sent Seth off to the school guidance counselor. Her prognosis? Seth was fine and adjusting as expected. That was hard for Pumpkin to believe after all the trauma Seth's father caused her. So, she sent Seth off to an expensive therapist who specialized in children from broken homes. His prognosis? The same. Finally, Pumpkin gave up and accepted that her kid just might be okay. And here lay further confirmation.

"I heard you talking on the phone to Auntie Ronnie about Prince Charming on a horse being the only one you'd give your heart to."

Okay. How does one explain sarcasm to an eight-year-old?

"I know grown-ups like having girlfriends and boyfriends." His little nose wrinkled at those two titles, and Pumpkin couldn't help but smile. "Auntie Ronnie and Auntie Tommie have lots of boyfriends. I think you should have at least one."

Huh. Kid logic. Was she really gonna try and argue that? Because, though Seth's father didn't break her heart in the philosophical sense, he did do a number on her head and its figurative sense of worth. Then again, it had been over three years. Maybe she was ready to move on and start dating.

"Tell you what, I'll think about it."

But one thing she didn't have to think about was the type of man she would date when she was ready. She knew, for certain, it wouldn't be some wolfish playboy who was only interested in a fling, on his way through the woods.

CHAPTER TWO

CRACK!

ARMAND "MANNY" CHARMAYNE'S FACE burned from the impact of the palm colliding against his cheek. Who knew petite Honey Timmons packed a strong, right hook. She stood before him, in a yellow sundress and black stilettos, vibrating with indignation and fury. Manny blinked his right eye and flexed his jaw, his teeth still rattling. It wasn't the first time he'd been slapped, but each time it happened came as a surprise.

"You led me on," Honey accused.

Those words echoed what Rachelle Simpson had shouted at him their junior year in college. During that summer, both Manny and Rachelle worked at the same summer camp that took inner city kids into the Driskill Mountains for character building and goal setting activities. Manny and Rachelle continued to keep each other warm in the cold mountain nights. When summer ended and senior year began, with an influx of new coeds, Manny ended things. Rachelle's manicured talons streaked across his face before he'd gotten out the phrase "We can still be friends."

"I thought you were the one," Honey pointed her finger, red and shaky from assaulting his face.

Shanti Rodriguez had thought that, too. Shanti and Manny had been assigned to the same Malawian village during Manny's year in the Peace Corp. They'd met during his last few months there and spent their days working to build schools for the children. Inevitably, they ended up spending their nights together. Manny enjoyed their time together and felt he'd met a kindred spirit. He was certain the two would remain friends throughout their lives. Only, Shanti had assumed their lives would be spent together. The slap she'd delivered him continued to ring in his ear after he'd crossed the Atlantic on the plane ride back home.

"You won't find another woman like me," Honey declared before storming out the door.

The problem was Manny wasn't looking for another woman like her. Unlike regular people, love wasn't a Hasbro guessing game for Manny. He wouldn't need to ask a bunch of questions or flip a playing card to know if he'd met his match. Like every Charmayne man or woman in history, when Manny's true love finally showed up, he'd know for certain.

If she ever showed up.

Though Manny had no need for the adolescent Matching Game, as a red-blooded man he took a great interest in The Dating Game. With one major rule change.

He'd been dating Honey for nearly three months now. Well, technically it had been five months if you counted the first time they'd gone out together. And Manny was sure Honey counted that far back. Rule number one: Manny kept his relationships on the underside of three months, because after that women got serious. He didn't want to lead anyone on when he knew after that first glance if the relationship would last a lifetime. But he'd been traveling across the state for the last two months, testing the waters for this new venture in his life. And he hadn't broken it off with Honey in time.

"You okay? We could hear that slap all the way in the other room." Darrell Walker poked his head in the door.

"Yeah, I'm good," Manny answered, rubbing his still sore chin.

He looked up at his friend. Darrell stood basketball player tall with long limbs and big hands. Only, Darrell lacked any coordination that the sport required. In exchange, Darrell had been blessed with the gift of brains and strength.

"You sure? I could give you a quick spinal adjustment. Sounds like she may have knocked you out of alignment."

Manny had met Darrell after a minor fender bender. He entered Darrell's chiropractic offices feeling mangled and tense. Darrell cracked him straight in just five minutes.

"I think the best thing I can do for my health is to swear off women for a while."

Darrell shook his head. "Trust me, that won't make it better."

Unlike Manny who never lacked for company, Darrell, with his gangly height and proclivity for shyness around the opposite sex, was perpetually single.

"Well," said Manny, "at least until the mayoral campaign is over. I don't need any new distractions."

"You're really doing this," Darrell dropped a stack of papers on the desk.

Manny looked down at the fliers. "Charmayne for Mayor," they announced in royal blue. Across the middle, in red accents, it proclaimed he was "Putting the Community Back Together." The candid photo captured Manny smiling proudly in profile with a hammer in his hand as he helped to rebuild a home damaged by the storms.

"Looks like it," Manny answered looking out the window of his new campaign headquarters. He'd chosen to house the "Charmayne for Mayor" offices in the market district. At the top of Market Street loomed executive offices for manufacturing, refineries, tech companies and banks. Farther down, an outdoor flea market burst with activity in the middle of a lush green park that ended at the docks. Manny had situated himself at the cross roads of the concrete enclosures of business and open booths of the community. Hello, capitalism; meet communalism.

"I'm still surprised you're taking this on," said Darrell. "You could spend the rest of your life running the charitable arm of Charmayne Industries."

Manny had been the face of the Charmayne Charitable Foundation even before graduating college. Both of his parents had been successful in the corporate world, but as a child, Manny saw brightness in both of their eyes when they extended a hand to the less fortunate. Manny believed his parents were more proud of his philanthropy than any of his other accomplishments. And Manny was proud of himself, but helping a handful of troubled kids in the summer, building a woman's shelter that could only house ten families at time, was no longer enough. He wanted to make a bigger impact. To establish a road between the haves and the have nots. There were so many unheard have-nots, and not enough haves to listen, or more importantly, act.

The flaw with social programs is that the poor start to believe they can't do for themselves without it, and the rich believe the poor can't act without their help. It winds up being a vicious cycle with each side resenting the other.

He recalled her view of the world... Malika was her name. Or was it Pumpkin? Her view of the world was unlike the one he saw framed outside his window.

"Darrell, you do a lot of work down at the community center, right?"

"Yeah."

"Do you ever feel that people there are resentful?"

"Resentful how?"

Manny turned and rested a hand on his desk. His fingers grazed the Faberge egg that was the color of his birthstone. "You grew up in that neighborhood and now you're a success. Do you ever feel that people in the community resent you for that success?"

Darrell opened his mouth to answer, but then paused to think. "Well, there are always those who feel they're entitled to whatever you have to give, without doing anything in return."

Manny could understand that mentality. He'd endured enough over the top birthday parties as a kid where an heir or heiress threw a tantrum if the presents weren't big enough, or weren't better than the Jones'. He'd attended his fair share of excessive, socialite soirees as an adult where he couldn't meet the eye of the Average Joe serving his appetizer.

"But," Darrell continued. "It's been my experience that anyone who wants to succeed will take all the help they can get, and be thankful for it. Where's this coming from?"

"Just working out my stump speech," Manny shrugged. "I've gotta get to the board meeting at Charmayne Industries."

"They haven't endorsed you yet?"

"It's just a formality." Manny grabbed his suit jacket and walked Darrell out.

It was a sunny afternoon and Manny decided to walk the mile to the top of Market Street to the offices of Charmayne Industries. Entering the glass doors, he was hit with a wave of nostalgia. He'd spent much of his childhood in this place. Hiding in empty offices, sending slinkies down the marble staircase, playing in the corner while his dad negotiated business deals on the phone.

"Armand, it's been too long." Ed Satterfeld shook Manny's hand as he entered the boardroom. It was more of a jiggle than a shake as Manny's firm hand met with the excessive pudge of Satterfeld's palm.

Satterfeld had been a junior partner when Manny was in high school. During his father's time, Charmayne Industries supplied a great deal of jobs in the community to the upper, middle, and lower classes. Under Satterfeld's leadership, many lower class jobs had been outsourced, pay cuts shoved out many of the middle class, but the executive suite had plush, new carpeting and upgraded fixtures.

Manny looked around the square table at the heads of six men in various stages of balding.

"We think it's a great decision for you to run." Satterfeld levered himself into a seat at the head of the table, the seat that once belonged to Manny's father. "Your father would be proud. This will look good for the company, having the Charmayne name in politics."

"I'm not doing it for the company," Manny said taking a seat. "I'm doing it for everyone in the community: businesses, the middle class, the poor, the children. Everyone in our community needs a voice, someone to listen to them and be their advocate."

There was dead silence at this. Then—

"Put that in a speech and it'll get you elected," Satterfeld grinned, white teeth flashing like a shark. "But if you're naive enough to believe you'll get there with the people alone, you're living in a fairytale, son."

A chorus of unintelligible grumbles rumbled around the table, reminding Manny of the adults in the Charlie Brown cartoons.

Manny didn't respond. He wasn't naive. Though he didn't prefer the boardroom, his father had taught him the rules of this game. This was the part where the men in power would haggle for the little man's soul. Manny crossed his arms over his chest, like armor, and waited to see if he could stomach the price.

Satterfeld steepled his pudgy fingers and rested his double chin at the bridge. "You've always been an honorable man, Armand. Just like your father. But the unions are bleeding us dry, son. We've had to cut so much already."

Manny looked around the room at the nodding heads inside of tailored designer suits.

Satterfeld continued, "If the demands of the masses eat up the foundation, who will hold them up? Without Charmayne Industries there'd be no jobs. Any pilot worth his salt will tell you that you have to put the oxygen mask on yourself before you save anyone else. We just want to survive. We need to know you have our interests at heart."

"That's what I want, too," Manny reached for the common thread. "Us all to survive and prosper. So I can count on your endorsement?"

"Of course, son. You thought you even had to ask?" Satterfeld flashed his whites again.

It couldn't be this easy. Could it? If these were the terms, ensuring that the company survived and thrived, Manny would take the deal. Everyone would succeed under his leadership, and without any flaws or cycle of resentment. He'd make sure the haves and the have-nots saw that they needed each other in order to survive.

"Just one more thing," Satterfeld held up his index finger.

Manny felt his soul take a step backwards into himself and curl around his heart.

"Though we feel that your philanthropic reputation is infallible, we are concerned that your social life leaves much to be desired. And it's not just the board, there are many families and religious-minded voters in this community. We feel you should... tidy that up."

"Tidy that up?"

"With marriage. The public trusts a man on a ball and chain more than one who's free."

The ball and chain joke brought forth laughs and a few comments from the men around the room on their second, third, and fourth wives.

Manny's brain tried to unscramble the cartoonish walla around him. "You're saying you want me to get married?"

"Oh, no, no. Just engaged. For now." And then Satterfeld clarified, "To a woman of quality. You're pitting yourself against Preston Whitely. A family man who's older, with more experience, and more ties to the business community. You've spent a lot of time flitting around the world —doing admirable things, yes, I know. But while you've been home, you've been in the social section of the papers with a different girl on your arm every few months. That doesn't scream stability. You will get the youth vote, if you can get them up after their hangover. You will get the lower class vote, if you can get them to the polls after a day standing in the welfare and unemployment lines. But if you want the establishment vote, you need to show that you can make a commitment. The best way to do that is to tie yourself to a woman of quality."

Satterfeld stuck out his hand to shake on it. Manny's empty palm lay frozen on the cold, marble table.

CHAPTER THREE

"WHAT DID YOU DO TO my son to make him behave this way?"

Pumpkin tried to stay in the present, and not flash back to the last conversation she ever had with her mother-in-law. Mrs. Colson, the woman who currently sat before her, was in her early forties with perky boobs, further perked up with help from Victoria's Secret. Her wrinkle-free face was set in a scowl and her blue eyes were intent on Pumpkin.

"Mrs. Colson," Pumpkin began. "Tyler has to accept some of the responsibility for his actions."

Tyler sat beside his mother, a smirk on his face. Arms crossed over his chest in a nonchalant manner that broadcasted confidence that he could sit back and relax while Mommy bailed him out of trouble.

Yeah, serious deja vu.

"He did the assignment," said Mrs. Colson.

"He turned it in late."

"My son had extenuating circumstances."

"Contracting... an STD does not preclude someone from writing a paper. And I really don't think it appropriate for you to have shared that information with me."

"Tyler's been sick."

"He's been at school every day since I handed out the assignment, with no side-effects from the non-life-threatening virus you too vividly described to me. He's simply chosen to not do the work."

"Well, he's done it now," snapped Mommie Dearest. "Why are you being such a hard ass?"

Pumpkin counted to five. As she did, she watched Tyler's lips curl in amusement. Pumpkin pinched the bridge at her nose and continued to ten.

"You know what? I'll just take this to the Principal," Mrs. Colson threatened. But instead of getting up to storm downstairs to the administrative suite, she crossed her arms over her chest and stared Pumpkin down.

In today's world, it'd become all too common for college educated quarter-lifers who didn't hack it in their major to step backwards into teaching. Common enough that public school administrators across the nation created accelerated "how to teach" courses for those professionals who failed to make it in the real world. The courses amounted to customer service training where they pound into your head the old adage: the customer is always right.

In today's academic arena, teachers are supposed to meet children at their level. They're supposed to give them as many chances as they need to get the right answer. And a whole bunch of other baloney that will cause kids to fail in the real world.

So, staring between Mrs. Colson and her spawn of a son,

Pumpkin knew what she was supposed to do.

"You're right," Pumpkin began with a serene smile.

Tyler stiffened. His smirk turned to suspicion. He knew something was up. He really was a smart kid, just lazy and used to getting by on his charm.

"I'll accept the work on one condition," Pumpkin said. "In the last month, Tyler hasn't turned in any of the classwork I've assigned. If he can make it all up in two weeks, I'll accept the paper with no late deductions."

"Fine, with me." Mrs. Colson shrugged and grabbed her purse. Her work here was done.

Tyler, on the other hand, was finally getting started. "That's not fair!"

"What?" Pumpkin shrugged her shoulders in false incomprehension. "I'll grade your work, if you'll complete mine."

Tyler stared her down, searching for a way out. With his mother's back turned, Pumpkin dropped her innocent smile to glare. Gotcha! It was childish, she knew, but there were so few perks in teaching high school English.

The door to the classroom opened before Mrs. Colson reached it. A girl with a mop of straight black hair poked her head in. Pumpkin's student teaching assistant, DaeHo. Pronounced just like it reads, unfortunately.

DaeHo had been the name of a revered ancestor. It meant "great" and "goodness." Her family bestowing it upon her was a great honor. Only, when her parents brought their family over from Korea, they had no idea what lay in store for their good, little girl. Imagine the fun she had growing up in the halls of American public schools.

"Oh, I'm sorry Ms. Tavares," said DaeHo. "I didn't know you had a meeting."

"We're done here, Dae. You can come in."

Pumpkin took her gaze away from Tyler's blue eyes and smiled at DaeHo. Then, he did the same. And Pumpkin never saw it coming.

"Hello, DaeHo," Tyler took special care to include the "a" sound in her name.

DaeHo froze under the brilliant spotlight of his smile. "H- Hi, Tyler."

Tyler had the same icy blue eyes as his mother, only his shaggy blonde hair fell forward to hide the mischief in them. "I was wondering if you might be able to help me with something."

It was the beginning of the day and Pumpkin had skipped breakfast trying to help Seth with his science fair project. That was the only excuse she could come up with for why it took her so long to realize what was happening.

"I need to make up a couple of assignments," Tyler continued shining the full force of his lazy charm on poor, helpless DaeHo. "And I don't think I have all the notes. Do you think you could walk me through them? It would really help me out."

"Wait! No!" Pumpkin finally found her voice.

DaeHo didn't look at Pumpkin when she responded; her eyes locked under Tyler's smile. "I don't mind, Ms. Tavares."

"But, DaeHo," Pumpkin racked her brain for a way to save her favorite student. "You have a lot of your own work to do. A—and we still need to work on your college applications."

"So, you have the time to help me with the make-up work, Ms. Tavares?" Tyler turned his attention back to Pumpkin. Unlike with DaeHo, the smile he turned on her was a sneer. "I figured you would be too busy. And since DaeHo is the class TA…"

That slimy toad!

"I don't see what the problem is here." Mrs. Colson, who stood with her hand on the door, decided to play at parenting again.

And then Pumpkin's favorite student turned on her as well, when she said in that sweet, naive voice of hers, "Ms. Tavares, really, I don't mind."

Pumpkin was beat. But, she wasn't down.

"Great. You guys can work together during class. That way, if you have any problems with your work, Tyler, I can be there to make sure you get it done."

Tyler held Pumpkin's smiling glare for a second before nodding, and finally joining his mother on the other side of the door. Pumpkin let out a sigh.

"What's the problem, Ms. T?"

Pumpkin glanced over at DaeHo. They could have been sisters from another mother. Two book smart girls, not unattractive, but not popular either. Quintessential, textbook, good girls. The kind who peer from behind Jane Austen books to sneak looks at the most popular guy in the school. The kind who pray, with eyes and palms squeezed so tight, for a fairytale ending to their uneventful beginnings. The kind who cross their fingers until the blood drains, for Prince Charming to ride up on his white horse and choose them.

"Be cautious of him, Dae." Pumpkin inclined her head to the now closed door.

"Who, Tyler? What? Like he's the Big Bad Wolf or something."

Not far off the mark.

"Trust me," Pumpkin said. "Girls like you and I need to go after the Ducky's."

"The who?"

"Ducky. From Pretty In Pink." Seriously, what did teenage girls watch these days? "Do you know the television show, Two and a Half Men?"

"Oh, yeah. With Charlie Sheen. Winning!" DaeHo giggled.

"You remember his brother, Alan?"

DaeHo nodded.

"Well, Tyler is a Charlie. A no-good womanizer, who will never settle down or get a decent job. Whereas, girls like you and me, we should go after Alan."

"You mean the divorced moocher?"

Pumpkin sighed again.

"Ms. T, I'm just going to help him study. I'm not embarking on some great romance. As if he would even be interested in me."

"Oh, Dae," Pumpkin shook her head. "Guys like that are always interested. But it never lasts."

"Well, I'll keep that in mind as I help him correct his dangling participles."

DaeHo giggled again, and this time Pumpkin let loose her stern teacher face.

"Oh, I almost forgot." DaeHo reached into her bag and pulled out a manila folder. "I wanted to drop these essays off before I went to the school assembly."

"Are these for Sarah Lawrence?"

"Louisiana State, actually."

Pumpkin's alma mater! "I'll look at them today."

"You coming to the assembly, Ms. T?"

"Yeah, I'll be down in a sec. Who's speaking, again?"

"One of the candidates for Mayor. I'm hoping to volunteer for his campaign. It'll look great on my college applications."

Pumpkin smiled again. "Good girl. I'll see you down there."

Pumpkin arrived downstairs to a packed auditorium. She crammed herself backstage with the rest of the faculty members and the visitors of the guest speaker who addressed the crowd of students. It was both his words and his voice that caught Pumpkin's attention.

"Sometimes, you might feel you're out in this world alone."

She knew that voice. The timbre of it called up the faint outlines of hazard signs at a clearing in a forest.

"You might feel that no one hears your voice or sees you when you walk past. But I see you, and I want to hear what you have to say."

There on the stage, dressed in dark slacks and a collared shirt without a jacket or tie, stood Mr. Smokey Eyes from the DFACS voter registration drive.

"Some of you may be thinking: Hey, this guy was raised with a silver spoon in his mouth. He doesn't have time for me."

A light rumble rippled through the crowd. That's when Pumpkin realized who he was. Armand Charmayne, son of Gerard Charmayne. The Charmayne family had old money. They owned tons of land and had their hands in all kinds of businesses across the entire state.

The young Charmayne continued, "That's not true. Well, the silver spoon is true. My mother loved fancy cutlery."

Light laughter came from the adults backstage.

"There are a lot of stereotypes of the rich. That we get everything we want, with little to no work. Like most stereotypes, there's some truth to those ideas. But if you believed those ideas about every wealthy person, you would be mistaken. If you believed every racial stereotype, every sexist stereotype, every cultural stereotype, you would be mistaken.

"My father put me to work at the age of thirteen. I got things wrong, made mistakes. But as long as I didn't give up, as long as I was willing to try again, there was always a second chance for me. My father always backed me as long as I tried my hardest. That was the greatest lesson that I learned from him."

He paused here, possibly for dramatic effect, but then he looked to the side of the stage to someone just beyond Pumpkin. Only his eyes never made it past her. They locked on her. He blinked. Then blinked again before that wide, wolfish grin spread across his face.

"I believe there's enough success to go around for all of us. That if you work hard enough, you'll find that there are enough fish in the sea for everyone to be bountiful, but sometimes we need a hand in making a catch."

Pumpkin was immobile. He blinked once more, or was that a wink, and then he turned back to the crowd.

"As you move into the world and try to catch your own dreams, you might mess up. Don't let that stop you. Get up and try again. Make your voices heard. And the best way you can make your voices heard; the best way you can be seen is to stand up for what you believe in. If you're eighteen, register to vote. If you're not, go out and volunteer for a cause you believe in. Thank you all for your time."

Wow, that actually got a round of applause from the apathetic teenagers. Some students were even on their feet. Pumpkin never saw this much enthusiasm outside of a pulled fire alarm during finals.

Mr. Charmayne turned and shook the hand of the Principal. The two moved off the stage and into a crowd of smitten faculty members, mostly women. He moved through them with ease, offering that charming smile, spending just enough time with each, and winning them over. Winning.

Pumpkin took a step back, and promptly bumped into someone. "Oh, I am so sorry." She turned around. "My feet don't always look where they're going."

The man she bumped reached out a big, strong hand to steady her. He stared. After a beat too long he said, "Oh, you're joking."

"Yes," Pumpkin smiled. "Because feet don't have eyes."

He nodded. "But starfish have eyes in their arms."

Now, Pumpkin stared at him quizzically.

He rushed on to fill the awkward silence. "But butterflies, butterflies have taste buds in their feet."

"Oh," Pumpkin nodded. "What?"

He scrunched his face in embarrassment and shook his head. "I'm sorry. I'm really bad with humor. When I try it, it just winds up being facts that are just plain weird."

"Oh, you were making a joke." Pumpkin smiled and then let out a chuckle.

"And now you're laughing at me."

She shook her head "no," but wound up saying, "Yes, I am."

He cracked a grin. "I'm Darrell." He extended his large hand again.

"Malika."

Darrell's handshake was warm and gentle. "That's a beautiful name," he said.

"It means princess."

Darrell smiled again. He had a really nice smile. Open. Not over-confident. His hazel eyes were focused on her, but they were hooded; not allowing her to see too deeply. That he had his guard up made Pumpkin feel oddly safe.

"My friends call me Pumpkin."

Darrell was slow to release her hand this time, when he did, Pumpkin slowly took it back.

"Are you a volunteer with the campaign?" she asked.

"Yes, I was actually Mr. Charmayne's chiropractor before he convinced me to come on board his mayoral campaign."

"Chiropractor?"

"Yes, it's a back specialist—"

"I know what a chiropractor is," Pumpkin said. Ducky—well Alan, John Cryer's character on Two and a Half Men, was a chiropractor.

"Well, hello there, Malika."

Pumpkin turned at the sound of that deep voice that had visited her dreams last night. Beside her, she felt Darrell take a step back.

"You two know each other?" Darrell said.

Unlike Darrell's smile, Mr. Charmayne's smile was confident and a tad proprietary.

"We weren't formally introduced. Armand Charmayne."

"Mr. Charmayne." Pumpkin took his hand. His palm was hot, his fingers firm as they gripped hers.

"My friends call me Manny." He grinned his wolfish grin.

A thrill went up Pumpkin's spine. "That's good to know, Mister Charmayne."

His grin widened, boa constrictor wide. "I hear your friends call you Pumpkin?"

Pumpkin looked into his smokey eyes, expecting leering. His friendly smile confused her.

"What did you think of my speech... Pumpkin?"

Was he baiting her? "You have a great delivery."

"Thank you, Pumpkin. Do you think I got my point across?"

She started to tell him what he wanted to hear. To politely agree, but for some reason she spoke the truth as she saw it. "It's what they're used to hearing. You can get whatever you want —eventually. No matter how many times you screw up. Everyone gets a trophy just for participating. There are no losers."

"That's not what I said." His eyes widened along with his grin. "I just gave a rousing speech about perseverance in trying to achieve your dreams."

"Having the courage to reach for your dreams is one thing, a noble thing," Pumpkin conceded. "But they need to try to succeed on the first attempt, not fumble their way through life until someone gives them the correct answer. Everyone doesn't get a second chance. There are no heroes there to catch them if they fall."

Mr. Charmayne jerked back as though she'd slapped him. His grin turned into a frown. "So, people aren't allowed to make mistakes?"

"One or two maybe. But in the real world, the one without the silver spoons, not everybody's cut out to be at the top. There are winners because there are losers."

He crossed his arms over his chest and studied her. Well, his eyes were on her, but they were unfocused. He was doing it again, turning her words over in his head. He was about to say something else when a manicured hand snaked around his shoulder.

"All right Armand, you've locked down the fry jockey, movie usher, and camp counselor vote. Can we go sit at the adult table now? The lobbyist meeting starts in thirty minutes." The manicured hand belonged to a pair of long, shapely legs and a perfectly coifed bun that Pumpkin's unruly hair could never manage in a million years.

The hand gave a proprietary squeeze to Manny's arm. He blinked, and then smiled down at the hand's owner —it was the wolfy grin. When he turned back to Pumpkin, his smile was once again polite.

"It was nice seeing you again, Pumpkin." He looked just beyond her. "Darrell, we gotta go."

Darrell. The chiropractor. She'd completely forgotten he was there. Darrell gave Pumpkin a small smile and stepped up beside Mr. Charmayne, who hesitated and turned back to her.

"You know, Pumpkin," Mr. Charmayne said. "I could use someone like you on this campaign."

"Me? But I disagreed with everything you just said."

His smile widened, his eyes flashed. The temperature went up ten degrees backstage. "Yeah," he shrugged, and the room instantly cooled. Mr. Charmayne's smile was polite, professional once more. "Half the electorate will disagree with me. Maybe I need someone to remind me of that. Plus, you know how to run a successful voter registration booth."

The long-legged bun gave Pumpkin a once-over, but it was just one glance. Its quick assessment of Pumpkin's worn slacks, scuffed shoes and droopy shirt: Pumpkin was no threat. Pumpkin's eyes darted to Darrell.

Darrell smiled his guarded smile at her again.

When she answered Mr. Charmayne, it was him, Darrell, that she looked at. "I'll think about it."

CHAPTER FOUR

THE MOON SPOT-LIT MANNY from his place before the balcony's open doors. He stepped to the side to avoid the pale glow on his back, but he couldn't escape the sea of sparkling lights that spread out before him. Pale, blue dots zeroed in on the expensive linens that covered Manny's broad shoulders. Doleful, green orbs fluttered as they tracked his fingers loosening his collar. Heated, brown disks arrowed straight to the front of his fitted pants. Dozens upon dozens of women's eyes twinkled at Manny from every corner of the room. All trying to catch his attention.

"I heard that his family was cursed by love." The sultry voice came from the balcony exterior over his shoulder. "Something about when he kisses a woman for the first time he'll know she's The One."

"It's not a curse," a second voice replied in a dreamy tone. "I heard it's some kind of psychic power or something."

"Or maybe it was after he had sex with her," drawled Sultry Voice.

"I think it's romantic," Dreamy Voice sighed. "Like a real live fairytale."

"Or, he made it up to get in women's pants," said Sultry. "A man who looks like that, with that many zeroes in his bank account, could kiss me anywhere he'd like."

Manny stepped away from the balcony doors and peered out a window. Out on the water, the sky was inky dark and the stars looked as though they'd been poked through with a pencil.

For the most part, the two women on the balcony were right. There were only a few holes in their story about him. When Manny met The One, he would know it for certain, that part was true. But it would be before they slept together, before they even kissed. When Manny came face to face with the woman he was meant to spend the rest of his life with, he'd know her by sight.

The Charmaynes descended from gypsies. They'd come from the border between France and Spain and settled in Louisiana. Their "second" sight had made the family rich on the Continent. That wealth doubled when they reached the New World, because the sight enabled some in the family to make accurate predictions in business dealings. The sight enabled every member in the family to make an accurate prediction about love.

Every Charmayne, male or female, was able to spot their true love on first sight. When they saw The One, that person would be surrounded by a golden glow that only they could see. Manny's father had seen that glow around his mother when he was sixteen. They'd married the day she turned eighteen and never spent a night apart until she passed away.

Growing up in the midst of that powerful love, Manny had been excited about finding his own true love, for as long as he could remember. He looked hard at every girl who came his way, but he never saw so much as a spark.

By eighteen, with no light in sight, his hormones took over and Manny began turning a blind eye, in exchange for companionship. He was always sure to keep things casual with his companions in anticipation of the day he spotted his true love —thereby came the three-month rule.

Only now, at thirty and still single, his belief in the family sight had waned. Nearly every Charmayne had been happily married with children by this point in their life. Manny was beginning to think that maybe it wouldn't happen for him. Maybe he had no true love. Maybe he'd missed her. Maybe the sight that had guided so many of his family to the gift of love was actually a curse.

Manny turned his attention back to the ballroom. The theme of the evening's charity event was The Wizard of Oz. Yellow bricked plastic lined the marble floor. Gray streamers hung from the ceilings to look like a tornado. There were Tin Men in actual tin, others in silver suits and painted faces. There were orange faces made up to look like lions, and straw under hats to resemble scarecrows. Some younger men wore the rags and kinky dreads to resemble Michael Jackson's scarecrow.

The women sparkled in their glittery dresses as the Good Witch. There were far more dark cloaks and pointy hats from the West. You could tell the generation of the witch based on if she was cloaked with a crooked, green nose from the original Oz or a fashionable pantsuit and overlarge black hat a la Mila Kunis. Manny had considered going with Richard Pryor's robed version of the wizard, but decided to stick closer to his peers and donned James Franco's top hat and tails.

"There you are, Manny, my boy."

Manny cringed at the sound of Satterfeld's voice, more at the use of the endearment than the older man's perpetually smug tone.

When he turned around to greet Satterfeld, Manny felt the blaze of a thousand suns once more. Women eyed him at every turn, seeming to crowd him in. Satterfeld led one woman closer, cornering Manny. In this world, Manny was the Wizard everyone sought, with his powerful name, troughs of gold, charming looks, and magical love at first sight gift-curse. And like the story, they all wanted the fantasy. None cared to pull the curtain back to see the man behind the myth.

"Armand, you haven't met my daughter, Sophia." Ed Satterfeld was dressed in the checkered green of a munchkin. His daughter wore the royal blue of Dorothy, her thick hair in two glossy pigtails woven through with blue ribbons.

Satterfeld pushed her forward as though she were on a platter. Sophia looked up at Manny with the same light in her eyes that all the women around him had.

Manny looked down at Sophia. One second passed, then another. Manny blinked away the familiar disappointment, took her hand in his, and kissed it.

"It's so good to finally meet you Armand," Sophia said, her voice sultry and familiar. "Father talks about you incessantly, I thought you might've been some fairytale."

"No," corrected man. "Just a regular guy."

"Sophia's just graduated from Princeton," Satterfeld said. "She's taking over the United Breast Cancer charity here in Louisiana. Why don't you take a moment and get to know each other, before your speech."

Armand looked down into Sophia's smiling face that was so full of invitation. She was a beautiful woman; dark hair, tanned skin, intelligent eyes, and charitable inclinations. She was the total package. Would it be so bad to settle down with a woman like her?

There were plenty of marriages of convenience. A large part of the planet still had their marriages arranged based on expert observers. Most of those experts nowadays were computer programs running in the US, matching users, promising harmony based on comparable algorithms and personality profiles. Perhaps he should do the same with his choice of wife. Write up the details and negotiate the terms of the relationship. Stop with this love-at-first-sight business that had not worked for him.

Manny led Sophia Satterfeld around the room as she chattered on, each statement either a thinly veiled qualification for matrimony or a not too subtle innuendo for intimacy.

They stopped at a window just before the stage. Manny saw Cypress trees dotting the shoreline. The strong proud trees were his mother's favorites. They covered the property of Charmayne House and were visible from every window, including his mother's bedroom window, where she'd spent the last few months of her life. In the moon's light, Manny spotted the dark slick on the trees' bark, evidence of the oil spill that ravaged the state and its wildlife. Even through the presence of the toxins, the trees' roots held firm.

"What do you say we get out of here?" said Sophia, in her sultry voice.

It would be so easy to say yes. He'd said yes so many times before, with the full knowledge that it wouldn't last, with the secure belief that he'd get another chance. The knowledge that the right choice was out there somewhere, waiting for him to see it.

A safety net that allowed him to risk other women's hearts when he knew he would not be sticking around because he'd always get another, and then another chance.

"I can't," Manny said. "I have a commitment to keep."

He turned to the stage and climbed the steps.

The Mistress of Ceremonies hurried through her introductions and then the microphone was in Manny's hand, but he didn't take out the notes of his prepared speech.

"Many of you knew my mother," he began. There was a murmur of nostalgic assent throughout the crowd.

"You may not know that after her diagnosis, she spent most of her days watching romantic comedies. She believed she could laugh the illness out of her body. Her favorite moments in these films were something called the Grand Gesture. That scene just after all hope is lost because one of the lovers, normally the guy, has done something stupid that's led to the end of the relationship. So he thinks up this bold, romantic move to get the woman back."

A glance around the room told Manny that he held the largely female crowd in rapt attention.

"An example of a grand gesture would be a guy telling his estranged wife that she completes him in the midst of an angry mob of women. Or rescuing her underwear from the class geek and returning it to her at her sister's wedding. Or holding a boom box over his head, in front of her bedroom window, early in the morning, while blasting the song that was playing as he deflowered her."

A different wave of nostalgia swept through the crowd this time as they remembered these treasured moments of Hollywood Cinema.

"In the real world, some people might call these behaviors creepy, or stalker-ish. But not my mother. She loved them. She believed in love, believed that when you loved someone you said it loud, you showed it often, and you never gave up."

Manny paused here, partly for effect, mostly to collect himself as visions of his mother's joyous face played in his head. He rubbed the heel of his hand against his chest.

"The national divorce rate is 50 percent."

There was no surprise in the room, where most of the men were older and the women on their arms were younger.

"There's never been a divorce in the Charmayne family. Not one recorded anywhere in our family line."

The sparkle of young women's eyes threatened to blind Manny from where he stood on the stage.

"What that means is when a Charmayne gives you their pledge, they are committed."

The decision was a split second one, but once Manny made it he stuck with it. He stepped around the podium, mic in hand and dropped to one knee. The gasp of every woman in the room was near deafening.

"To earn your vote, I will do whatever I have to, including blast Peter Gabriel in the streets. Charmaynes don't quit. I'm committed to this, to the people of this town. I hope that I can count on your vote."

The room erupted in thunderous applause, and the women's eyes sparkled even brighter.

CHAPTER FIVE

"WHY WOULD HE WANT YOU?"

"He probably just wants to get in her pants."

Pumpkin gave herself credit for being intelligent. She'd graduated first in her high school class and Summa Cum Laude from a prestigious college. But this one lesson, one that she'd known since elementary school, she simply could never retain; never bother to tell her family about anything good going on in her life.

Pumpkin's memory lapse started right before dinner when LaRon began telling them all about her latest conquest at a local bar that men in the Armed Services frequented. LaRon's latest victim, a pilot, was headed out to Afghanistan in two months.

"Perfect timing," chuckled her mother, LaVerne.

The two actually high-fived. Pumpkin couldn't imagine another mother approving of, let alone encouraging, her never-married daughter's ambitions of seducing men in the Armed Service with the intent of getting knocked up and then hitting them up for child support. And the beauty of their plan? The men would ship off or fly out and LaRon wouldn't have to deal with them.

Her son LaDan's dad was in the Army, deployed now for five years. He still wrote her love letters, which LaRon cackled over with her mother and sister.

The twins LaShawn and LaSean's dad was in the Navy. He was married. He sent no letters, only checks.

Needless to say, LaRon planned to nab a Volunteer from every branch of the military.

Not to be outdone, LaTom updated them on her latest catch: a car dealership owner. Her mother's eyebrows rose at this. There was such pride there. Her baby girl had graduated from a Mustang with her daughter LaNick, to a Miata with her oldest boy LaCarl, to a Porsche with little LaRico's dad, and now an owner of a Honda dealership. Unlike LaRon, LaTom liked to keep her men and be kept by them.

Pumpkin watched as her aunt leaned towards her daughters, hands clasped at her heart, pride in her eyes. And then, somehow, Pumpkin opened her mouth to tell them about being asked to work on the Armand Charmayne mayoral campaign.

"Why would he want Pumpkin when he barely glanced at us?" said LaRon.

"Yeah, I think he might be gay," said LaTom.

"Now girls, I think we should give your cousin some credit."

Pumpkin's head jerked up at her aunt's words.

"You know his family's got money," Aunt LaVerne continued. "Old money, too. And I think he's an only child, so all that money will be coming to him. Now, if she could manage to get him in bed, which let's face it..." Aunt LaVerne looked Pumpkin up and down with doubt. "Well, you do have your mother's ass, so you probably could get him there. But, how to get rid of the condom?"

Aunt LaVerne continued to study Pumpkin. LaRon and LaTom joined their mother in this puzzling problem of her lack of sexual espionage. Pumpkin inhaled under their scrutiny and inwardly chided herself. Why had she even bothered saying anything?

Usually when Pumpkin came to family dinners with her aunt, cousins, and their gaggle of children, she kept her mouth shut and her eyes straight ahead. Otherwise, her eyes would be rolling and her mouth chiding their antics. Pumpkin did her time and then got out. The only reason she did her time? Well, they were the only family she had.

The three women launched into a series of condom-evasion tactics that had worked well for them. It was kinda of funny, in a really twisted way. For once in her life, they were actually trying to help her. Or so they thought.

"But I don't think she can do that," LaTom was saying. "She's such a goody-two-shoes."

It didn't matter that Pumpkin sat right beside her. LaTom always talked about her like she wasn't there.

"Well, she did land Anthony," LaRon offered. "And none of us thought she'd pull that one off."

Pumpkin flinched at the mention of Seth's dad. He too had been from a well-off family. And just like now, her family had been astonished at the possibility that someone handsome, wealthy, and from a respectable family had been interested in her.

"Well, she couldn't hold onto him, now could she?" Aunt LaVerne looked at Pumpkin again with disdain, then disappointment. "And then she never went after him for child support."

Pumpkin bit the inside of her lip to keep from defending herself and her decision to not force someone who didn't want her or her son, to take care of them. She didn't want any one's pity or charity.

She could handle things herself.

But they did have one point.

Armand Charmayne was an A-story guy. A-story guys were Pumpkin's weakness. Fitzwilliam Darcy, Jake Ryan, Lloyd Dobler.

As a girl, Pumpkin dreamed of stepping out of her B-story subplot and into a main character's storyline. There were enough examples of a story like hers working: orphaned girl, neglected at home, brilliant in her own right, attracts the prince or popular guy who sees her —really sees the gem behind her rough edges— and swoops down to rescue her away to an HEA, a Happily-Ever-After. There're tons of these stories on the bookshelves and On Demand. And Pumpkin was so sure she was going to get one of her very own.

So the first A-story guy who looked her way, she leaped.

And boy did she fall.

Hard.

On her ass.

But Pumpkin was a smart girl. She learned her lesson. She wasn't destined for the A-track. She was a sidelines, subplot, B-story kinda girl.

"I'm not trying to date Mr. Charmayne," Pumpkin assured her family. "I'm just trying to help him on his campaign."

They all looked at her as though she'd spoken German. "Would he be paying you?" asked LaTom.

"No. I'd be a volunteer."

Now, not only was she speaking German, she had antennas growing out of her head like some alien.

"I believe in what he's saying." Wait, no she didn't. She hadn't agreed with a word he'd said thus far. But his efforts intrigued her. If only she'd had someone like that in her corner while growing up.

She'd had that for a few years. Two people had loved her

unconditionally for six years. Pumpkin had been with her aunt and cousins at the time it happened.

"We'll return before midnight, otherwise our little Pumpkin will turn back into a carriage." Her father had kissed her on her forehead, then took her mother's hand and left through her aunt's front door.

Pumpkin had waited by the window impatiently for her parents to return from their date night and rescue her. They never returned. A drunk driver took them away forever.

Pumpkin turned away from her aunt's stare and looked out the same window. When she was six, her aunt's house felt like a punishment. Now it contained the only link she had left to her mother and father. And they were staring at her like she was a German from Mars. All in all, it was a typical Sunday night dinner. Her cousins were being praised for their trifling behaviors, while Pumpkin got scolded or ignored for her socially acceptable achievements.

Pumpkin didn't have a chance to respond because Seth entered into the room. "Excuse me, Mama? Can I go into the car and get my homework packet?"

"Sweetie, aren't you watching television with your cousins?"

Seth shook his head. "They're watching a show that I'm not supposed to watch."

LaRon poked her head into the living room. "They're watching The Family Guy. It's a cartoon."

"It's an adult cartoon," Pumpkin corrected her.

LaRon shrugged. "It's on Cartoon Network. Your old boss."

"No, I interned at Jukebox TV, where they made actual children's programming. Anyways, I think we'll be taking off now. It's way past his bedtime." Pumpkin figured both she and Seth had had enough exposure to Adult Swim.

"It's only ten o'clock," said her aunt.

Pumpkin simply nodded and grabbed her things to go. She didn't need a lecture on her parenting skills from this bunch —again. She was already at her wits end with them bringing up her least favorite topic in the form of Seth's dad; better known as the frog prince who turned into a snake.

Her family may not think her smart, but Pumpkin was no longer naive. Love was a fairytale. The stuff of imagination that only lived in songs, books, and the Disney vault. Very few stories featured heroines of color. No stories were told about heroines who were mothers who got rescued by a hero on a white horse. Here Pumpkin stood, a black, single mother.

She knew she wasn't meant for a man like Armand Charmayne, but she also knew she wasn't meant to be typecast under the social stigma that the women of her family portrayed.

As she buckled Seth in, she caught a glimpse of her family framed in the window. Pumpkin stood on the outside looking in at her cousins laughing, as her aunt bounced one of her grandchildren on her knee; a queen on her throne inside her government assistance home.

Pumpkin ducked into her driver's seat and pulled onto the street. They'd barely registered her departure.

CHAPTER SIX

"I FIRMLY BELIEVE THAT MOTHERS hold up this world."

Pumpkin watched from the edge of the park as candidate Armand Charmayne held court in the midst of a mommy group. The ringless moms of the group wrangled their way to the front. The married ones fidgeted with their sparkling bands or stuffed their left hands inside designer jean pockets.

"I wouldn't be the man I am today without mine," Armand continued.

"So, you're a mama's boy," said one mom.

"Proud of it," he grinned. "Mothers are the bravest, strongest creatures on the face of the earth. If elected I will fight for equal pay and paid family and medical leave."

And just like that, the Saint Anne MotherBoards', a collective of mommy bloggers, vote swayed his way. He could've stopped his speech right then and there, but he continued.

"What little boy doesn't think the sun rises and sets on his mom?" Armand raised his head and found Pumpkin's eyes on him.

"I'd storm the castle, vanquish the wizard, and slay a dragon for my mom." His grin widened and his gray eyes twinkled just as they had when Seth asked him if he were a prince last week.

The people and scenery all around Pumpkin went fuzzy as she stood there in the beam of that grin. In film there's a phenomenon called figure ground. In a scene of loud sounds, like the dance club scene in The Matrix where Neo first meets Trinity, the booming bass and treble of the speakers at the underground club magically dim and the hero and heroine begin an intimate, whispered conversation that anyone who's been to a club knows is impossible to do without shouting. But the audience doesn't question the aural impossibility of this whispered conversation because they, like Neo, want to know "the question."

No, not What is the matrix?

The question Pumpkin asked herself: Is Armand Charmayne hitting on me?

Her heart thudded so loudly in her chest at the possibility. But her brain came to the rescue and gave it a mental shake. There were no fairytales. She'd read the papers, she knew his reputation. He just wanted to get her into his bed. She'd been down that plot-line's road before. She knew where it led. She knew where she belonged. Pumpkin looked away from him.

"He's cute," a woman approached the voter registration booth Pumpkin manned.

"I guess," Pumpkin refused to be swayed by a thousand watt smile, a well-placed compliment, and a cinematic trick of perspective. Any swaying on her part would be based on substance.

"What's his stance on Issue Nine?"

"Um... I'm not sure..."

The potential voter wrinkled her nose and turned to leave.

Pumpkin turned to Darrell. "I'm not doing a very good job."

"It's okay," he assured her. "It's really all about name recognition. She won't remember you. She'll just remember the name of that cute guy who's a mama's boy."

"Yeah, I know the type."

"He's not a bad guy," Darrell insisted. "In case you're... interested..."

"Interested?"

"In him."

"What makes you think that?" Pumpkin asked.

Darrell shrugged. He looked at her with that guarded expression, as though unsure how much of himself he was prepared to reveal. "You two just seemed... friendly back at the high school."

Darrell was right about that. In their two encounters, Pumpkin and Armand did have a Maddy and David, Moonlighting, thing going on. But that television relationship had major issues because glamourous Cybil Shephard and gruff Bruce Willis' characters were in two entirely different leagues.

"He's not my type," Pumpkin proclaimed.

"I'm not his type either."

Pumpkin's mouth slacked open. She'd never had a good gaydar.

Darrell's hands came up. "No, no. I mean. I'm not like him. I didn't mean to imply... I mean..." He took a breath and reset. "I'm not smooth. I don't always know the right thing to say—obviously. Unless it's a diagnosis."

Darrell chanced a grin. Pumpkin realized he'd made another failed attempt at humor.

"I'm sorry," he said. "I armor myself with my intelligence when I'm nervous."

"Me, too."

"So... what is your type?" he hedged.

Her type? She hadn't done much dating before Anthony. Actually, she hadn't done any dating before or after Anthony. Her type had been characters from books and screens. But that was the old Pumpkin.

From yesterday.

This new Pumpkin —of today— she had her head out of the clouds. She made rational, sensible choices in life and love. She was no longer looking for some epic, fairytale fiasco. She was looking for a strong, steady, supporting male lead. She opened her mouth to tell Darrell just this.

Before she could get her new manifesto out, his phone rang.

"I'm sorry," Darrell said. "It's my office. I need to take this."

She hung back for a bit, eager to declare her new intentions out loud. After a while, it sounded as though Darrell's call was going to take longer than he expected. The next shift came to the table and Pumpkin decided to explore the outdoor flea market adjacent to the park.

It was a typical outdoor market. People selling manufactured and homemade goods. People offering services like food, fortune telling, and of course people pushing ideals on policy and social welfare.

Pumpkin skirted by the table of Armand's opponent, Preston Whitely. Where the Charmayne volunteers were college kids and young professionals, Mr. Whitely's people were an even mix of retirees and suits. Whitley's agenda pushed less regulation, defunding social programs, and lower taxes on the rich. Unlike Armand, Preston Whitely was not present shaking hands with the mommies, the coeds, and the other regular folks in the park.

"Tell your future?"

Pumpkin turned and came face to face with what could only be described as a gypsy woman, dressed in a flowing skirt and scarves. Rays of silver sprang out from her radiant face. She looked to be in her early fifties maybe?

Pumpkin didn't care to have her fortune told, but she did want the name of her moisturizer. "I don't believe in magic."

The woman grinned. "Humans are energy beings, dear. Energy can be moved and it can be measured. I'm very sensitive to that energy."

When put like that the woman's proclaimed abilities sounded both sensible and rationale. Right in line with the new Pumpkin.

The gypsy woman squinted. "You look familiar."

"I don't think we've ever met."

"No, not in person," she cocked her head to one side. "Your energy is familiar. I've seen your aura before."

From across her draped table the woman put her hands up, feeling the air just in front of Pumpkin. Pumpkin looked down at herself, actually expecting to see some rays or something emanating off her person.

Nada.

The gypsy woman gasped. The sound rang with delight. "Your core is golden."

Something about that proclamation made Pumpkin happy.

"People with golden auras are a dying breed. That means much is expected of you."

They say psychics figure out how to tell a person what they want to hear. Well, this one hit the nail on the head with Pumpkin. All her life she'd grasped high, aiming for good grades, a dream job, that fairytale love.

The fortuneteller concentrated once again on that space just before Pumpkin. Pumpkin held still, completely taken in. Until, the woman frowned.

"But your gold is so faint now. And the colors around it are muted. Your green, that's the color of your heart's aura, there are dark shadows surrounding it." She looked up at Pumpkin in confusion. "But your heart hasn't been touched. It looks to me like those shadows are protection."

Pumpkin's hands rose to her heart. In defense of those assumptions? To hide from the exposure of those words?

"Sometimes the heart and the brain get their signals crossed," the woman continued. "Sometimes the heart tries to give love to someone the brain knows is wrong for us. Sometimes our brains tell us to love someone who makes sense but is truly not in our hearts. It looks like you tried the former."

Pumpkin's back stiffened at the all too accurate diagnosis. The gypsy woman sighed at Pumpkin's posture, but there was no disappointment. No pity. She looked compassionate.

"It can change," she assured Pumpkin. "If you let it. You chose wrong that first time. I can still see his signature on you, but it's fading. You don't have to let him, or that decision, affect you any longer."

The woman smiled at Pumpkin and it completely disarmed her. Those light eyes scanned Pumpkin's face left to right, reading the story of her life. Then Pumpkin realized that she'd seen that smile before. Seen the twinkle in gray eyes similar to that.

"Auntie Gale, are you harassing my staff?"

Pumpkin turned towards the sound of that deep, male voice.

"Do you need to be rescued, Pumpkin?" Armand's gray eyes did that twinkling dance as they surveyed her.

"She's a kindred spirit, Manny."

Manny walked over and gave the woman —Auntie Gale— a kiss on the cheek. They both turned and smiled at Pumpkin. Auntie Gale's smile was thoughtful; Armand's apologetic. Pumpkin looked between the two of them. The features were strikingly familial, now that they stood side by side.

"This is my aunt, Galinda," Armand said.

"Like the Good Witch of the East?" Pumpkin blurted.

Armand burst into laughter. "It depends on which book you read. The Wonderful Wizard of Oz or Wicked."

Galinda gave him a dirty look, which he only laughed at again. Pumpkin looked at the table of tarot cards and crystals.

"I don't understand how this is your aunt? You're rich." God! She really needed brain surgery. This problem with words that skipped from the top of her head straight out of her mouth needed to be corrected. But it only seemed to happen around this man. Pumpkin was horrified at what she had just said, but the relatives in front of her burst out laughing.

"I think she's insulting you, auntie," said Armand.

"Because she thinks I'm a lowly street beggar?" said Auntie Gale.

"No, no, no" Pumpkin stammered. "That's not what I meant." Pumpkin turned from Armand to his aunt. "I don't think of you as a beggar."

Gale shrugged. "I didn't give up my inheritance." A secret smile spread across her face, as she continued to assess Pumpkin. Looking more in front of her than at her.

"She told you that you had a golden core, didn't she?" Armand asked.

Pumpkin's heart skipped a beat at the possibility that she'd just been had by a fraud. What if Gale told everyone they had a golden aura? What if Pumpkin wasn't special at all?

Armand smiled, not the wolf grin. It was his genuine, thoughtful grin. "I believe it."

"Didn't peg you as the type to believe in magic, Mr. Charmayne." No, she pegged him as the stuff of magic.

"It's Manny," he insisted. "And I don't need magic, I can look at the evidence. The first day I met you, you were helping out the less fortunate."

"No, that was indentured servitude and—"

"The second time I met you, I learned you're a teacher fighting the battle to uplift the minds of the future generation."

"Uplift is a strong word—"

"And now, you're here. Volunteering at my campaign to help me make the community a better, fairer place for all. Ms. Tavares, I'd say you were the golden champion of Saint Anne's Parish."

He was grinning, but his eyes twinkled with mirth. Pumpkin couldn't tell if he was being serious or poking fun. Gale stood beside him, a cosigning smile on her own face. They couldn't be serious. None of that stuff about her was true. Well, there was a kernel of truth in each statement. She had helped her cousins. She was a teacher. She was volunteering to help on the campaign. Only, he embellished the facts. They both had. Both Armand and Gale saw extra things in her, things that just weren't there.

Pumpkin shook her head, ready to launch into a protest, but before she could, a manicured hand snaked around Armand's bicep. Armand blinked, turned his head to the tight-bunned beauty, and smiled. A gush of air left Pumpkin's lungs. She hadn't realized she'd been holding her breath.

"Hello, Auntie Gale," said the bun. "How's business today?"

Gale's smile was barely cordial. "It's Galinda, dear. And I don't do business. I provide a service." Gale indicated the sign that said "Free Readings."

The bun's smile faltered. Armand narrowed his eyes, chastising his aunt. But Gale ignored it.

Gale continued. "I believe when you've been given a gift, you should share it with the world. You can't charge for something that was given to you freely." Then Gale turned to Pumpkin with a mischievous smile that she had spied before, on her nephew. "Besides, I'm rich. I don't need the cash."

Pumpkin couldn't help but grin back at her. There was something intensely likable about this woman. Her eyes were a lighter shade of gray than Armand's. They matched her hair color. Her peasant blouse was a loud rainbow of colors. She reminded Pumpkin of a flamenco dancer, but with a new age twist.

Armand turned to Pumpkin. "Lorielle, have you met our newest volunteer, Pumpkin?"

"Pumpkin?" Lorielle wrinkled her nose as she said the name.

"It's a nickname. My given name's Malika."

"Pumpkin is a writer," Armand offered.

"Well, I used to be a screenwriter," Pumpkin corrected.

"Screenwriter? You didn't tell me that," Armand looked impressed.

"Any movies I'd know?" Lorielle interjected.

"Well..." Pumpkin hesitated, then decided against opening up old wounds. "No."

Lorielle's smile was polite and dismissive.

"But I did win some competitions." And lost more than she'd bargained for, in exchange.

"That's perfect," Armand said. "You could help with the radio ads and television commercials."

"Well, I've only ever written for kids and teens."

"And they have the shortest attention spans," said Armand. "If you can keep their attention, you can keep the adults'."

"Well," Pumpkin said. "I suppose so."

"It's settled then," Lorielle interjected. "Malia—"

"Malika," Pumpkin corrected, but Lorielle didn't hear.

"—can get to work on the spots for the campaign. I'll have the office put you in touch with our ad agency." She turned to Armand. "Armand, I need to talk with you about the fundraiser."

"Oh, right." Armand looked past Lorielle at Pumpkin and Galinda. "Excuse me Pumpkin, Auntie Gale." He started to leave, but turned back a second later. "Hey, Pumpkin. We're all going to grab a drink after we close the booth. You should come."

His smile was once again genuine, all traces of the wolf gone. But still, Pumpkin knew this part of the plot. It was the Call to Adventure. He was inviting her into his Special World. It was a journey she'd taken before and it hadn't worked out for her.

Armand Charmayne was so obviously a hero. Just look at his name! It was full of 'ahs.' She could hear legions of women calling out his name across the moors, from a high tower, in his bed. Armand Charmayne was going to have an amazing story, but Pumpkin would be watching from the sidelines where she belonged.

"Thanks," Pumpkin said, "but I have to go and pick up my son."

"You mean little cupid?" he asked with merriment in his gray eyes.

Pumpkin's face slipped into mortification, but Armand only chuckled. "Why do I get the feeling you're the type of person to not let a conversation like that go?"

"A conversation like what?" asked Lorielle. But she asked as though she were less interested in the answer and more concerned that she was being left out of the conversation.

"Nothing," grinned Armand. "Just a son looking out for his mother. It was precious."

"You make him sound like Golem from the Lord of the Rings," Pumpkin countered.

"Says the woman using her kid to pick up men."

"I did no such thing!"

"I thought single folks used dogs to pick up dates, not kids—"

"And now you're calling my kid a dog?"

"I didn't know this was the new trend. It's fascinating."

"Mr. Charmayne—" Pumpkin started, but stopped when his good humor sobered.

"I told you to call me Manny."

Gale looked between the two of them with sly amusement, Lorielle with wary impatience. Pumpkin looked at Armand — Manny— whose frown reminded her of Seth arguing about bedtime after a long day of work when she was exhausted. Pumpkin couldn't win arguments after the sun went down. Apparently she couldn't win arguments after Armand Charmayne looked at her all wounded either.

"Fine. Manny," she conceded.

"Thank you," he said with a restored grin. "And I'll keep my eye open for any princes."

Pumpkin shook her head. "I'm not interested in princes. A regular guy will do just fine for me."

Manny opened his mouth to say more, but then—

"Armand," Lorielle said with an impatient tug at his attention.

"I'll see you soon, Pumpkin."

The two stepped off to the side, out of earshot. They looked like a live action version of Ken and Barbie. Armand in a white collared shirt that stretched across his broad chest. Lorielle in expensive pumps and a pencil skirt. It was time for Pumpkin to take her jeans and sneakers and exit stage left.

"It was nice meeting you, Galinda."

"It's Gale, honey."

Pumpkin paused. Looking back at Lorielle, then back at Gale.

"Don't forget what I told you," Gale said. "One bad move doesn't knock you out of the game. Don't kiss any more frogs with royal expectations. That goes for pawns and bishops, too."

"Um... okay. Thanks. Gale."

Pumpkin ducked away quickly. The registration booth was just a few tables away. She grabbed her bag from beneath the table. As she turned to go, she bumped into Darrell, literally. She'd forgotten he was here.

Darrell's hands steadied Pumpkin before she toppled over. "You're leaving?"

"Yeah," Pumpkin said. "I've got to pick up my son from Chess Club at the community center."

"Bayou Chess Club? I was in chess club when I was a kid. It made me very popular with the ladies."

He said it deadpan and Pumpkin chuckled. "Now, that was actually funny, Darrell."

"Only because it bore a kernel of truth."

Pumpkin smiled again. Why wouldn't a girl want a man like Darrell? Kind. Smart. Employed. Darrell had a gentle, albeit awkward, way about him. He was a total Ducky. Right up her alley.

"Malika..." he began. And she immediately knew where this was heading. Pumpkin hadn't been on a date since Seth's dad left. When asked, she'd always turn guys down. But mostly, she just didn't get asked.

From the corner of her eye, Pumpkin saw Manny had an eye on her and Darrell while nodding at something Lorielle was saying. His expression, so open just moments ago, was now unreadable.

"...I was wondering..."

Gale, too, was watching with interest. What had Gale just told her? One bad decision doesn't knock her out of the rest of the game.

"...if you're not busy..."

Pumpkin didn't hear any of the details of Darrell's request. She looked back at him and said, "I'd love to."

Score one for her.

CHAPTER SEVEN

"ARMAND CHARMAYNE IS WITH A different woman each week."

Dozens of newspaper clippings of Manny with a different girl on his arm flickered across the television screen to illustrate the narrator's scripted words.

"Does our city need a playboy who makes empty gestures?"

Shaky cellphone footage of Manny down on one knee at the charity ball materialized next.

"Or does our city need a man who'll keep the city and its people moving steadily forward."

Preston Whitely stood proudly with his Stepford Wife and Disney kids.

"On election day, don't fall for the playboy on his knees. Vote for the family man who's stood strong on two feet for this community. Vote for Preston Whitely."

With the click of a button, the television flashed off. The silence it left behind was dark and heavy. In an attempt to clean up his playboy image, Manny had stopped dating completely. But taking himself out of the marriage mart may have very well taken him out of the running for office.

"With that ad, Whitley just got a five point bump in the latest poll." Lorielle paced the length of Manny's desk in her heels. The red underbelly of her stilettos flashed angry as she turned and paced the other way.

"He's just picked up Region's Bank," said Heather, Manny's chief statistician. "Add that to Anchorage Industrial and Backwater Corp and we're way off projections."

"You need endorsements, Armand," Lorielle's heels flashed at him. "Voters have a herd mentality. They look to their immediate leaders for what to think. Or their heads swing to who shouts the loudest on television."

Lorielle grabbed the remote from his desk and turned the television back on. It didn't take many clicks to get to a channel running Preston Whitely's smiling, mature face. That face was so fake. For the two terms that Whitely had been mayor, the city had seen a decline in the employment rate, but an increase in wealth. The wealth was concentrated at the top with a promise to trickle down if only the masses were patient.

"Preston Whitely has the leaders of our community behind him," the narrator of the new ad proclaimed. Graphics of big named companies popped up on screen, most notably one with Manny's last name. "If the company you run isn't behind you, what does that say about your leadership? Vote Preston Whitely. Trusted. Proven. Leadership."

Lorielle clicked the remote again. The screen went black, but Manny could see that the wheels in her head were turning. He trusted that, true to her profession, Lorielle was figuring out a way to make this work in their favor. "I can spin this," she said. "Heather get me the numbers on how many women Whitely has staffed in high positions. I'm sure it's low."

Heather tapped on her handheld. "You're right. He's never had a single woman in a high level position."

"We can turn this back on him," Lorielle continued. "He won't extend a hand to women where Armand believes in equal pay and equal opportunity. Mayor Charmayne will staff his cabinet full of female advisors and key officials. But—"

Lorielle rounded on Manny, a manicured talon pointed at his chest. He should be afraid, a weaker man would have been, but he'd known Lorielle since high school. He knew her bark was worse than her bite. Most of the time.

"But if you want to be a leader," she said, "there have to be people behind you, following you. And not just women, youth, and minorities. You're going to need some heavy hitters if you want to be taken seriously."

"We just have to get the people's ear," said Manny. "Once they hear my platform they'll see that I have the best plan for everybody."

"They won't know it if they can't hear it," Heather tapped her computer pulling up more numbers. One of the reasons Manny had hired Heather was because of her objectivity, her ability to speak numbers. But now he wished she caught on to the emotional part of his argument.

Lorielle's heels tapped the floor louder as she paced faster, sounding like an army march. "We need to start focusing on your ad campaign. I've set up a meeting with Gulf and Foster's Creative for tomorrow. They have some suggestions for you—"

"Pumpkin's writing the ad," said Manny.

"Who?" Lorielle stopped her pacing and faced him.

"Malika Taveres," offered Darrell.

Manny turned at the sound of Darrell's voice. For such a tall guy, he was easy to forgot. Darrell sat in the corner with his long legs scrunched into a small chair.

"She's an English teacher at the local high school," Darrell continued, a small smile played at his lips.

"You need someone professional," Lorielle insisted.

Darrell opened his mouth, but took a look at Lorielle's stance — hands on hips, head high, jaw set firm— and he closed it.

Manny couldn't take his eyes off Darrell and the ghost of a smile that had briefly touched his friend's lips. He knew Darrell was interested in Pumpkin. What red-blooded man wouldn't be? The woman's body was shaped like a female comic book heroine's; two-handfuls of breasts, a small waist, and flaring hips. She had lips full enough to leave a man indecisive over whether to watch her talk or to kiss her into submission.

But he wasn't going to get his hands on her breasts, or kiss her. He wasn't doing that with any woman right now. He just enjoyed talking to her.

Arguing with her was more like it. He'd known plenty of women who disagreed with him. He'd dated women on the opposite side of his political views, social stances, and economic status. Pumpkin wasn't any different from the rest.

As that statement sank down into Manny's gut it left a fiery trail that didn't sit well with him.

"Armand, did you hear me?" Lorielle's voice called him back to the present. "I said you need someone professional."

"I want Pumpkin."

Both Lorielle and Darrell looked over at him sharply.

"To work on the ads," Manny amended. "People are tired of the same old messages. You can shout all you want, but people can still tune you out. She has a unique perspective." One that challenged him to see things in a new way, and opened his mind to a new way of thinking. "I want her to be my voice."

Lorielle sighed. "Fine, Mallory—"

"Malika," Darrell corrected quietly.

"—will draft the first ad, but we'll send it over to Gulf and Foster's for polishing. You need to start winning some high level endorsements, and soon, if you have any hope of staying in this race."

Lorielle was right. If it was just a matter of money, Manny had enough to throw at the problem. But this wasn't a problem money could solve. He needed people. And not just the little people.

"All right," Manny looked up at his team. "Who do I have to schmooze?"

Lorielle and Heather read him their list of names and outlined each group's needs. With their strategy firmly in place, the team adjourned for the day. Lorielle and Heather click-clacked out of the room, both zeroed in on their tablets while holding on to their conversation.

"Hey, D. You got plans for tonight?"

"Uh, yeah." Darrell patted his jacket pocket and then his pants.

Manny waited a moment, and then prompted his friend. "So, what you up to?"

Darrell looked up distracted. "Oh, just dinner." He produced his cell phone from his jacket pocket and headed towards the door. "I'll be a little late to the registration booth tomorrow."

"Sure," Manny waved to his friend as he left his office.

Manny sat on the edge of his desk, alone. He looked out his picture window. The golden light of the sun was setting, the gold mocking him as it went in and out of the clouds.

CHAPTER EIGHT

"LARON, YOU CAN'T CANCEL ON me! He's supposed to be here in fifteen minutes."

"Look Pumpkin, it can't be helped."

Pumpkin pulled the phone away from her ear and glared at it. "How many times have you dropped your kids off to me at the last minute for a couple hours? And then, not come back until the next day?"

"Girl, Seth is what? Seven? He can stay by himself."

"He's eight and that's how Child Protective Services wound up at your house last year."

"Whatever, Pumpkin-Head," she snapped. "It's a Basketball Wives marathon going on right now and I don't want to miss it."

"But you've seen them all already."

"Not back to back. Besides, I'm expecting some company later."

The real reason finally shines through. "Let me guess, the pilot?"

"Who? Nah girl, this guy says he's a Navy Seal, from Seal Team Six. You know, the ones that captured Bin Laden and shot him in the head. Can you imagine the child support check?"

"Aren't their identities classified? And they're sworn to secrecy by the President?"

LaRon paused. "Whatever, Pumpkin-Head. Just take the kid on the date. Or better yet, put the kid to bed and try to do the same with the... what did you say he was again?"

"A chiropractor."

"What? Oh, wait. That's the door. I gotta go." LaRon disconnected.

Pumpkin stared at the phone. Unbelievable. She rarely asked her family for anything, mainly because of the total lack of support they'd given her over the years. Secondly, because any —no every— time she did ask them for something, they would always let her down.

"You okay, mama?" Seth asked from the living room. Pumpkin stood in the dining area staring incredulously at her cell phone.

"Yeah, baby. Unfortunately, Auntie LaRon's not gonna be able to hang out with you tonight."

"That's okay," he shrugged. "Auntie Ronnie smells like smoke anyways. Can we watch a movie instead?"

"Sure, honey. Just let me call my friend to—" The doorbell rang. Uh, no!

Sure enough, Darrell was on the other side... with flowers. No one had ever brought her flowers.

"Oh, Darrell. I'm so sorry."

His face fell. "Oh, no. Are you allergic?"

"Allergic?"

"To flowers?"

Pumpkin frowned. "No."

He frowned. "Then why are you sorry? You look beautiful by the way."

"I do?" Pumpkin glanced down at herself. She'd dug the dress out from the back of her closet. The bodice was a peasant blouse that added a cup size to her girls. The waist was cinched in with a belt hiding her muffin-top. "Thank you."

"Are you ready?"

"No. My sitter just cancelled."

"Oh." Darrell's face fell. And then his eyes focused below her breasts. "Hi."

Pumpkin looked down her body and saw Seth peering from behind her.

"Hi," Seth said.

"I'm Darrell." He offered his hand.

Seth's hand disappeared into Darrell's. "I'm Seth. Nice to meet you." The kid looked to his mom for approval at his manners. Pumpkin smiled and winked.

"Are you hungry, Seth?" asked Darrell.

Seth shrugged.

"Well," continued Darrell. "I was gonna take your mom out to dinner. Would you like to go with us?"

Seth looked at Pumpkin. Pumpkin looked at Darrell. "You don't have to do that," she said.

"Why?" Darrell smiled mischievously. "Is he a heavy eater?"

Pumpkin cracked a smile. Darrell's sense of humor improved each day she knew him. Still, she wasn't sure if she should expose her son to her dating life. In the end, Pumpkin threw caution to the wind and they all went out the door.

Darrell had reserved a table at a really nice French restaurant. The menus were the kind that were reprinted every night on expensive card stock. The items were listed in French and the prices were not listed at all. They did not have a kid's menu.

Pumpkin ordered a pasta dish. Darrell ordered a steak dish. Seth had the equivalent of a hamburger. Well, a hamburger that was upscale with French flare. The burger was huge with a beef steak tomato on baguette bread instead of rolls. Like that Cosby Show episode where Cliff took Rudy and her friends to an upscale restaurant. It was the same monster burger with fancy potatoes instead of French fries.

Seth poked at it suspiciously.

"Just try it," Pumpkin urged.

The kid looked doubtful. "I don't think I can fit it in my mouth."

Darrell looked at Pumpkin apologetically. "I can get him something else."

"No, Darrell, really."

"I don't mind. It looks like it'd be great in my lunch tomorrow."

"It looks like something the Gorgon Hound in Beast Quest would eat," said Seth.

"Beast Quest! I can't believe those are still around." Darrell beamed at Seth.

Seth eyed Darrell in a new light. "You read Beast Quest?"

"I read the whole series when I was a kid."

"Really? I'm only on number seventeen."

"Well, I think I may have the books packed away in my attic. I could let you borrow them."

Seth's eyes went wide. The Beast Quest books, which were a re-release of an old series, were now being released every other month. "That would be awesome!"

"I hear you're into chess."

The two launched into a discussion on offensive techniques in the game. Pumpkin didn't bother trying to join in. She was a truly lousy chess player. From time to time, Darrell would glance up at her and smile. She'd smile back.

Darrell and Seth completely hit it off. Pumpkin felt a sense of ease. Maybe Gale was right. Maybe she could have a second chance after all.

Later that night, after Pumpkin ushered Seth inside and closed the door to their apartment behind him, she stood on the threshold and faced Darrell. She had made her decision.

"Thank you," Pumpkin said. "We had a really, really nice time."

"Good..." Darrell's eyes dipped to her lips and then back up. "I'm glad. He's a great kid."

"Yeah, I think I'll keep him."

Darrell chuckled.

Pumpkin waited. She watched Darrell take a deep breath, summon his courage, and lean slowly in.

It was nice, the kiss. His lips were soft, malleable. He pulled away and smiled, pleased with himself. Pumpkin smiled back.

"Good night, Malika."

"Good night, Darrell."

She slept well that night, having made her decision. In the morning, Pumpkin called the school, telling the Front Desk that she would be late, and requested a substitute.

Around 8 a.m., she pulled into the courthouse. It had been raining the last time she was here, too. Seth had been the size of a pea inside her belly.

"May I help you?" asked the clerk behind the desk.

"Yes," Pumpkin said. She took a deep breath. "I'm here to file for divorce."

An hour later, Pumpkin walked into the school feeling empowered. It wouldn't be difficult to get a divorce from Anthony.

He'd abandoned them over three years ago.

Pumpkin doubted she'd have to do much in the way of due diligence in trying to locate him. She wanted this divorce done quickly, and most importantly, quietly. She called herself taking a chance with Darrell, but the truth was that Darrell was taking a chance with her. Only he didn't know it, and Pumpkin intended to keep it that way.

Single mothers weren't exactly a hot commodity in today's dating pool. Add "married" to the single mother title and Pumpkin was sure she swam up stream alone. Darrell was the second chance at happiness that she never expected to get. She'd gone blindly into her relationship with Anthony. Not this time.

She had her eyes wide open with Darrell. He was responsible, smart, kind, and not bad to look at. Darrell wasn't the type to cheat, lie, or steal. And he'd be a good role model to Seth. Yes, this was the sensible choice. Her head knew it and her heart would climb onboard.

Feeling good about her decision and life's new trajectory, Pumpkin walked into her classroom. The first thing she saw was DaeHo and Tyler. Their heads together in a tete-a-tete that was more intimate than academic. At that moment, Tyler looked up. The demon raised one eyebrow in a challenge, and then returned his attention to DaeHo.

"Ms. Tavares," called Mrs. Beard the substitute.

Mrs. Beard was often Pumpkin's sub. She had the unfortunate luck to marry a man named Beard as well as have whiskers growing out of her own chin. Pumpkin used to feel sorry for her.

Used to.

"Is everything okay with your boy?" Mrs. Beard asked.

"He's fine, thank you for asking."

"Such a shame that he doesn't have a father to train him up properly."

"Hmmm," was Pumpkin's noncommittal response. "I've got it from here." Pumpkin side-stepped the older woman before she tried to set her up with her forty-year-old son who had failed to launch from his mom's basement.

Pumpkin set her trajectory for DaeHo and Tyler. DaeHo had her head bent over Tyler's notebook, striking through words on his paper.

"Ms... uh?"

Pumpkin turned and focused on another student. It was Stanley Marshall. The poster child for why, for some, marijuana was a dangerous drug.

"Uh... hey, Ms... uh..."

"What is it Stanley?"

"Huh?"

They both waited for the other to speak.

"Stanley? You had a question." Pumpkin saw his dilated pupils try to focus.

"Oh, yeah," Stanley slurred. "You know that paper about that book that we read?"

"Yes."

They both waited.

"What about it, Stanley?"

"What about what, Ms..."

This was going to take a minute.

"You know, Stanley," Pumpkin steered him toward Tyler and DaeHo. "Why don't you get some help from the T.A."

"The who?"

DaeHo and Tyler looked up at their approach. "The teaching assistant," Pumpkin clarified.

Stanley's dilated pupil tried to focus on DaeHo. "Oh, you mean The Hoe."

"Watch it, stoner."

Pumpkin's head whipped to Tyler.

Stanley seemed to clear up for just a second. "Oh, sorry man."

"Not to me," insisted Tyler. "To her." Tyler inclined his head toward DaeHo.

"Oh, yeah. Sorry Day-Hoo."

Dae gave the pothead a weak smile. "I'll be over to your desk in a second, Stanley."

Stanley nodded and then walked off bewildered.

"If I were you, I would let him fail," said Tyler. Tyler's eyes were intent on Dae.

Dae diverted hers shyly. "It's my job. Besides, if I were that picky I wouldn't be helping you."

Good girl!

"You're too good." Tyler's tone was serious, but his smile rubbed Pumpkin the wrong way, especially when he turned it on her. "Ms. Tavares, I just wanted to thank you for letting Dae help me. She's been instrumental in catching me up."

Pumpkin's smile to the imp was tight. "Don't mention it."

Tyler walked away and Pumpkin turned to Dae. "You're not writing his papers for him, are you?"

"What? Of course not. You're wrong about him. He's smart and he's actually really nice."

"Oh, Dae," Pumpkin sighed. "Guys like Tyler are only nice when they want something. Then, once they get it they abandon you."

DaeHo's chiding turned serious. "Look, Ms. T., I'm doing my job here. I'm not comfortable with you delving into my personal life."

"So you're saying it's gotten... personal?"

"No!" DaeHo shifted uncomfortably. Her eyes ducked away.

Pumpkin followed her gaze to Tyler. He was chatting up two other girls. Pumpkin turned back to say something but the bell rang. Dae grabbed her things and shoved them into her backpack.

"Dae, I'll see you later at the registration booth for Mr. Charmayne?" asked Tyler. He had his hand on the back of one of the girls as they sashayed out the door. The girl turned and frowned at DaeHo. Her eyes, which glanced DaeHo up and down, dismissed Dae as competition, and the girl continued out the door.

Dae put on a smile. "Sure. I'll see you there."

"I can take you, if you'd like."

DaeHo's eyes lit up. "Really? That would be great."

"No, no. Dae, I can take you," Pumpkin said.

DaeHo looked between her teacher and Tyler.

"Well, Ms. T, I really enjoyed what Mr. Charmayne had to say the other day during the rally here, and DaeHo has been telling me about her volunteer work. It all sounds really interesting. I thought I could get involved." He turned back to Dae. "So, I'll meet you in the parking lot after school?"

"Yeah," said Dae. "That would be great."

"Are you headed to the library?" asked Tyler. "I could walk you."

"Oh, sure."

They headed out the door.

But then Tyler turned and waved at Pumpkin. "See ya later, Ms. T," he grinned.

Cheeky spawn!

CHAPTER NINE

PUMPKIN STOOD BEHIND THE VOTER registration booth, but instead of working, she watched DaeHo and Tyler. DaeHo stood on the sidewalk, diligently flagging passersby down, steering them towards the voter registration table. Tyler stood beside Dae watching women walk by, watching cars go by, and watching Dae's backside.

"You know there are daggers shooting out of your eyes right now?"

The market was crowded this warm, sunny afternoon. A light breeze carried both air and sun rays over bare limbs. The shouts of men, squeals of women, and cries of children all blended together like the walla of a sports arena until none were discernible. Yet, that voice found Pumpkin in the cacophony. It coursed through her like an electric charge.

"What did he do?" Manny stood behind her and looked over her shoulder at Tyler.

"Nothing," Pumpkin said. "Absolutely nothing."

Manny turned to face her with that magnetic grin. Every one of Pumpkin's synapses fired with the same instruction: closer.

"And he got away with it? There is no justice in this world."

"That kid's a slacker in school and now he's trying to seduce my teaching assistant."

Manny spied DaeHo and nodded in approval. "She's cute."

"She's smart!" Pumpkin's head whipped around and now her eyes shot daggers at him.

Manny put up his hands to fend off the attack. "So, smart girls are off limits to slackers?"

"Yes," Pumpkin nodded firmly. "I'm sure it's written somewhere."

"You don't think she could rub off on him?"

"I think he's going to veer her off her path and she'll wind up forfeiting all her dreams. Then when he leaves, she'll be left with a broken heart."

Manny's smokey eyes turned to soft wisps. "That what happened to you?"

"Like I said the other day, my heart didn't break," Pumpkin held her head high. Maybe a little too high as she started to feel light-headed from the thin air in the altitude of wounded-pride. "It just confirmed my disbelief in fairytales. It's biologically impossible for ducks to turn into swans. And Prince Charming only marries Cinderella after she wipes off the soot and dresses up in a magic corset with matching shoes."

Pumpkin's breaths were heavy when she finished speaking, like, when you awaken from a nightmare and try to clear your brain; reminding yourself that none of it was real.

"He really messed you up, didn't he?" Manny's voice was gentle. His eyes full of compassion. "Cupid's father?"

There was a moment of silence while Manny studied Pumpkin.

It felt like he was reading her, seeing her past in her words. Pumpkin wanted to close herself off, she felt so exposed. Instead, she balled her left hand into a fist. The fourth finger had been barren for years, but Manny studied her so hard she feared he'd see the ghost of the indent of her ill-fated marriage.

"I don't need rescuing," Pumpkin insisted.

"I don't have a horse," Manny countered.

That startled her. She snorted. Not a dainty intake of breath that hits the back of your throat and makes an unladylike noise. More like a-

"What the hell! Did Eddie Murphy just sneak up on us?"

Pumpkin tried to stop, but she couldn't help it! More sounds erupted from the back of her throat. This time they were no longer snorts, more like wheezing. Like a dying hyena.

Manny doubled over laughing. "I can't even," he said between howls of laughter.

Pumpkin covered her mouth to stop the sounds from coming out. Never in her life had she made sounds like these. Never in her life had anyone made her giddy one moment and ready to flee the next. The polar opposites were taking their toll on her.

Finally, she got herself together with a deep cleansing breath, but Manny grabbed for her hands.

"Come on," he teased, "do it again."

Pumpkin reached out and shoved him in the shoulder with her right hand, putting her left hand behind her back. "Why are you hanging around me? Shouldn't you be out kissing babies or something?" The shove she gave him didn't budge him in the slightest and she wound up stepping into his personal space.

If you've ever played with magnets then you've tried to see how close you could get them while still keeping the two charges apart.

You've felt the two pieces pull to one another as your fingers fought to maintain their distance. That was fun and games. When we were young.

Pumpkin's eyes were level with Manny's mouth. She tried to inch her way back from him. She tucked her chin. She sucked in her gut. The problem was that he wasn't taking any of the same measures. In fact, it looked like he was leaning in. He exhaled and Pumpkin tasted his warm breath on her tongue. The air between them positively pulsed.

"I like hanging around you." He shut his mouth abruptly, as if those words had escaped without his permission and more were close on their heels.

Pumpkin knew she shouldn't look up. Looking up into those gray eyes would be a colossal mistake.

She looked up, and felt pulled in closer.

There was an inch between them. He made no move to close it, but she could tell that he wanted to. Hell, she wanted to. Pumpkin thought he could tell that, too. She saw a vein in his bare bicep twitch, his fingers clench. But he stayed in place. Letting her make the decision on whether to move or not.

Well, he had been letting her make the decision, but now he stepped in. The buckle of his belt brushed the wrist of her right hand. There was an electric charge.

Snap, crackle, pop. Pumpkin jerked her hand up from the metal of his belt and it landed on his warm chest.

"You're so easy to rile up," he said. "I find it endlessly amusing."

Pumpkin swallowed. It was a clear invitation. Her right hand lay on his chest, her left hand hid behind her back. One foot was on the ground, the heel of the other was raised and the ball of her foot poised to move forward. Pumpkin had no place to retreat. She didn't have enough desire to retreat. It was then that her rescue came.

From the corner of her eye, she saw a tight bun headed towards them. A tight bun, on top of a perfectly made-up face, in a designer suite, catwalk strutting in six-inch heels.

The positive charge she'd been feeling turned negative and Pumpkin broke away. Taking a step back she said, "Don't you find Lorielle amusing?"

Manny frowned, his hand still on her elbow. "Lorielle?" A light of mischief rose up in those gray eyes. "She'd never lower herself to snort."

Pumpkin jolted. Her arms wrapped around the loose-fitting, Old Navy t-shirt she'd gotten off the sale rack, and out of his reach. "Oh," she nodded, eyes focused on her scuffed Payless brand flats. "But I would?"

"What?" Manny reached for her elbow, but Pumpkin was beyond his sphere, out of his league. He placed his hands on his hips, knuckles on the waistband of his dark slacks.

The move reminded her of Super Man. Lana Lang had only been temporary in Clark Kent's life. Just someone to pass the time until the heroine made her entrance and captured the hero's unwavering attention.

A wayward curl of hair popped into Pumpkin's eye. She swiped at it uselessly. Terri Hatcher's Lois Lane had perfect hair. So did Margot Kidder in the original movie.

"Why do I feel like we're having two different conversations now?" asked Manny. A smile played on his lips, encouraging her to come back inside his bubble and play. "You know there's nothing wrong with snorting. I'm sure you could be treated for it. One of those infomercial tablets where the contraindications might be worse than the cure." He took another stab at humor, but Pumpkin wasn't playing any longer.

"Am I interrupting something?" Lorielle's hand snaked around Manny's bicep, staking a claim. Pumpkin needed to let her know she wasn't prospecting.

"No—"

"—Yes."

Lorielle looked between Manny and Pumpkin after they'd both spoken at the same time.

"I think Pumpkin might need medical attention," Manny deadpanned. "It appears she suffers from a rare syndrome. Murphyena."

Lorielle's eyes went narrow in dubiety Pumpkin's rolled in ambivalence.

"I do not laugh like a hyena," Pumpkin said. And then she added, "Normally."

"You know, the first step is admitting you have a problem." Manny's eyes pleaded with Pumpkin to play. No longer serious. Just playful Manny.

She didn't take the bait. She couldn't. She looked away.

Manny sighed as though she'd knocked down his playhouse. Pumpkin refused to dwell on the fact that he could read her so well without words. Maybe that was his superpower, reading B-story girls so that he could swoop down and have his way with them until the main attraction arrived. Or maybe that was Pumpkin's kryptonite, being transparent for A-story guys to deduce they could take advantage of her.

"Yeah. Okay." Lorielle turned and stepped into Manny's eye line. "Armand, I thought we were meeting inside the HQ? I just finished a conference call with some potential donors. They've agreed to come to the charity ball this weekend, but they want a face-to-face first."

Manny winced an apology. "Sorry, Lor."

"E-elle," Lorielle smiled tightly.

Manny bowed his head in a mollifying nod. "Sorry, Lorielle. I've been out checking in on staff, meeting potential voters."

Lorielle clicked on her phone, eyes on the screen as she spoke. "Looks like you're fraternizing with the help."

"Pumpkin's a valued member of the staff."

"Who?" Lorielle turned to Pumpkin, but her head was still focused on the screen of her phone. "Oh, the one who's working on the ad? How's that going?"

Pumpkin opened her mouth to speak, but—

"Oh, good," Lorielle turned back to Manny. "They said they can squeeze us in tomorrow morning."

"I can't," said Manny. "I'm meeting the fisherman's union in the morning."

Now, Lorielle looked up. "Why?"

"You said I needed to get bigger endorsements. The fishing industry is a large part of my constituents. They've been hit hard by the hurricanes and the oil spill."

"They don't have much money," Lorielle countered. "Their profit margin has dipped a few points after the oil spill."

Manny opened his mouth to say more, but Lorielle's phone rang. She put up a finger to ward Manny off and turned into the phone. Manny looked at her back as she walked away, a frown on his face.

"She's right, you know," Pumpkin said. "A few big endorsements would basically buy you the election."

"Money doesn't solve problems," said Manny. "People do. If I take their money and turn my back on the people, I'm no better than Whitely."

Manny looked up into the sky, brows drawn in his thinking face. Another person would've lied to get what they wanted, but not this man. He kept defying each of her prejudgments about him. Pumpkin had to remind herself that he wasn't all crowns and carriages.

"So... you're girlfriend's nice."

Manny turned to her and stared. He blinked once, understanding dawning in his light eyes, a sly smile spread across his face. "Lorielle isn't seeing anyone," he took a moment for that to sink in. And then, "In case you're interested."

Pumpkin's eyes went wide. "Me? No... I..."

He chuckled.

Pumpkin reached out to shove him again. "You are such a child!"

Once again her shove did nothing except put her in his personal space. He caught her left hand in his own, cradling her knuckles. His thumb rubbed the center of her palm, tracing the longest of the three lines there. The life-line it was called. He traced it from its beginning to its end once... twice.

"Hey, guys."

They both looked over to see Darrell approach. Pumpkin nearly jumped away but caught herself deciding it was more adult to simply pull her hand away and put her back to Manny. It also looked less guilty. Not that she had done anything wrong. With Manny, at least. Pumpkin's left hand felt swollen and obvious and she hid it in her jean pocket.

When Darrell came up next to her, he didn't appear to notice either her offensive hand or her proximity to Manny.

Darrell leaned forward slightly toward Pumpkin's cheek. Thought better of that and reached his hand out to rub her shoulder. But by then Pumpkin was leaning in. In the end, they exchanged an awkward hug.

"Here you go, Manny." Darrell handed him a package.

Pumpkin felt Manny's eyes on her as he stepped forward and took the package. She didn't look at him.

"Thanks for picking these up D. We were low on fliers."

Darrell turned to Pumpkin and handed her a package as well.

"I brought these for Seth."

They were a bunch of worn, first editions of the Beast Quest chapter book series.

"He's going to flip when he sees these," Pumpkin said. "Thank you, Darrell."

Manny stood by for a second looking between Darrell and Pumpkin. Pumpkin glanced up and their eyes connected briefly. She couldn't tell what passed through Manny's. He'd shuttered them.

Good. He was getting the message.

"I'll catch up with you guys later," Manny finally said, and walked off toward DaeHo and Tyler. When he reached the two, Tyler jolted to action.

The lazy leach.

"I had a really great time the other night," Darrell said.

Pumpkin tore her gaze off Tyler who was now chatting with Manny. "Oh, yeah. Me, too. Monster burger aside, of course."

Darrell frowned. "Monster burger?"

"Never mind."

Tyler laughed at something Manny said.

"I was hoping we could do it again. Maybe just you and me this time... Although Seth is great!"

Now, Manny had a hand on Tyler's arm as if in confidence. Two magnets.

Pumpkin turned and gave Darrell her full attention. "I'll work on getting a sitter."

"Great!" He smiled. "I'm sorry. I have to get back to the office."

He leaned in hesitantly, but this time Pumpkin met him halfway and gave him a quick peck at the corner of his mouth. He smiled down at her again, then walked away.

Pumpkin was quite pleased with herself. At this point in the plot, an underdog heroine would've brushed off the well-meaning nerd and capitulated to the hunky jock character who would lead her on a road toward heartbreak, and a too-late realization. No, thank you! Pumpkin would keep her ducks in a row, her eggs all in one basket. She would not be another cliché.

She spied Gale arriving and sauntered over to her table.

"Hello, dear," Gale greeted her with a welcoming smile.

"Hi, Gale."

"You're looking red today." Gale looked at the space in front of Pumpkin's belly.

"Is that bad?"

"Only for whoever it's directed at," said Gale. "Red is the color that belongs to your root. It's the house of our most base intentions."

"Like anger?"

"Red is not just for anger, dear. It's for passion as well."

Pumpkin looked over at Manny in the distance.

"You don't want any of your colors gone. You just want them all in balance. So that your golden nature can shine through."

"Were you always able to see these things, Gale?"

"The normal spectrum of auras, yes. The gift runs in my family, though sometimes lately it skips a generation." She glanced over at Manny who was still chatting with Tyler. "My father could see auras, and his mother before him. It goes way back to the old country. The Charmayne's were Gypsies. We told people's futures by reading their auras."

"That sounds like a fairytale."

Gale only smiled. "You ever get a feeling about someone? You just know that they will make a great friend, or that they are someone you can't trust."

Pumpkin looked over at DaeHo. She'd liked the young girl on first sight. As she got to know her, Pumpkin saw that they were so very alike. Her eyes shifted over to Tyler, whom she'd had the exact opposite reaction to. Tyler reminded her so much of Anthony that Pumpkin struggled to be civil around the kid.

"When my family got to the new world," Gale said, "we stopped cultivating the talent, and the children stopped seeing. My own sight was weak until I met my true love. That was the first time I saw a golden light."

Gale's eyes went hazy with memory. "I didn't know what it meant, that beautiful golden color. But I knew he was special because most people don't shine gold at their core."

"But you see that in me?"

Gale nodded. "I see it in you and Manny both."

Pumpkin turned once again to look over at Manny and Tyler. Just then, as though he sensed Pumpkin's eyes on him, Manny looked up and smiled at her.

"The shadows are moving away from your heart, dear. Slowly, but they're moving."

Pumpkin smiled weakly at Gale. She wanted to believe her future was grand, but she couldn't shake off her shabby past. More than that, she had no desire to reach high and fall prey to the giants who resided up there.

She'd been on top before. It wasn't all yellow brick roads and crystal coaches.

"I'm just going to go and check on my students."

Gale smiled and nodded. There was a conspiratorial air to her grin. Pumpkin turned and headed over to the others. They were all laughing as she came up.

"Hey, guys," Pumpkin said, unable to hide her suspicion. "What's going on?"

"Oh, hi, Ms. Tavares," said DaeHo. "Mr. Charmayne was just telling us about the underside of high school politics."

"Underside?" Pumpkin asked.

"Yeah," said Tyler, his eyes uncharacteristically bright and alert. "In high school, Mr. C. worked in the Main Office for the administrators that approved and copied student government campaign fliers. He made a little edit to his opponent's flier so that instead of saying "Vote for Troy Cox" it read "View Troy's Cox.""

Pumpkin turned to Manny.

"It's not like I went Tracy Flick on him," Manny said.

Pumpkin couldn't help but crack a smile at the Election movie reference.

"Who's Tracey Flick?" asked DaeHo.

"What are you teaching these kids, Ms. Tavares?"

"I think what you did was pretty bad ass," grinned Tyler.

Pumpkin's head whipped around to the boy like she was his mother. Well, maybe his Guidance Counselor.

"It didn't end well for me though, Tyler." Manny jumped in before Pumpkin could chastise Tyler.

"You won the election," said Tyler.

"Well, yes." Manny glanced over at Pumpkin.

Pumpkin decided to make use of their non-verbal communication abilities. Her eyebrows rose, trying to tell him to figure out a consequence to his actions.

"I got a hefty punishment," said Manny, "and in the end I learned my lesson." It was more of a question aimed at Pumpkin than a statement to Tyler.

"Which was?" Tyler's voice was a challenge directed more at Pumpkin than Manny.

Manny thought on this for a second, obviously caught in the headlights, trying to make a lesson out of his intended sabotage.

"I think the point is that Mr. Charmayne has figured out that he has to use more than his wit to win a campaign."

They all turned to look at DaeHo.

"He has a solid, fiscally responsible, and socially conscious platform that will help him win," DaeHo continued. "And you won't always win if you don't play fair."

"People don't always play fair," said Tyler.

On that Pumpkin could agree, just look at her cousins, and her soon to be ex-husband.

"But you're a decent guy, Tyler," DaeHo said. "A good guy."

Both Tyler and Pumpkin's eyebrows rose at this.

"You are," Dae insisted. "Which is why you're going to help Mr. Charmayne in his campaign, because he's a good guy, too, and he can actually do something to change things."

Manny smiled at this. "Well, thank you, DaeHo."

"You're welcome. Now, come on Tyler. Let's get back to passing out fliers. And this time, it would be more helpful if you actually handed out the fliers instead of checking out every woman who walks by." DaeHo tilted her head at Tyler and turned on her heel.

Tyler smiled after her and followed. Then he actually started handing out fliers and engaging people. Pumpkin stared in awe after them.

"I don't think he's as terrible as you think."

Pumpkin blinked. "Who?"

Manny grinned at her dumbfounded expression. "Tyler. I think he's a good kid, too. He just needs some direction."

"From the devil, so he can get back to where he came from."

Manny gave her a dramatic gasp. "Ms. Tavares! Aren't you supposed to be leading the next generation onward?"

"I... don't know what I'm doing teaching. It's not where I'm supposed to be." Where did that come from? Maybe all the talk with his aunt was really getting to her.

"Where are you supposed to be?"

Pumpkin looked into those gray eyes. There was open curiosity and genuine interest. "I was supposed to be a screenwriter. I even won an award for one of my scripts. It was for a teen drama about a young girl. She was an oracle who was meant to save the human race from enslavement by computer programs, but she fell in love with one of the cyborgs."

"That sounds like a really good story. Did it get made?"

"Sort of."

"You know," Manny looked off into the clouds with what Pumpkin now called his thinking face. "It sounds like that movie that came out a few years ago. What was it?"

She didn't answer. She waited to see if he'd make the connection.

"Oh yeah, The Source Code." He smiled, proud of his memory. "Only that movie was more about a young man as a hero. The man was the savior of the human race, not a young girl. But there was an oracle in it, too."

"Yeah..." The original story had been about a strong, idealistic young woman who would be the savior. Pumpkin should have known that kind of story wouldn't fly in Hollywood. Her heroine had been reduced to a helpless pawn and the male lead had been pushed forward to take all the credit.

"It sounds like you have real talent, Pumpkin. Have you written anything else?"

"No, not really." Pumpkin had tons of stories, but they all stayed safe in her head now. She no longer committed her ideas to paper where they could be taken away from her.

"So," Manny hedged. "You and Darrell?"

"Yeah. Me and Darrell."

"You find him endlessly amusing?"

"I... He and I are on the same storyline."

Manny looked Pumpkin straight in the eye. His pupils roving hers in minute flicking motions like a sensor trying to detect... something. "I should've called dibs." There was a mix of humor and disappointment in his voice.

Pumpkin stood by speechless.

Manny grinned, it was the wolfish grin. A second later, he released her from observation. But then he paused, and looked at her once more. No, not at her. In front of her like his aunt always did.

"What?" Pumpkin brushed at her shirt.

Manny shook his head. "Nothing," he frowned.

"Have you ever seen auras? Like your aunt?"

Manny chuckled uncertainly, then gave a firm shake of his head. "No. It looks like I didn't get the gift. Auntie Gale said I could see when I was a kid. But I don't remember. It's supposed to come back when I meet..." He stopped and looked away.

"When you meet who?"

Manny turned back, a hesitant smile on his lips. "The One." His smile faltered as he squinted at Pumpkin once more.

Pumpkin held perfectly still. She held her breath for a reason she would not name. And then the moment was gone. Manny's grin was back in place, playful once more.

"It's family folklore," he said. "Likely my ancestors' version of abstinence for their hormonal teenagers."

"I suppose that didn't work on you."

Manny burst into laughing. He shook his head in response. Then he sobered. "It's time I stop believing in fairytales, too."

Manny now stood a respectable distance from Pumpkin. Not close enough to tempt a charge.

"I'll see you around," he said.

He departed with a friendly nod. Friendly, playful, without advance, and no positive charge.

CHAPTER TEN

MANNY THRUMMED HIS FINGERS ON his steering wheel as he eyed the zooming cars zipping down the highway in the single-file, fast lane. Just one lane to the right, he felt like he was sitting in a metaphor; stuck standing still while the partnered people in the HOV got all the breaks.

Preston Whitely still killed him in the polls by running that family ad day in and out.

Manny had been surrounded by couples his whole life. His parents, aunts and uncles, most of his cousins, all were partnered up and moving along at the speed of life. He'd dated more women than he could remember, rarely spent a night by himself, but he'd always felt alone. Stuck, standing still, and waiting for the signal to move over into the next lane.

Up ahead a flash of garish orange caught his attention. The color and shape reminded him of a pumpkin. And then he saw her.

The traffic edged closer to the orange car. He saw a puff of smoke come from the hood. A pair of legs stuck partway out of the vehicle. The legs straightened and the full length of Pumpkin Tavares emerged from the car. She was dressed in casual slacks that fit snuggly over her ample ass and a loose fitting shirt that, sadly, hid the curves of her breasts.

Manny steered his Mustang over to the shoulder, ignoring the blares of angry horns.

"Pumpkin?" he called from the driver's window.

She turned around, startled. "Hi."

They stared at each other for a moment.

"Is everything all right?" Manny asked.

"Oh, yeah," she shrugged. "Fine. My car is just letting off some steam."

Manny chuckled. He put his car in park, brushed a hand down his unwrinkled, finely tailored suit, and stepped out of his car. When he strode toward her, she backed away, out of his reach. The palms of his hands began to itch.

"What are you doing here?" Pumpkin asked.

"I have to give a speech at the Fisherman's Union."

"Mama, is everything okay?" a small voice called from the back seat. Manny peered inside and saw Little Cupid.

"Yeah, sweetie." Pumpkin rubbed her fingers over her temple. "I've got it all under control."

As if on cue, the car coughed up more smoke.

Manny walked around to the back of the car and lifted the hood. More smoke billowed.

"There were no indications of anything going wrong," Pumpkin joined him. "The check engine light was off. I changed the oil exactly when the sticker told me to. There's over half a tank of gas left. She was running perfectly up until this very moment. She's always gotten me exactly where I needed to be."

"Mama, I'm gonna be late," her son called from the back seat. There was panic in the kid's voice as he clutched a cardboard box to his small chest.

"I'm sorry, sweetie, I'm doing the best I can."

"Have you called your road-side-assistance service?" asked Manny.

"No, I was hoping the car would get over its tantrum and start working again."

Manny grinned. Then he ducked his head under the hood before asking his next question. "You call Darrell?"

Radio silence crackled beside him. He snuck a glance at her. The look on her face told him that the thought of calling Darrell for help never entered her mind. He wondered if she would have called anyone for help if he hadn't happened upon her.

Manny straightened and shut the hood. "Give road-side-assistance a call while we drop Cupid off at school in my car. You have to be here when they come to tow it?"

"Yes, but you have your speech. I don't want you to be late."

"I'm not leaving you two on the side of the road. I'll let the union know I'm running late."

Pumpkin hesitated.

"You know," said Manny, "I've got a ton of quips ready about how this is not a rescue, and you're an independent woman who 'don't need no man' and all that." He snapped his fingers in time to each word. "But the fact is you'd really be helping me out. See, I have this really fast car and I never get to drive in the fast lane because I'm usually on my own."

Pumpkin rolled her eyes ready to deliver a witty comeback. But then her eyes landed on the panicking boy clutching his project in the back seat of her smoking car. "Okay, fine. Let's HOV it."

Manny's eyes wrinkled with mirth. "Oh, that was just awful. You must've been a dramatic screenwriter, not a comedic one."

They piled into his Mustang and took off. Pumpkin called her school and let them know she was having car trouble. Then she called a tow service who said they'd be able to come out in ninety minutes.

"Cool project," Manny observed.

"It's a solar oven," said the boy, who introduced himself as Seth. "I used it to bake cookies."

"You made food in that?" Impressed, Manny's voice rose an octave.

"Yes," Seth pulled out the plastic baggy of chocolate chip cookies. "It took an hour but I was able to save energy and reduce my carbon footprint."

"Wow... that's... Wow. I was on volcanoes at your age," offered Manny.

They pulled into Seth's school moments later. Pumpkin got out and walked her son to the door, his little legs scurrying ahead of his mom to get to his classroom and show his work.

Manny toyed with the cellphone in his hand. He knew Darrell wasn't in the office yet. His friend's hours typically had him in between 9 a.m. and 10 a.m. Manny could call Darrell and hand Pumpkin over so that he could get to his meeting on time. After all, it was the union he was trying to impress.

The door to the school opened. Manny pocketed his phone.

"You still have over an hour before they come to pick up your car," he said.

Pumpkin opened her mouth to assure him that—

"I'm not leaving you alone on the side of the road. You're just going to have to play the part of damsel for an hour."

She shook her head. "That's not the role I'm meant for."

"Pumpkin, everyone needs a helping hand now and then." He held his hand out for her, to hand her into the car.

She surprised him by actually obliging and putting her hand in his. The itch in his hand went away and was replaced by a tingling buzz. So, he was attracted to the woman. He wouldn't deny it. He placed his other hand at the small of her back, and delivered her into the vehicle. She tucked herself into the bucket seat.

Manny shut her door and climbed into the driver's side. "So, if you're not a damsel, then what are you?"

"I'm a B girl."

"Like break-dancer?"

The car's engine roared to life, the sound like stallions rearing up on their hind legs.

"No, a B-storyline is the secondary story in a movie. It's a subplot usually featuring a supporting character."

"You're a supporting character? In whose story?"

"Yours, of course. Face it, Manny. You're the hero of this story."

"I wasn't aware I had been cast," Manny laughed. He pulled onto the highway and slipped easily into the fast lane.

"This is totally your story," she said. "Armand Charmayne, along with an untried group of volunteers, fights to win the mayoral seat against the corporate machine."

"I like this movie."

"Of course, you do. You're the star: handsome, strong, charismatic." Pumpkin paused before allowing the next words out. "And you're very generous."

"You say that like it's a bad thing."

"No," she shook her head. "Just unexpected."

"Because I'm wealthy."

Pumpkin turned to him. Manny's fingers clenched hard on the

steering wheel trying to calm the itch that rose once more.

"No," she said. "I wasn't talking about your money. You flit around the community trying to save everyone just because you think it's the right thing to do. That's your super power."

"Yeah," Manny sighed. "That is a pretty awesome power."

"You say that like it's a bad thing," she mimicked.

Manny shrugged as he signaled out of the fast lane. "It's just... sometimes being a hero isn't all it's cracked up to be. You do all this amazing work for others, you are put on a pedestal, and you're all by yourself up there. There're not many people like you. Not many people understand the hero. Not many people care to. They just want the work done, the miracle performed."

Manny wondered if she noted the change from the first person "I" statements to the second person "You" statements as he spoke. In the few conversations they'd had, Pumpkin had changed his perspective on things.

"You're not alone," she said. "You have supporting characters."

"Like you?"

"Yes," she nodded. But then quickly continued. "Me. And Darrell. And your aunt." She rubbed her arms. "And Lorielle and the whole staff."

It was a crisp Autumn morning. The sun was out, but a light breeze wafted through the air.

"Are you cold?" Manny used one hand to reach into the back and grab a thin jacket. He handed it to her. He didn't fail to notice that she inhaled deeply. She was probably sniffing it to make sure it was clean, but still, the thought of Pumpkin inhaling his scent forced him to shift in his seat.

"Better?" he asked.

She dropped the fabric. "Yes, thank you."

Manny shifted again. "You said that you and Darrell are on the same plot line."

"We're the subplot characters, the B-story. We have a bit of backstory, but only so much as it ties into your storyline. Darrell was your doctor and he's involved in the community you're trying to affect. I add a bit of dimension to you because I've challenged your worldview. I'm like the best friend the main character calls on as a sounding board."

Manny pulled into the union's parking lot and put the car in park. She sure did challenge his worldview. But—

"Best friend," he said. "In most movies doesn't the hero see that he wants the best friend who understands him and has always been there for him?"

Pumpkin shook her head, avoiding his eyes. "I learned a long time ago that I'm not A-story material."

"I think you sell yourself way too short, Pumpkin."

"No, I tested the theory. My... Seth's dad was an A-story kind of guy. At least he appeared that way in the beginning. I cast him wrong."

"What happened there?"

"It was just so clichéd, that relationship. Good girl falls for bad boy."

"You, I assume were the good girl."

"Ha ha," she deadpanned.

"Darrell's a good guy." Manny picked at a non-existent spec of dirt on his suite.

"Yeah, he is." Pumpkin became incredibly interested in her nail polish.

"You know, I talked to that kid you were about to murder the other day."

"Who? Tyler?"

"Yeah, that one."

"I wasn't going to murder him. I don't think..."

"He's a good kid."

"That's only because you haven't asked him to do anything."

"Actually, I did," said Manny. "Apparently, he's good with computers and web design. So, I asked him to help with my campaign web site."

"Get an under construction banner ready."

"Hey, aren't teachers supposed to inspire the young to greatness?"

Pumpkin looked over at him with her eyebrows raised. "Have you met kids from this generation? They have this sense of entitlement and no work ethic."

"I met DaeHo."

"Well, she's an exception."

"I think the two of them, Tyler and DaeHo, are good together. They balance each other out."

Pumpkin turned to him in absolute horror. "No. Absolutely not. I just told you that whole myth of good girls and bad boys getting together and working like a yin-yang team is complete bull. He'll only bring her down."

Manny shrugged. "Maybe you've cast him wrong."

Before she could respond, he opened the door and got out of the car.

They were greeted at the door by a man who looked like he'd walked out of Moby Dick. He had on a navy blue pea-coat with a gold seal. His beard was a mixture of salt and pepper, his skin varnished black.

"Mr. Jackson?" asked Manny.

The old man nodded. "Mr. Charmayne, so nice to meet you."

Manny stuck out his hand and gave a vigorous shake. "Thank you so much for taking the time and allowing me to come speak."

"Well, we are hoping you'll hear what we have to say after you speak." Mr. Jackson turned to Pumpkin. "And this is your wife?"

"No, no," she said, a bit too vehemently for Manny's tastes. "I'm not his wife. He just rescued me. Well, not rescued, because I'm independent. I mean, I'm his support."

Both men looked at her as she rambled on. Mr. Jackson in confusion. Manny, in amusement. She was too adorable when she got flustered. Her lips kept working, alternately forming words and getting caught between her teeth. Manny wanted to catch her bottom lip with his tongue. Instead, he cleared his throat.

"Mr. Jackson, this is one of my PR staff members, Malika Tavares."

Mr. Jackson stuck out his barnacly hand and engulfed hers. "It's nice to meet you Ms. Tavares."

Mr. Jackson released her hand and led them down a hallway. Manny bumped his shoulder against Pumpkin's as they walked down the hallway. When she glanced over, he tried to keep a straight face. She rolled her eyes and bumped him back. They went back and forth like two children for a couple of steps until Mr. Jackson looked back at them with a crooked smile.

Manny straightened up. He probably should stop playing around with her. But on second thought, they were friends now. Best friends, she'd assigned them. Might was well act the part.

The room they entered looked out onto the docks where a number of boats swayed in the water. On the walls hung pictures of men in fishing boats from way back when. All of them brown-skinned.

"We are an old organization," said Mr. Jackson. "One of the first to unionize."

The pictures told the story. There were black and white prints where you could see men in boats wearing overalls and working with crude tools and rickety boats. Gradually the pictures went from sepia to full Technicolor, and the tools and boats became more modern.

"How have you faired since the storm?" Pumpkin asked.

"The last storm took much from us," Mr. Jackson smiled sadly at her. "The oil spill nearly wiped us out. Fishing is one of the largest industries in the state, but my men can't work until the waters are clean. My men want to get back on the waters, but we don't see any progress in the clean-up process. I believe that Charmayne Industries has been placed in charge of the funds given by the government for the clean-up process." Mr. Jackson glanced over at Manny. The look was more an admonition from an old grandfather than a dig from a disenfranchised fisherman.

Manny met his gaze. "I'm not much involved in the corporate dealings of Charmayne Industries. My life has been spent working for the Charmayne Foundation. My belief is that we need to protect our natural resources as well as our people. Regardless of whether I'm elected or not, I promise you that I will look into this matter."

Mr. Jackson nodded. "I'm glad to hear it, son. We think more can and should be done."

"I'm ready and willing to listen to all suggestions, Mr. Jackson."

Mr. Jackson stopped before a door, appraising Manny. Manny held his gaze. He saw the wheels turning in Mr. Jackson's old eyes. Manny felt a sense of pride at the spot where they landed.

"I do think I believe you will," was Mr. Jackson's verdict.

They entered through another door. It was a conference room. All of the seats were taken, and many people were standing. It took

Manny by surprise, the number of people who were there. He was used to boards being a small number of people, not having everyone involved. He paused in his stride for just a second, causing Pumpkin to bump into him. Their bodies touched. Her breasts to his broad shoulders. Their hands met somewhere in the middle. And there it was again; that spark of electricity, like the humming "om" of peace.

A wave of comfort washed over him, of rightness. He looked back at her, expecting, hoping... but no. He was met with a smile. No light. Just belief. Pumpkin believed in him. Believed he had the words, the ability to do what was right. More than anything Manny didn't want to disappoint her.

He did it before he'd even decided he would do it. Manny entwined his fingers with hers and gave her hand a gentle squeeze. Their eyes locked for a second. Pumpkin returned his gentle squeeze. He let go and strode forward. She stayed behind, at the side of the stage.

Manny addressed the crowd with what could have been called his stump speech. He would be a voice for the unheard. He could get inside the system and work to change it so that it was fair for all. It brought to mind DaeHo's impassioned explanation to Tyler the other day. Manny talked about his privileged upbringing, that there was enough to go around. Which made him remember the first time he met Pumpkin outside of DFACS.

He called to mind their conversation earlier in the car. She'd likened him to a hero fighting without a mask or a cape. His greatest strength... his strong belief. Manny did believe what he was saying. He believed it was possible. And slowly, these people began to believe him, too. Most of them.

"Why should we believe you," one man shouted. "Preston Whitely came in here five years ago, got our votes, got into office, and then forgot about us. Ya'll all the same."

For a second, Manny was lost. Like back outside the DFACS when he tried to convince Pumpkin of the benefits of a tempestuous social system. Like backstage at the high school where he'd tried to convince her that everyone would have more than one go, more than one shot at their heart's desire. She hadn't believed him then. Truthfully, he'd been a flounder in a sea of doubt since.

"That's not Mr. Charmayne."

Everyone turned to stare at the owner of the voice.

"He told me the same spiel when I met him," Pumpkin continued. "It sounded like a fairytale: there's enough for everyone, we should all share and get along. The thing is, not only does he believe it, he lives it.

"He's got money. He could live comfortably doing nothing for the rest of his life. Or working for his family. But he's out here doing the work. He listens to people, thinks about what they say..."

Here she stumbled for a minute, her eyes connecting with his. Manny's entire body itched to pull her to him. But she looked away from him, and went on.

"Preston Whitely has corporate sponsors backing him. But Manny, Mr. Charmayne, he's got people backing him. If he says he's going to do it, he does it. That's why I support him. And that's why you should, too."

Everyone paused and considered those words, her words, the words of his supporting character. Suddenly the room broke out in applause.

Manny went to her then. Stood beside her and pulled her into his side. She fit perfectly. His arm slid around her waist to rest at the small of her back. The smile on her lips was uncertain. He was tempted, to lean down and crush them with certainty.

Instead, he dipped his head and spoke into her ear. "Pumpkin, you're my hero." She may not have been bathed in a golden light, but Manny felt a connection to this woman.

A flash of yellow light blinded them both. Manny put up his hands reflexively to protect Pumpkin.

"Is this your new girlfriend, Mr. Charmayne?" The photographer took another photo, the flash blinding Manny once more, stunning him before he could gather his wits to speak.

A bark of laughter sounded beside him.

"Don't be ridiculous." Pumpkin laughed, stepping away from his side. "I'm just a volunteer. And I have a boyfriend. Well, he's not my boyfriend yet. But I'm dating him. Someone else, not Mr. Charmayne, I mean."

Manny watched her fluster, and inside he felt a flutter of something. What was so ridiculous about her dating him? He looked up at the reporter. The man's camera was holstered, his pen and pad now aimed at Manny waiting for comment. The whole room seemed to wait. He looked over at Pumpkin who appeared to shrink under the scrutiny. She'd said earlier that she didn't need to be rescued, but her eyes begged a different story.

"Malika Taveres is a very talented and valued member of my team. As for my social life, it revolves around the campaign at this moment. I don't have time to devote to any one person as I'm fully committed to winning this seat and serving all the people of this great community."

The reporter went on to ask Manny a slew of other questions. Manny answered them all with carefully prepared statements that Lorielle had drilled into him. From the side of his eye, he noticed that Pumpkin had slipped away from his side and into the back of the room. He stood in the middle of the room alone. His side felt cold.

He watched as Pumpkin looked around the room, her arms crossed over her middle, one hand subconsciously rubbing at her elbow. She pulled her lower lip into her mouth as she looked down and shuffled her feet. Then she looked up, directly at him.

When she looked at Manny, her entire expression changed. Her arms came away from her middle and her back straightened. She let go of her bottom lip and smiled at him. It was a small smile on her lips, but it was genuine. That up-tilt of her lips spoke of allegiance, certainty. Manny felt warmed through. He turned back to the room, abandoned Lorielle's notes and spoke from the heart. When he finished, the reporter took a photo of Manny shaking the hand of Mr. Jackson, whose union pledged to endorse the Charmayne campaign.

CHAPTER ELEVEN

"THERE'S NOTHING WRONG WITH IT, ma'am." The burly mechanic rolled his eyes at Pumpkin for the third time.

This was one job she wished Anthony was still around for, dealing with mechanics, construction workers, or handy-men, or any male-dominated field where they could use their knowledge to make women feel small.

After the union meeting, Pumpkin and Manny had shared a quiet ride back to her car. The silence between them reminded Pumpkin of her favorite comforter. It felt like a warm, sweet spot that she didn't want to leave. But all too soon, they were back at her car where the tow service arrived just a moment later.

Manny gave her his cell phone number and made her promise to call and let him know if she needed him to get Seth from school, or if she needed a ride home after visiting the mechanic. She took down his number and shoved the scrap of paper deep into the recesses of her purse, where she'd have to dig if she ever needed it. Manny climbed into his white Mustang and rode off into the sun.

And now she stood before the mechanic in front of her purring car. Pumpkin narrowed her eyes at the fickle vehicle. She took great care of it and it had never given her problems before. With this mild tantrum over, she grabbed her keys from the annoyed mechanic and got behind the wheel.

She ran a couple of errands now that her day was free. Three-o-clock came quickly, though, and she hit the road to get Seth. That's when she noticed that she still wore Manny's jacket. She hadn't called him to let him know the car was okay.

An image of him worrying over her popped into her mind. She wanted to doubt that he'd given her another thought, but everything she'd witnessed from him in the short time that she'd known him told her otherwise. Instead of digging into the recesses of her purse, she found herself in the market district without remembering how she got there. She figured she'd just stop by the campaign headquarters, return the jacket, and let Manny know she was fine.

Pumpkin and Seth climbed the stairs to the campaign headquarters. A few volunteers she knew came out of the door as she climbed the lasts few steps. They exchanged quick greetings and then she made her way into the offices. The first person she saw was Gale.

Gale met Pumpkin's eyes with a bright smile. "You're radiant!"

"Really? I've had a pretty crappy day. My car broke down, but your nephew showed up and rescued me."

Gale raised her finger, pointing it skyward. "That explains it."

"Explains what?"

"He was pretty golden this morning, too."

Pumpkin's heart kicked her chest cavity. Was Gale trying to say that both she and Manny had golden glows because of each other? Maybe Gale could see that, but didn't Manny have to in order for it to mean something. And he didn't see that in Pumpkin.

Which was fine. Because she was seeing Darrell and focused on legally excising Anthony from her life. Pumpkin knew Manny liked her. They got along so well. Better than she got along with anyone.

Just then, the door to Manny's private office opened. He spoke quietly with someone behind the door. Pumpkin saw a tall woman in a tight dress. The young woman oozed money and class. Her smile was an invitation and her hands tapped Manny's chest, looking for a place to stake a claim.

"I don't think that bit of gold you saw in him had anything to do with me," Pumpkin said to Gale.

The woman's hands now climbed up to Manny's neck and tugged his head down for a kiss. The move caught Manny by surprise but he didn't resist. The two of them were picture perfect. They made a much better picture than he and Pumpkin made when they were taken by surprise by the reporter at the Fisherman's Union. She'd backed away from his spotlight not wanting to tarnish any of his shine.

"Ahem" Gale cleared her throat.

When Manny looked up, his eyes immediately caught Pumpkin's. She looked away.

"Hey, Pumpkin. Hi, Seth."

"Hi, Mr. Charming," said Seth.

"It's Charmayne, honey," Pumpkin corrected.

Manny chuckled. "I get that a lot."

"Don't encourage him," said Gale.

"Well, he is charming." That came from the woman still attached to Manny's arm.

"Aunt Gale, Pumpkin, this is Sophia Satterfeld. Her father is Chairman of the board at Charmayne Industries."

Sophia gave a polite nod of deference, but didn't extend her hand.

Pumpkin extended her hand with Manny's jacket in it. "Um, Manny, you forgot your jacket this morning."

Sophia's eyes narrowed on Pumpkin.

"Oh, no, no," Pumpkin backed away. "He picked me up on the street."

Now, one of Sophia's perfectly plucked eyebrows rose.

"I wasn't on the street —like street walking. I was on the side of the road."

Now both of Sophia's eyebrows rose.

Oh, god! Why could she not shut up? Pumpkin looked over at Manny for help. He watched her gleefully, barely holding in his laughter. He reached out his hand and took the jacket.

"Thank you, Pumpkin," Manny said with mischief in his gray eyes. "This morning was amazing. I've never gotten a woman to the place she needed to be so fast before."

Playfully, Manny peered out at Pumpkin. He'd fed her a line. His gray eyes had no doubt Pumpkin could take it and run with it, just like a good little sidekick.

A wave of adrenalin rushed through Pumpkin's brain at the invitation to play her part in his story. A myriad of lines from a hundred movies went through her head as she watched the quirk of Manny's lips, anticipating what she would say.

"That's life in the fast lane," Pumpkin began innocently. "But I don't believe that was the first time you took a girl shopping on Rodeo Drive to cover up her hooker clothes?"

The side of Manny's mouth trembled, and then quaked. His laughter burst forth.

Pumpkin couldn't help but join him, pleased at her own performance.

From the side, she saw Seth eying them quizzically, as he often did adults who made no sense to him. Gale watched with a wise smile, like she knew something they didn't, and was quite pleased with the knowledge. Sophia, however, was not pleased.

"It's a reference to the movie Pretty Woman," Pumpkin said after she gathered herself enough to speak coherently. "When Richard Gere's character takes Julia Roberts out shopping after the snobby sales women were mean to her."

Sophia looked Pumpkin over from head to toe as though she found her current wardrobe wanting.

Pumpkin sobered. "My car broke down," she admitted. "And Manny happened to pass by. We were able to get into the fast lane because there were two of us in his car. Nothing happened between us. I went to the Fisherman's Union with him until the mechanic came."

"The Fisherman's Union?" Sophia said. "What were you doing there?"

Manny's expression turned wary as he now sobered from playtime. "I sought their endorsement."

"But they're in direct opposition to Charmayne Industries over the oil spill."

Manny nodded. "I'm looking to serve the entire community. That means I have to look out for everyone's interest. I can't take sides."

"Taking sides is exactly what politics is all about," said Sophia.

"That's not what it's supposed to be about." Pumpkin closed her eyes since she couldn't keep her mouth shut.

When she opened them again, Sophia Satterfeld had turned her disapproving glare onto Pumpkin. Everyone in the room looked at her with interest.

"Well... it's true," Pumpkin said. "The original purpose of politics was for people to be able to collectively achieve goals. It's the leaders who are supposed to act as the bridge between."

The entire room went silent.

"Well said, Pumpkin," Manny grinned. "I hope that's going in my ad."

Right, his ad. That she was supposed to write in order to help him advance in the polls. Pumpkin had seen Preston Whitely's ad that tore Manny apart for his youth and single status. She'd been thrown into the role of ad writer, yet she hadn't picked up a pen or sat at a word processor in years. She had to tell him that she wasn't the person for the job. But when she opened her mouth to speak, her phone rang.

"Um, excuse me." Pumpkin stepped away, placing the phone to her ear. "Aunt Verne?"

"Pumpkin?" LaVerne sounded taken aback by Pumpkin's voice.

"Yeah, it's me, Aunt Verne. Did you mean to call LaTom or LaRon?"

"No, I just thought you were working and I'd get your voicemail."

The silence seemed to hang there like an accusation. And then Pumpkin felt like she could read the future. She knew what was coming next.

"Look, Pumpkin. Something just came up..."

Pumpkin stopped listening. She'd heard this spiel too many times before. She didn't know why she'd even bothered asking her aunt to babysit for her date tonight. No one in her family ever came through for her.

Pumpkin hung up the phone a moment later. Her face must've looked the way she felt because Manny looked up from his tense conversation with Sophia Satterfeld.

"Pumpkin? Is everything okay?" His face was full of concern.

So, was Gale's.

Sophia's was annoyed.

"Yeah, my aunt just cancelled on me for my date tonight with Darrell."

Manny reached out and rubbed her arm. "I'm sorry."

Pumpkin had to stop her feet from moving into the comfort of his broad chest. "It's not your fault. It's mine for asking my family. They're not the most dependable bunch."

"No, I mean I'd help you if I could," Manny said, "but I'm having dinner with donors tonight."

Manny looked at her earnestly. Pumpkin wasn't used to having people offer their assistance. She didn't know how to respond. "Thanks." It came out with an uncertain question mark dangling on the end.

"You sound surprised," he grinned. "What kind of hero would I be if I didn't support my sidekick?"

Manny's arm was still at her elbow, his grip warm and gentle, a comfort. He smiled at her and she felt cocooned in that cloudy gaze.

"I'm not busy." They both turned to Gale. "As long as Seth doesn't mind helping me mix up a dragon-slaying brew."

Seth's eyes went wide, and then narrowed in suspicion. "There're really no such things as dragons."

Now, Gale narrowed her eyes at him. "Really?"

Seth inhaled loudly, his eyes going wide once more. "Mama, can Ms. Gale please come over, please?"

An hour later, Gale was propped on Pumpkin's bed while she modeled a series of dresses.

"Earth tones are your colors, dear." The latest dress was a sweater dress that was a muted orange. It came down to just above her knees.

"Black heels or brown?" Pumpkin asked.

"Let's see one of each."

Pumpkin was having a great time. She'd often watched LaTom and LaRon get ready to go out, but the amount of make-up they put on and the little bit of clothing they wore out of the house never really inspired her to ask for their advice, and they never offered. This was the first time Pumpkin had actually gotten ready for a date with another woman's help.

"Auntie Gale!" Seth came in out of breath. "We don't have fresh basil leaves, but we do have crushed dried basil." He held up a spice jar. "Will that work?"

"That's actually better because we were going to have to crush the basil ourselves. Dragons smell the fresh leaves from miles away, but when you let it dry and crush it up it's harder for them to detect."

"Okay, okay," Seth held up the list of ingredients for the dragon-slaying elixir.

Gale had said it was an ancient potion, but it was written on the back of a memo pad page from Manny's campaign office.

Seth ticked items off using his fingers. "I just have oregano, garlic, and parsley left. Oh, wait. Mama, aren't I allergic to garlic?"

"No, sweetheart, that's your dad. You're allergic to nuts."

"Great!" Seth took off again.

"Gale, are you two making spaghetti sauce?"

"It's my mother's secret sauce. So, you should feel privileged."

Pumpkin burst into laughter.

"The black ones," Gale pointed to a kitten-heeled pair of black shoes. "Unless you have a brown belt. Then I would say the brown ones."

Pumpkin turned into her closet. It was mostly work blouses and casual pants with a couple of dress pants and a few dresses. "No, no brown belt."

Pumpkin slipped on the second black shoe and sat down at the vanity mirror. Her make-up holdings were just as scarce as her closet collection. She opened an eyeliner pen and began drawing a line. From the mirror's reflection, Pumpkin saw Gale frowning.

"No, no dear. You need to put the eye shadow on first. Here let me." Gale took the pen and reached for the shadow, smiling. "Didn't your mother teach you how to put on make-up?"

"No, she passed away when I was very young."

"Oh, I'm sorry dear."

"I could tell you any fact you need to know academically, but there are a lot of gaps in my social education."

"Like what?"

Pumpkin closed her eyes as Gale started to apply the shadow. "Like dating, for one. I didn't know how to spot the frogs from the princes."

"Seth's dad was a frog?"

"Warts and all, but I kept on kissing him."

"You think your mom could've steered you clear of him?"

"I'd like to think so."

Maybe it was because Pumpkin had her eyes closed as Gale applied the shadow that she was being so open. Maybe it was just because it was Gale, and Pumpkin found her so easy to talk to.

"I think I just wanted so badly to be loved," Pumpkin continued. "My aunt and cousins... they made it very clear that I was an unwelcome guest, a freeloader who was infringing on their lives. I just wanted to belong somewhere, to someone.

"Anthony, that's Seth's dad, he was needy. But I didn't understand that was a bad thing; a red flag that a mother would've caught. Or so I'd like to think. I bent over backwards trying to keep him happy. And sure enough, he walked all over me until he walked out the door."

Pumpkin opened her eyes. She no longer expected to see pity when she talked to Gale or Manny. They both seemed to understand her.

"I know you think Darrell is me settling for... a less vibrant aura. But he's a decent person. He's honest and he's kind. And really, Gale, I don't have many options as a single mother. I can make this work."

Gale put the top on Pumpkin's eye shadow. "You can't make a thing work when you're hiding something else, dear."

The older woman said she wasn't psychic. She said she only saw auras. But she had seen the muddy colors Anthony left on Pumpkin's aura. Perhaps she also saw their marital ties, as frayed and weak as they were.

"You think there's someone else?" Pumpkin held her breath and waited for Gale's response. Their eyes caught in the mirror's reflection.

The doorbell rang and Gale released Pumpkin from her gaze. Pumpkin left her bedroom with a clouded mind, shaky legs, and a heavy heart.

Gale did Pumpkin up pretty good, enough so that when she opened the door to Darrell, he took a moment to glance her up and down before greeting her with words. They left Gale and Seth to mix potions in the kitchen. Potions that would surely feed a hungry, Italian dragon.

Italy must've been in the air because tonight Darrell took her to a really fancy Italian restaurant. Pumpkin ordered a pasta dish. Darrell ordered a steak dish.

"De ja vu," she said when their food came.

"What was that?" He looked up.

"They must've changed something in the matrix," Pumpkin laughed. Darrell looked at her in utter confusion.

"It's what Trinity said to Neo in the movie The Matrix."

He looked even more confused.

"Because we just ordered the same dishes that we had in the French restaurant."

"Do you want something different?" He raised his hand to signal the waiter.

"No, Darrell. I was just making a joke."

"A joke?"

"Yes."

"Oh. Okay."

His brow crinkled as he forced a smile. They both picked up their forks and began to eat.

"So, tell me about your day, Darrell."

Ten minutes later and Pumpkin still didn't understand what they were talking about. Some guy had gotten into an accident and there was something wrong with his T's, which apparently had something to do with his back, and Darrell was trying to align them or cross them or something. She nodded during pauses, said hmms and ohs where she felt they were appropriate, but she felt her eyes glaze over.

Gale's voice popped into her head. You can't make a thing work when you're hiding something else.

But she wasn't hiding Anthony. He'd left years ago and she didn't know where he was. If anything, he was the one hiding and she was cutting the remaining ties.

Pumpkin decided to focus on Darrell's lips while he talked. Darrell had really nice lips. When he had kissed her the other night it had been nice. Nice. Not passionate. Not magnetic. But who needed passion when you had consistency. Darrell was consistent. He was kind. He was attentive. Though he didn't seem to notice that her attention was wandering. And he wasn't trying to get closer to her. But he had lit up when he saw her earlier. There was something there. Fires didn't start themselves, after all. You needed to kindle it. Pumpkin put her hand on the table, palm up. Maybe he would reach out and hold it.

Her hand sat there for five minutes, then ten, untouched while he went on about a woman with scoliosis.

Come on, Darrell, she urged. Give me something more to work with here.

Darrell reached out and touched her hand lightly. "I'm boring you, aren't I?"

Pumpkin perked up. "No... Yes."

Darrell smiled. See, nice lips. All warm and soft. "Tell me about your day," he said.

"My day?" Her day. With Manny. Somehow Pumpkin did not think Darrell would appreciate the hooker by the side of the road joke. "I had some car trouble. Took my car into the mechanic. But they couldn't find anything wrong with it. And now I'm back on the road."

"Well, that turned out well," Darrell said.

"Yeah."

They sat there in silence for another moment. It wasn't one of those comfortable silences where they were staring into each other's eyes. They both searched for something else to say. Darrell still had a light grasp of her hand. Pumpkin stared at their touching fingers. No sparks flew between them.

It didn't matter. She wasn't giving up on this guy because her psychic friend told her to go after a man with a golden glow that neither he nor she could see. Women who followed their psychic's advice never ended up happy. They ended up broke. Pumpkin had been there. Done that. Without a psychic. She was not going back again.

Pumpkin took her hand back from Darrell and twirled her pasta. The long stretches of silence between them, she decided, were amiable and adult.

Darrell dropped her off at her door and she held still for the kiss.

He parted his lips, but words came out. "Listen, Malika."

A stone plopped into her gut. Had he been bored on the date too? Was he about to call it quits?

"I really enjoy spending time with you."

Oh no, wasn't that the kiss of death before getting dumped?

"I don't date a lot so I don't know all the rules. But I wanted you to know that I'm only dating you. Exclusively."

Darrell's pause was a heavy one, but she was certain the weight only rested on her shoulders. He wanted to know if she was seeing anyone else. The truth was she hadn't been on a date in years, but that was only part of the truth. The rest of it, her marriage, her impending, uncontested divorce on the basis of abandonment, was too complicated to explain on her doorstep. When she did finally explain it she wanted to only say, 'Oh by the way, I was married before. But he abandoned us and I haven't seen him in years.' She didn't want to talk about the whens and how longs. She was an English teacher not a Math teacher; semantics she could handle.

"I'm not seeing anyone else either, Darrell."

He let out a breath and grinned. It was an unguarded grin, the first she'd seen from him. "Were you thinking about going to the charity ball this weekend?"

Manny was having a fundraiser where everyone in the community was invited. Everyone included the poor, the workers, the unions, and the corporations. It was Manny's attempt at big tent politics.

"I'd love to go."

"Great, then I'll see you this weekend."

Darrell smiled and leaned in. Pumpkin concentrated so hard on trying to seek out the slightest sensation of a spark that her lips pursed. When they met his, Darrell didn't seem to notice. After the kiss, he pulled away smiling and told her good night. The other half of the truth that hadn't left her lips rose in her throat and tasted like bile.

When Darrell was gone, Pumpkin slumped against her door. A moment later, it unexpectedly opened and she fell backwards into someone's arms. Nice strong arms attached to gray eyes, looking down at her in concern that quickly turned to amusement.

"Hey Pumpkin. Fancy meeting you here."

It was Manny. What the hell?

CHAPTER TWELVE

MANNY SLOWLY RIGHTED PUMPKIN. SLOWLY because she was a sight to behold dropped back in his arms. Her eyes wide, her lips parted. He had complete control of her body and he liked it. His fingers press into her waist, testing the flesh of her curves. He'd always liked a girl with a little meat on her bones.

Pumpkin used his arms as leverage and righted herself. "What are you doing here?" She stepped back, putting a friendly amount of distance between them.

Manny stepped around her and closed the door. "My aunt called. Said she had some emergency she needed to tend to."

"Is everything okay?"

"It's nothing to worry about." Gale's excuse was flimsy at best. He saw right through his fortune-telling aunt. But he decided not to clue Pumpkin in on the fact that his aunt was trying to play matchmaker between the two of them.

Gale didn't interfere in his love life much, unless she thought the girl was all wrong for him, which was always. Come to think of it, this was the first time she'd tried to shove a woman towards him.

"She shouldn't have taken you away from your meeting."
Pumpkin grimaced, biting her lower lip.

Manny tried to tear his eyes away from her plump lips. He had to
swallow a couple of times before answering her. "It was no problem,
really."

"But it's not your responsibility."

He did tear his gaze off her lips then. Manny looked at her and
saw her crystal clearly in that moment. "You came when I called; to
help out with my campaign." He reached for her shoulder, cupping
his hand lightly on her shoulder cap. "Why wouldn't I do the same
for you?"

Pumpkin leaned into his hand for the barest of moments. In that
moment, Manny felt the weight that rested on her slim shoulders.
Here was a woman ready to offer support to others, but relinquishing
none of her own weighted load.

Pumpkin took a step back, out of his reach.

"She should've called me," she said. "I'd have come home early."

"You deserved to go out and have a good time."

She averted her gaze and turned away from him. He tracked her
movements as she removed her wrap and hung it in a closet.

"So, did you?" he asked. "Have a good time?"

Manny's chest tightened as he waited for her response. It felt like
hours waiting for her to turn around, to open her mouth. He couldn't
decide if he wanted her to turn around and gush at him about her
date, like they were school girls; or if he wanted her to turn around
and spill all the sordid details, like they were sorority sisters.

In the end, he got neither because Seth called out to his mother.

Manny followed Pumpkin down the hall to the kid's bedroom.
"I managed to get him clean —mostly. And in his PJs—well, just the

bottoms actually. We couldn't find the matching top, so we settled on an undershirt. When I heard you at the door, we were working on selecting a book to read for the night."

Pumpkin had a fit of giggles at Manny's recap.

Manny laughed at himself. "I have a new respect for mothers."

"Twenty-four seven, dude!"

Seth hopped off the bed when he saw his mother.

"Hey, buddy."

"Hey, mama."

Manny watched the two embrace as though they hadn't seen each other three hours ago. Hmm, a three hour date. If Manny had taken Pumpkin out, he certainly wouldn't have let her go at the three hour mark.

"Did you have a good time with Auntie Gale?" Pumpkin asked her son.

"Yeah," Seth grabbed a vial off his bedside table. "We made the dragon elixir. Wanna smell?"

The pungent smell reached Manny from his place in the doorframe.

Pumpkin put up her hands in protest. "No. No, thank you. I can believe it works."

"But then she had to go," Seth said, "and Mr. Charming came over."

"Charmayne."

"He said I can call him Manny, but I told him I have to ask your permission first."

Pumpkin glanced over at Manny with an appreciative smile. "It's okay with me. Did you have a good time with Manny?"

"Umm, hmm. Is Mr. Darrell here?"

Pumpkin's back stiffened. "No, sweetie. He went home for the evening."

Pumpkin's wasn't the only back that stiffened at the mention of Darrell's name. What would Manny have done if she hadn't come home until later, much later? What if Darrell had insisted on coming in? The thought galled Manny.

The fact that it galled him irritated him. He should be happy for the two of them. Darrell was a good friend, and Pumpkin was fast joining those ranks.

No, she wasn't joining Darrell at his rank, she'd surpassed him. She'd skyrocketed to the top of Manny's friend list in only a matter of days. She'd connected with him on a level that most people never had. But Manny had to cap her advancement. He'd sworn off getting involved with random, non-glowing women during the campaign. Although Pumpkin didn't glow, she wasn't random. Manny didn't like the thought of not seeing her again after three months.

"When is Mr. Darrell gonna come over?" Seth asked.

Pumpkin ushered Seth's little body into his bed. "Um, maybe we can have him over this weekend."

"Cool. I wanna show him my science project."

Pumpkin nodded. "All right, buddy. Let's choose a book. It's bedtime."

Seth grabbed one of the Beast Quest books from the package Manny had seen Darrell give to his mother.

If the bro-code hadn't entirely convinced him before, the sight of the book clutched in Seth's hand did it. After a moment of watching mother and child go through their bedtime rituals, Manny pushed away from the doorframe.

He returned to her living room and began tidying up her apartment. He placed the dishes in the dishwasher. Scrubbed down the table. Straightened the pillows on the couch. Then he went to her mantel where a number of pictures and plaques rested.

Manny had lived a life of privilege. Portraits of family members in groups dating back centuries hung in hallways and great rooms. On Pumpkin's mantel, pictures of Seth at various ages dominated the space. There was one sole family picture. A young woman, with a wild mass of hair, bounced a gap-toothed toddler on her lap. The toddler sported the same wild mass of hair. Behind them stood a dark-skinned man with a proud glint in his eyes. These were Pumpkin's parents. He knew she'd lost them at a young age.

Just behind this picture was a plaque. It read "Affinity Films' Rising Star Screenwriting Competition." Below the announcement of first place was Pumpkin's given name. Manny knew Affinity Films was a highly successful production company in Hollywood. They'd made decades worth of summer blockbusters, including one of his favorite films The Source Code. If Pumpkin had won an award with this company for her writing, he couldn't understand why she was here in Saint Anne's parish teaching high school English instead of in California penning more scripts.

"You're still here?"

Pumpkin stood in the hallway entrance. Gone were her date clothes. She was in pajama bottoms and a tank top. Braless, in a tank top.

Manny tore his gaze away from her breasts.

Pumpkin crossed her arms over her chest. "I thought you'd left."

Manny frowned. "I wouldn't leave without saying goodbye." He picked up a VHS box from her shelf of movies. And raised his eyebrows.

She shrugged. "What can I say? I'm an old fashioned girl. I got a couple of Betamax tapes in the closet too."

Manny chuckled and turned the title over. Bringing up Baby, it read. "This was one of my mom's favorites."

"She liked impossible match ups too?"

"Impossible match up?"

Pumpkin bit her lip, avoiding his eyes as she spoke. "A super smart paleontologist and a scatterbrained socialite fall in love while wrangling a pet leopard, sounds pretty impossible to me."

Manny wanted to tilt Pumpkin's head high, tug her lip free with his own. He placed the movie back on the shelf. "My father was an industrialist. Mother grew up in a hippie commune on land that my father's family was trying to acquire to build a shopping mall."

"You're kidding," Pumpkin gaped. "I thought your mother was a socialite."

Manny shook his head with a laugh. "My mother was a barefoot, dreadlocked, tree hugger when she met my father. She believed that love was the strongest magic in the world. She believed it would cure her cancer. It didn't."

Pumpkin's smile vanished and Manny felt the loss.

"She loved romantic comedies. Her favorite movie line was, 'Death cannot stop true love. All it can do is delay it for a little while.'"

"The Princess Bride."

Manny grinned at Pumpkin's correct identification of the movie line. "She lived longer than the doctors expected. Smiling, laughing, holding hands and kissing my dad. She died in his arms. Barely a month later, he passed away in his sleep. They said it was a heart attack. He was in his forties and in perfect health."

"I lost my parents too."

They stood there frozen for a moment, both lost in their own sense of loss. Then Pumpkin's eyes traveled around her apartment.

"Manny? Did you clean my kitchen?"

Her tone sounded incredulous, or perhaps angry that he'd touched her things.

"Yeah," he hedged. "I didn't want you to have to clean up after a long day."

Pumpkin shook her head, incredulity written across her pretty face.

"Thank you, Manny." The words sounded forced. "I really appreciate this." Her tooth captured her lip once more.

"It was no problem," he said.

"No, you had your own stuff to do tonight and—"

Manny interrupted before she could take back on any of the load he'd just lightened. "Today, at the Fisherman's Union, when they nearly turned on me, you saw that I needed a hand. You didn't ask if you could help me out, you just did. Your support has been monumental to me. In this campaign."

Pumpkin bit her lip again. Manny was coming to know the habit. It signaled that she was unsure of herself.

She looked down shyly, uncertainly. A stray curl from her messy ponytail fell in her face. Manny's palms began to itch again. He wanted to assure her that she had nothing to be shy about with him, no reason to be uncertain. She released her lip, signaling that she'd gathered the courage to speak her mind.

"I came up with an idea for your ad campaign," she began. "Whitely has been attacking your character in his ads. He's cast you as a playboy, as a prince of society, for getting down on one knee for votes. I say we beat him at his own game. First, we target women with a line like 'Tired of kissing frogs?' And next we target male voters with a line like 'Been tricked by a wolf in sheep's clothing?'"

Pumpkin looked up at him, her eyes trying to gage his reaction.

Manny wondered if that was how she saw him? As a frog or a wolf? Some animal lying in wait to trick her.

She continued her pitch. "The tagline would be 'Then vote for the real deal.' That would be you, of course, because you're the real deal."

Pumpkin went on to detail more lines of script along with visuals. She stopped speaking and looked at him for a verdict.

Manny swallowed a couple of times before speaking. "You think people would believe that? About me?"

"Of course, I do. I've watched you prove each of your talking points. We've got tons of pictures and footage to accompany each line. None of it would be a lie."

Her smile was the brightest thing Manny had seen in days, years, maybe.

"I think it's a great idea," he said. "Write it up and I'll show it to the agency."

Her smile faltered.

Manny regarded the woman before him, cocking his head as she tried to puzzle her out. "I remember the day I met you. You thought I was a jerk."

"I was judgmental," she said. "We didn't give each other a chance."

"Now, look at us. Besties."

Pumpkin grimaced.

"What? Are you recasting me?" He wondered if she heard the hint of hope in his voice.

"No. Besties is good."

Her smile was back. He wanted her to smile always. He wanted to be the one who made her smile. The faces of Honey Timmons, Rachelle Simpson, and Shanti Rodriguez flashed in his mind's eye. All angry, all ready to lash out at him because he didn't stay. Because they weren't The One. Pumpkin may not be The One for him, but she sure as hell was for somebody. He would have nothing less for her.

"You should recast yourself," he said. "You're a leading lady, Pumpkin, a princess. You're nobody's sidekick or supporting character."

She bristled.

"Hey," Manny put up an admonishing finger. "It's the truth. I have the pictures to prove it. Pictures from today at the Fisherman's Union. Pictures of you out volunteering. You're an important part of this story. You should rule in your own story."

Her eyes lit up so big. They looked like two hopeful saucers. Manny felt something stir inside him, something opening. He held his breath and stared at her, refusing to blink. But in the end, he only saw her. Her lovely brown face and untamed hair. The only light around her came from her eyes, not her person. Pumpkin didn't look so uncertain any more. She looked pleased, happy.

Good. That's the way she deserved to feel. Pleased and happy. Manny shoved his hands into his pockets and took a step away from her.

"I'm gonna go," he said. "I'll see you at the charity ball this weekend?"

"Yeah, I'll be there."

His hand escaped his pocket and reached out to her. He caught her cheek in his hand. Pumpkin's breath sailed across Manny's palm. Her eyes fluttered and locked on his. Manny pulled her forehead to him and kissed it lightly. His lips hummed as he pulled away.

"See ya, princess."

"Bye, hero."

Manny shut the door firmly behind him.

CHAPTER THIRTEEN

"ORANGE IS DEFINITELY YOUR COLOR, dear."

Standing before the full-length mirror in her bedroom, Pumpkin caught Gale's smiling reflection. Pumpkin rarely splurged on any purchase and never on something for herself. But when she'd looked in her closet a few days ago, she realized she had nothing that could pass as a ball gown. Not even an old prom dress. She'd spent prom night alone at the movie theater watching a romantic comedy double feature.

She'd been passing a dress shop in the market district when she saw it. The gown was a muted orange that befit her nickname. The tight bodice showed off her shoulders and lifted her boobs. The gown flared out at the waist, skimming over her ample bottom.

The dressmaker, a stylish woman who'd looked as though she belonged on a runway instead of inside a small shop tucked in the corner of the market district, had done the tailoring at no extra charge. The dressmaker pinned and hemmed until the corset's binding reshaped Pumpkin's curves into an artful hourglass.

"Every woman deserves a mirror moment," said the dressmaker.

Pumpkin was having one right now. She stared at the mirror in her bedroom in disbelief at her reflection. It was as though some fairy godmother had sprinkled her with orange fairy dust. She looked every bit the princess about to go to the ball and catch the eye and heart of the prince.

"Whoever made that dress is a regular Rumplestiltskin," Gale said. "They spun this cotton into gold."

Gale motioned Pumpkin to her vanity as she pulled out Pumpkin's now enhanced makeup kit.

"You won't need much makeup," Gale said. "The dress makes enough of a statement. Let me see the shoes."

Pumpkin sat down and lifted the dress to reveal a pair of uncomfortable heels. They were brand new, unscuffed and expensive. They were also a size too small but they matched the dress perfectly. She'd stuffed herself in, determined to make it work.

"You're practically Cinderella, dear."

"What is with you and your nephew? He called me a princess the other day."

The memory of Manny's lips pressed against her forehead, his fingertips brushing the small of her back, made Pumpkin's core warm and her heart skip a beat. For the past few nights she'd imagined what would've happened if she'd tilted her head up and captured his lips with her own.

Pumpkin shook the thought from her head. "Ridiculous, right?"

"Not if it's what you want, dear."

Gale's eyes met Pumpkin's in the vanity mirror. The twinkle of her gray eyes told Pumpkin she saw exactly what Pumpkin was thinking.

Pumpkin stuck her chin out. "I'm a grown woman, a working,

single mother." She smoothed down the fabric of the gown. "I don't have time for fairytales."

"Don't be ridiculous," Gale chided. "Every woman deserves her own fairytale. And you, my dear, are ready to play the part."

"It's just a dress, Gale. Besides, mothers can't be princesses. The fact that you have a kid immediately kicks you out of the running."

Gale frowned. "You seem to think that mothers aren't very special. I think your son would beg to differ. I think every kid in this world who looks up to their mother would beg to differ."

"You know what I mean, Gale."

"No, dear. I don't know what you mean. You seem stuck on this idea that you only get one chance to be happy in this life; that because you made a mistake you have to sit the rest of your life out and be unfulfilled."

Pumpkin opened her mouth to argue, to tell Gale that she was correcting her mistake. She'd filed for divorce. It would be final in just a matter of weeks. That she was going after another chance at happiness with Darrell.

"It's not unlike how my nephew thinks," Gale continued.

Pumpkin's heart sped up at the mention of Manny. She exhaled a long breath to try to slow it down.

"He won't make a commitment until he sees the proof," Gale shook her head as she placed a pin in Pumpkin's hair, which was being well-behaved under Gale's fingers. "He'd prefer to rely on 'the sight' more than his own judgment. Both of you are preoccupied with guarantees, but love is a leap of faith."

"I don't see why that's so wrong? Wanting to be sure before you make a commitment?"

Pumpkin had taken leaps of faith before. She'd leaped at the chance to work with Affinity Films, believing it was her big break, her shot at the big life she'd always believed she was destined for as an underdog. She'd even penned her script about an underdog who, against all odds, goes on to save the day. It was a fanciful idea, a young heroine saving the day, but Pumpkin believed it would be a success, just as she believed she would be a success. So, full of trust and bound by no contract, no commitment, Affinity Films snatched away her script and ran with it.

They bastardized her story and made millions after transforming her tale of an idealistic young heroine into The Source Code, where Pumpkin's heroine became the victim who could only be rescued by the young man whom she initially set free. When Pumpkin tried to speak up, to take the matter to the powers that be, she'd been a David facing Goliath with no sling-shot and no stone's chance in hell.

It happened all the time, she was told. She had no legal ground since she hadn't copywrited her script. She had no proof, only her word. No one was going to take the word of an awkward, black girl over a powerhouse like Affinity Films.

Then there was Anthony. She'd leaped again when he'd said some pretty words to her, enough for her to give him her virtue and plant a seed. Anthony had cheated on her, abandoned her and his child, and left her to pick up the pieces.

No, she did not want to leap anymore. She did not want to close her eyes, and jump, and hope someone would catch her. She stood with Manny on this one. She wanted a guarantee that she was not going to fall again.

Unlike Manny, she didn't have a psychic gift to rely on; she had her brain. Darrell was a smart choice. He had his feet firmly planted on the ground and he'd never ask her to leap. He was a guarantee.

"Oh, my dear, there's no such thing as a guarantee when it comes to love." Gale smiled sadly. Her eyes reading into Pumpkin's.

Solidifying that Gale saw more than just colors.

"Did I ever tell you about the man I was supposed to marry?" Gale continued. "We met when I was just a girl. He was older, more than was respectable. But we knew. From the first moment we met each other, we both just knew."

"He was like you?" asked Pumpkin. "He had the sight?"

"No," Gale smiled. "I saw his aura and I knew what that meant. He was drawn to me, but he denied it for the longest time because of our age difference. It wasn't love at first sight. The love developed over time. We got to know each other. I came to know that he was good and kind and funny and generous. He understood me in a way that no other person ever did. That's when I was sure that I wanted to spend the rest of my life with him..."

Gale trailed off, remembering. And that's when Pumpkin knew this story did not have a happy ending.

"What happened to him?" she asked.

"He died. He was killed. He played polo. He was trampled by a horse."

God, the irony.

"And you never had another relationship."

Gale shrugged. "I've never seen my shade of gold again. Our days aren't guaranteed, my dear. Manny's parents knew they were meant for each other at sixteen, but they got less than thirty years together. Happy years, but not ever after. I found my love at fourteen and he was gone before we'd ever even kissed. No one is promised forever. And sometimes people who care about each other make bad decisions. There are no guarantees. Only choices."

"And you think I shouldn't choose Darrell?"

"You're a smart girl, my dear. But love, true love, is a decision between the head and the heart. Not just one or the other."

Gale's eyes were misty. She turned away and stepped into Pumpkin's adjoining bathroom.

Pumpkin gave the woman a moment to collect herself from all those memories. She stood up and went before the full-length mirror once more. The sound of running water from the bathroom felt as though it washed away something inside her.

Choices?

She looked at the girl in the mirror with the corset and nice shoes. Then her eyes slipped off the mirror's reflection and caught on a picture frame on her dresser. It was a picture of her with Seth hanging on her leg. Her eyes swung from the mirror to the frame, like a pendulum perpetually in motion, not ceasing to rest in the middle.

Could there be a middle ground? A balance between who she was and who she wanted to be? If there was, she didn't see it.

The dress was just a dress. It was the only one she had, and she would take it off after midnight and return to her ordinary world the next morning. She could buy another gown and dress the part, but it was only a part and she wanted the whole thing.

Gale might see a golden light around her, but she was the only one who saw it.

The knock that sounded on her bedroom door made Pumpkin jump.

"Ms. Tavares?" DaeHo poked her head in the door.

Dae was here to babysit Seth for the evening. Pumpkin had learned her lesson and didn't bother to ask any of her family. This night was too important to have them squirm out of it.

"Wow! You look amazing, Ms. T. Mr. Walker is at the door."

"Oh, okay. Thanks, Dae."

DaeHo left out of the room.

"She's right," Gale came out of the bathroom looking refreshed.

"You look amazing, dear. Let's get you to your prince."

Pumpkin didn't meet Gale's eyes after the statement.

When she entered the living room, she saw Darrell in his tux. He looked very handsome. She willed her heart to skip a beat. It remained steady.

Darrell was deeply engrossed in a conversation with Seth about something science-y. Pumpkin waited a second for him to notice her, and then another.

"Ahem!" Gale cleared her throat, and then Darrell finally looked up and saw her.

"Mama, you look like a pumpkin princess!"

DaeHo laughed, turning to Darrell. "Just make sure you have her home before midnight or it'll turn to rags."

DaeHo, Gale, Manny and Pumpkin all laughed.

Darrell's brows drew in confusion.

Pumpkin opened her mouth to explain the movie reference to him, but at the last minute she closed her mouth and smiled instead.

"You do look stunning, Malika." Darrell came over and placed his hand on one cheek while kissing the other.

Her heart kept a steady beat, her eyes stayed wide open.

"You all ready to go?" Darrell asked.

"Yes. We don't want to be late for the ball."

CHAPTER FOURTEEN

LORIELLE OUTDID HERSELF, MANNY THOUGHT when he entered the ballroom. It was made to look like an eighteenth century ball. The color scheme mocked Manny and he frowned. The streamers were done in gold and white. The candles on the tables flickered, casting off golden flames.

The only modern touch was posters on the walls of him smiling. Below his face was his new campaign slogan, crafted by one Malika "Pumpkin" Tavares.

"Armand "Manny" Charmayne, a Prince among Men."

His guests stopped and admired the posters. It wasn't only the new posters and signs, it was the television and radio ads based on Pumpkin's idea. In the day since they'd released the ads he'd gained a five-point lead, and was still climbing. People were really resonating with the message. It was his message, spoken clearly, penned by Pumpkin.

Manny stood in the center of the room greeting his guests. Each time the doors opened his eyes swung to the entrance. He admitted to himself that he was looking for her. But it was just to tell her the news about the ads and thank her again. It'd been days since he'd seen or spoken with her. He didn't even know if she'd seen or heard the ads.

Manny looked around the room. It was filled with people from all walks of life, just like in his vision.

The first group of people gathered was the teachers' union, many of the teachers he recognized from Pumpkin's school.

He spied the mothers of the Mother Boards. So excited to be out amongst people their own age that they'd taken on some of the traits of their toddlers. They were in a herd, beaming brightly, talking loudly.

Gathered at a table, looking at all the splendor, were a few of the old men from the Fishermen's Union. They were dressed dapperly, the only ones who looked like they authentically belonged to this place from a time of old.

Mr. Jackson rose on creaky limbs as Manny approached.

"I'm so glad you could make it this evening, Mr. Jackson."

The old man's face wrinkled in a grin. "We don't get to get dressed up and attend a lot of fancy getups like this one. A lot of your guests don't like to get dirt on them."

"Everyone's welcome at my table," Manny said. "It's the only way for the community to move forward."

Mr. Jackson smiled that wizened smile. "That's exactly what we want, to move forward. But we can't do that while the cleanup dredges on slowly. Charmayne Industry is lining their pockets with the recovery funds while we sit by with our bellies empty. We deserve compensation. Now that you have our vote, we hope we can count on you."

Mr. Jackson's gnarled hands clasped Manny's shoulder with a

surprisingly strong grip. Before Manny could find words to respond, Mr. Jackson moved quickly back to his group.

Manny turned and looked to the opposite side of the ballroom. The businessmen and lobbyists wore expensive suits. The expressions on their faces looked like they had been tricked, like this was some joke they hadn't been in on as they looked around the room at all the commoners they were amongst.

Satterfeld came over. "Looks like you're up in the polls, son."

Manny winced at the word son.

"I have to tell you, I didn't think this man-of-the-people ploy would work, but it looks like they're all buying it." Satterfeld looked around at the mix of citizens gathered. "I see the Fishermen's Union is here. They've been raising some noise about the disbursement of the clean-up funds. Demanding that they be compensated for the loss of their income due to the spill."

"Well," said Manny. "Their livelihood has been affected."

"And you think ours hasn't? You don't see any of us asking for a handout. These things take time. They have to trust that we have their best interests at heart."

Satterfeld looked pointedly at Manny before continuing.

"You know Whitley could still clinch this thing. You need big business. Some on the board are unsure of your loyalty. If you keep our endorsement, you will be unstoppable. If only we had some type of commitment from you, I'd feel more comfortable convincing the board to keep our weight behind you instead of jumping ship to Whitely."

Satterfeld's gaze caught something behind Manny and he nodded. It was one of those nods that mafia men do in movies. When they were giving the okay for the deal to go down or for the kill shot to happen.

Manny peered over his shoulder.

Sophia Satterfeld approached them. She was breathtaking in white and gold.

"Sophia is a good girl to settle down with, make you look committed."

Satterfeld embraced his daughter and then left the two of them alone.

"My dad giving you a hard sell?"

Manny sighed.

"You're going to win this campaign," Sophia said. "My father knows it. You're the best man for the job. He wants what's best for Charmayne Industries. He also wants what's best for his little girl."

"I'm not the man for you, Sophia. I can't explain how I know, but I do know that for sure."

"It's true isn't it? The whole psychic sight thing." She huffed a laugh. "Marriage isn't magic, Armand. It's a contract, followed by a lifetime of negotiations."

Manny looked at her shocked. The pale gold of her gown suddenly appeared tarnished.

From the corner of his eye, Manny spied a different flash of gold. This one pure and bright. Her wild hair was tamed into a bun. Even from this distance he saw that her eyes were bright as they took in the splendor of the room. She looked every bit the princess he'd called her a few days ago.

"You could spend your life looking for some golden fantasy, or you could be sensible," Sophia continued. "You and I together, we make sense."

Manny unraveled Sophia's fingers from his arm. "Excuse me, I have other guests to greet."

Manny looked up, trying to spot Pumpkin again, instead he came face to face with Darrell.

"Big night," Darrell grinned as he reached for and shook Manny's hand.

Manny reached out his hand reflexively. Darrell's open grin caught him off guard. Darrell usually had a blank slate expression, but the open grin spoke of happiness.

"I thought I saw Pumpkin come in with you," Manny said.

"She stopped to talk with some teachers from her school."

"Thing's going okay with you guys?

"She's amazing," Darrell said. "I think she's the one."

"The. One?"

Darrell grinned sheepishly. "Listen to me sounding like you. I may not see a golden glow, but I can see myself with her in the future. We make sense together." Darrell looked over Manny's shoulder and his grin widened. "There you are."

Manny felt her before he saw her. His eyes focused on the floor as her gown came into view. He saw her heels peaking from the golden dress she wore. His eyes traveled up to the curves at her waist, the temptation of her chest. He lingered on her lips for a moment, watching them move and make words. Finally, their eyes locked, and everything came to a pause. His palms burned and he couldn't deny them any longer.

"Darrell, I'm going to take Pumpkin for a spin." There was no asking.

Manny took a bewildered Pumpkin's hand and led her onto the dance floor. When they were closer to the live band playing smooth jazz, he stopped and pulled her towards him, keeping the barest definition of a respectable distance.

Pumpkin pulled her lower lip into her mouth. "Lorielle outdid herself tonight."

"Yes." Manny didn't pretend to take his eyes of her lips. "It's a great turn out. But she can't take all the credit. A lot of it is due to you."

"Me?"

"Of course, you. The ad, it's been playing all over television, radio and social media."

"The ad?" Her face screwed in confusion, and then something close to dread. "But I didn't write it down. I only told you my idea."

"Yes, and I took the idea to the ad agency. They took your idea and made the television and radio spots, as well as new banners and fliers. I'm up in the polls. I just may win this thing."

Manny felt her stiffen in his arms. She wouldn't meet his gaze.

"Pumpkin? What is it?"

"You took my story?"

Her voice was barely a whisper. Manny had to lean in to be sure he heard her correctly. She stopped moving all together, as though the life went out of her.

"I can't believe you'd do that to me."

He gathered her body to him, the respectable distance gone. "I don't understand?" he said. "It was an amazing idea. They want to meet you, the ad agency. I'm sure they want to offer you a job in their media department. I told them they had to wait, that you were mine until after the campaign."

The words were out before he could retract them. Her body began to yield to him, her face regaining its light.

"You told them it was my idea?" she asked.

"Of course I told them. What did you think, I'd steal it and take the credit?"

Pumpkin bit her lip and looked away from him. Apparently, she did think that.

"Something like this happened to me before," she said.

"Someone stole your idea?"

"My entire screenplay."

Things began to click into place. The plaque shoved into obscurity on her mantel.

"Affinity Films?" Manny guessed.

Pumpkin nodded.

"Those assholes. And to think they made one of my all-time favorite films, The Source Code. They probably stole that too."

"Yes, they did. It was called The Oracle when I wrote it."

Manny blinked, then grinned. "I knew there was something special about you."

"It came from me, my mind, my imagination. But I couldn't prove it," she said, averting her eyes. "I didn't put a legal claim on the work, so they got away with it. My word against theirs, and they had a bigger voice."

Out of the corner of Manny's eye, he saw Darrell talking to another volunteer. Darrell had staked a claim on Pumpkin. As much as he wanted to, Manny couldn't hold on to her much longer. The song was nearly over and he'd have to return her.

Manny's fingers clenched the fabric of her dress. "You look stunning tonight."

"It's just a dress. It'll come off around midnight."

Manny's nostrils flared. "Maybe so, but I won't forget it. It's kind of cruel actually."

"Cruel?"

"You've come to my ball dressed like the woman of my dreams in a gold dress."

She frowned. "My dress is orange."

"What are you talking about?" Manny grudgingly let her go to look between them. "Gold is one color I definitely know for..."

Manny blinked. Before his eyes, he saw the color shift from a dusty gold to a muted orange. It was hazy, surrounding Pumpkin like a trick of light. Like golden dust floating in the air when a bright light was shined into an empty space.

It couldn't be.

His eyes started to go hazy, and the orange became stronger. His heart beat in his ears. He reached out to her, inhaled, stepped closer. He blinked, trying to capture the sight of her once more.

And there it was. His eyes caught the golden rays.

Manny looked away from her. Everyone everywhere else looked normal. He looked back at Pumpkin, at her face this time, and there it remained, a soft glow hovering just around her face. His heart fell to his feet and then rose to beat loudly again. His hands shook from the impact.

"It's you," he whispered. His eyes widened.

And then manicured hands reached between them.

"Armand," said Lorielle. "There's someone I need you to meet."

Manny was in so much shock that he didn't resist when Lorielle pulled him away, but he couldn't tear his eyes off the gold-dusted, Pumpkin princess who stared after him in disbelief. There was no mistaking what he was seeing.

CHAPTER FIFTEEN

"MALIKA?" DARRELL CAME UP BESIDE her. "You okay?"

Pumpkin nodded, slowly focusing on him. "Yeah. I mean, no. I think I need to use the bathroom."

"You're not feeling well?" Darrell's face filled with concern.

"I'm fine. I just need to freshen up a bit. I'll be right back."

But instead of going to the bathroom, where it was likely to be crowded, Pumpkin ducked into the Coat Room.

What had just happened?

No! It wasn't possible.

Was it?

Could she be? The One, with capital letters.

It had been her dream all of her life, her deepest desire. For there to be someone in her life who would love her, truly love her, and never leave. She'd stopped believing in dreams after Anthony abandoned her. Stopped believing in the magic of love. Instead, she focused on the practicality of partnership. She could have that practical partnership if she went back out the door to Darrell. Or she could take a leap, and believe in magic again.

Pumpkin took another deep breath and prepared herself to step out the door. When she opened the door, Manny was on the other side reaching for the knob. He stepped inside forcing her back in.

"How did you know I was in here?" she asked.

Manny closed the door behind him. "I could see you."

She knew, somehow, he didn't mean that he saw her come in moments ago.

Manny took a step closer, his eyes wide, his voice a whisper. "I can see you."

Pumpkin ran her hands over the bodice of her dress as though she could touch the magical thing he saw.

He smiled, his entire face lighting up. "It's beautiful," he said. "You're the most beautiful thing I've ever seen." He reached out and captured her face with one hand and brought his lips down to hers.

It was a soft taste-test that begged for more. It was an internal sigh that cried "At last!"

Manny broke away for just a second, barely an inch between them. He looked at her in wonder, then grinned and brought her to him again. This time the opposite hand came to her hip. He urged her body closer. Not much convincing was needed. Pumpkin came to him eagerly. His lips were at first gentle, probing against hers. But very soon, they turned urgent.

He delved deeper, tilting her head back to gain more access. She acquiesced with abandon, moaning slightly when his tongue retreated to allow the necessary function of taking a breath.

Her hands went inside his jacket seeking his chest. He inhaled at the contact and pulled her closer to him.

The hand that was on her hip traced down to her ass. Manny found the curve of her knee and raised her leg pulling her as close to him as he could get with her dress still on. At the rate they were going, that wasn't going to be very long.

Pumpkin's shoe slipped off her heel. It teetered on her toe, dangling in the air.

"Darrell have you seen Armand?"

Pumpkin's subconscious told her to pay attention to that high pitched voice, but her body did not want to be parted from Manny

"No, I was looking for Malika. She went to the bathroom," came the response.

The world around began to return to Pumpkin and Manny. Manny broke the kiss. Their eyes locked and their breaths held. But then there was a small crash to the floor. Pumpkin's shoe had fallen off.

The door to the Coat Room opened. Pumpkin knew she and Manny should have sprung apart. But their bodies were simply reluctant. So, Darrell and Lorielle got an eye full.

"What the hell!" Lorielle stood with her hands on her hips, taking in the scene. But it wasn't until Manny glanced over at Darrell that he actually began releasing Pumpkin from his embrace.

Pumpkin watched Darrell's face go from surprise, to hurt... to resignation. That sobered her up.

"Seriously, Armand," Lorielle's voice was more annoyed than angry. "If you want to traipse around with a low-class hood rat, fine. But I expect a little discretion. We have donors out there."

Three heads whipped around to stare aghast at Lorielle.

"Don't call her that."

To all their surprise, that came from Darrell.

Lorielle narrowed her eyes on him. "Really, Darrell? How dense are you? She's cheating on you in a closet."

Then came the flash of a camera. It blinded Pumpkin for

a second. Manny stepped in front of her to shield her with his body, but not before Pumpkin recognized the reporter from the Fishermen's Union behind the lens. Lorielle shooed the reporter away, following him down the hall making threats of lawsuits and bodily harm.

Darrell stood in the doorway looking between Manny and Pumpkin. He turned away and headed down the hall.

"Wait, Darrell." Pumpkin turned to go after him. But before she got to the door, she glanced back at Manny. He nodded for her to go.

When she got out the door, she felt something cold on her foot. Right, her shoe had fallen off in the closet. She caught up with Darrell who was nearly to the exit door.

"Darrell! Wait!"

He turned. Opened his mouth to speak, but then just closed it again. He shook his head. She felt like scum.

"Darrell, I'm sorry."

He held up his hand. "I'll take you home."

She walked with him, trying to hide her limping, shoeless foot. Darrell was a good guy. Such a good guy that he might actually turn around and go back in the closet to get the shoe, which was the last thing she wanted.

The drive home was awful. It was silent and tense. When Darrell pulled up at her door, he didn't turn the car off. He didn't get out to open the passenger door for her.

Pumpkin reached for the door knob, but then turned to him. He stared straight out the window with his hands on the wheel.

"Darrell, I'm sorry."

He said nothing.

"I didn't mean for that to happen."

"How long?" he asked.

"How long... That was the first time."

He was silent.

"I wanted it to be you," she offered.

Now Darrell turned to face her. "I was so certain about you," he said. "You and me together, we made sense. You and him? He's not gonna stick around longer than three months, you know that?"

Pumpkin looked into Darrell's eyes. There was still hurt there. Hurt that she had caused. And he wasn't going to let her do anything about it.

"Good night, Malika," he said quietly.

She turned the knob and climbed out the door. Darrell pulled off immediately after. Pumpkin stood there for a moment, the cold, gravely pavement under one foot.

When she went into her apartment, DaeHo was on the phone with a huge grin. Talking to Tyler, no doubt. The teen girl looked up surprised when she saw her teacher. Pumpkin told Dae she wasn't feeling well, and that got her out with little to no questions. Pumpkin checked in on a sleeping Seth, and then began undressing.

Freed from the binding corset, she stepped into a hot shower. She washed away Gale's transforming makeup job, but it did not wash away her guilt.

Now, back to her old self, she slipped on a pair of sweats and t-shirt and made herself a cup of hot cocoa, hoping that chocolate would cure the ache in her gut.

What had just happened?

The last couple of hours seemed like a faraway dream. Manny's lips on hers. The pressure of his hands against her thighs. The way he had looked at her. Like she was unreal. But she was all too real, with real baggage. A not quite divorced single mother, who had been seeing one of his close friends.

Darrell was right. Gold aura or not, Manny would high-tail it away from her the moment she began unpacking the details.

The doorbell rang and she froze. Her first guess was that it would be Darrell coming to make her feel more guilt. Or maybe to forgive her. Did she want to be forgiven?

Pumpkin peeped through the peephole and saw a pair of gray eyes staring back at her. She threw open the door. "What are you doing here!"

Manny's eyebrows rose, an uncertain half grin on his face. "Is this a bad time?" he said.

"Manny, you still have your event. What will all those supporters think? The funders? You can't just leave."

"I had something pressing to do." He stepped inside and closed the door behind him. From behind his back, he presented Pumpkin with her missing shoe.

She reached for it with a small smile. "You rescued my shoe. My hero."

"Yeah, I'm a regular Prince Charming." He smiled, glancing at her lips. He looked up at her, around her, and sighed.

The dress was off, her face wiped plain, her feet bare, but Manny looked at her as though she were the best sight in the world. Pumpkin warmed all over as though she could feel the impossible glow he saw surrounding her. All the jam-packed details she needed to tell him burned away under the heat of his stare.

"Darrell?" he asked.

"Gone." Pumpkin's feet seemed to move of their own accord toward him.

"Seth?" Manny placed a hand on the waistband of her sweats.

"Asleep."

In the space of a breath, his lips were on hers. He kissed her slowly, thoroughly. Not leaving an inch of her mouth unexplored. His free hand came up to the nape of her neck to angle her head for his maximum pleasure. The fingertips of his other hand slid just under the edge of her t-shirt, making direct contact with the skin of her back.

Pumpkin couldn't decide where to concentrate her attentions. She was completely lost. Lost in the scent of him, the feel of him, the heat of him. It was Armand overload, and Pumpkin couldn't get her fill.

But then he broke away.

"We should probably talk." He took in a shaky breath. "About... everything."

Her head was foggy. She concentrated more on his lips than his words, but some of that sank in. She had just ended a relationship and they were now very hot and heavy into something physical. The smart thing, the sensible thing, would be to take things slowly, sit down, and have a discussion.

She'd been smart and methodical and practical her whole life. Look where that got her.

Pumpkin reached up and pulled his head back down to hers. Just for tonight, she didn't want to think or analyze. She wanted to feel.

"Thank god," he said when he came up for air a moment later. "I've been dying to shut you up with a kiss since the first time you insulted me."

"It's not an insult if it's the truth."

Manny laughed at that, then watched his thumb as it traced across her lips. She glanced up into his eyes. They were so open with desire. A desire that wanted to do more than kiss her.

Pumpkin took his hand from her lips and stepped backwards

towards her bedroom. His eyes widened in surprise. He looked into her eyes and she clearly read his meaning. He wanted her too, but he would wait.

She knew this. Manny was a gentleman. It was one of the reasons that she wanted him so badly right now. When they got to her door, he stopped her. Taking her face in both of his hands, he kissed her gently. Then looked into her eyes once more.

Not too late, his eyes said. At that, she smiled even broader and turned the knob. He too grinned, brighter, and followed her lead.

But once in the room, Pumpkin lost her nerve. She was about to have sex. With Manny. She hadn't had sex in over three years. But it wasn't something you forgot how to do. Right? Should she take her clothes off? Or maybe he should do that? Should she take his clothes off? Maybe she should do a strip tease?

Manny watched her with a small smile.

"It's been awhile for me," she said without meeting his eyes.

"You and Darrell never..."

"No," she shook her head. "We'd only been on three dates."

"That actually makes me feel a little better."

Pumpkin cocked her head. "Well, I'm glad my lack of a sex life brings you pleasure."

"It's about to." His eyebrows rose mischievously.

She swallowed. Manny was far more experienced than she was. Was she gonna be able to keep up with him? To please him?

"Pumpkin," he embraced her lightly, his voice soft, his expression serious. "We don't have to do anything."

"I want to," she looked into his gray eyes. "I want you."

Manny dipped his head toward hers and began another slow exploration of her mouth, this time even gentler. "I want you, too," he whispered against her lips.

Pumpkin put her fears aside and unbuttoned his shirt slowly, not because she was trying to savor anything, but because her fingers shook trying to slip the tiny circles through the little slots. He waited patiently, raining soft kisses down on her forehead.

When the shirt was undone, Pumpkin gasped. Manny was truly a perfect specimen of man. And he was hers for the night. He stepped back and peeled the shirt off himself. She watched with hungry eyes as his muscles rippled with the movement.

With his shirt on the floor, he reached for the hem of her t-shirt. Capturing her lips with his own, he peeled the piece of cloth off her. His fingertips traced across her bare skin on the ascent.

When he got to her breasts, Pumpkin moaned. She wasn't wearing a bra. He pulled the shirt over her head and then captured one of her breasts with his hand.

A thumb stroked over her brown nipples, he bit down on his lower lip as he eyed it. Pumpkin could all but hear the thoughts racing through his head. And each of them was making her wet.

Manny tore his gaze away from her breasts and glanced up into her eyes. Asking permission to act on the thoughts in his head. Pumpkin couldn't form words. She could only swallow. She guessed in the language of lovemaking, that was a yes. And so, he descended on her breasts.

She felt the same rhythmic pulsing between her legs at the way his tongue worked on her nipple. Her breaths trembled, her knees knocked. She took a step backward to try to steady herself and came up against the edge of the bed. Manny caught her before she could fall and guided her gently backwards and down on the bed. Instead of coming with her, he knelt over her, grabbing the band of her sweats and tugging them off.

She glanced down and saw that she was nearly naked. All that was left were the cotton panties.

Dang it! Why hadn't she worn silk or lace! The lack of a thong became the least of her worries. For a moment, she was self-conscious. Her stomach wasn't as flat as it had been at twenty. There was a bit of cellulite on her inner thighs. She was sure that Manny was used to perfection in the female form.

"You're so beautiful," he sighed.

"You're blinded."

He raised his eyebrows.

"By a golden light," she clarified.

Manny skated his hands down her body, barely touching her skin, but touching something none-the-less. Pumpkin felt energy skate across her skin as his fingertips glided past the hairs on her arms. He stared at her middle just like his aunt always did. Then he looked into her eyes. Reverence was the word.

Manny prowled up her body, stopping at her thigh for a light kiss. Then her navel for a flick of his tongue. When he was just over top of her, he stopped and stared straight into her eyes, his expression inscrutable.

Manny descended on Pumpkin's lips again. This time more urgent, delving deeper. One hand cupped her cheek and pressed her lips closer. The other grabbed her thigh and urged her hips closer. She felt Manny's hard length against her thigh and she gasped out loud.

Manny froze.

Pumpkin caught her breath and then urged him on. "Don't stop."

He kissed her tenderly. His hips, she noticed, were slightly above hers. God, the patience this man had. He had a nearly naked woman beneath him who gasped and froze up at every turn.

Pumpkin let her knees fall open and then used her heels to arch her hips towards him. He released her lips, his eyes intent, looking for signs of distress. His hand trailed down her body, finding the cotton of her panties. She held her breath in anticipation. With his eyes still intent on her, he ran his thumb across the wet cotton.

Pumpkin sighed.

Manny smiled a very male smile, and then slipped his thumb beneath the cotton. When the pad of his thumb met her wet throbbing flesh, she cried out.

"Oh, god!"

"No," he withdrew his fingers. Waiting until he had a smattering of her attention, he said, "Say my name."

And then his thumb slipped beneath the cotton once more. This time parting the damp folds he found there.

"Manny!"

"Yes, Malika."

Two fingers snaked around the fabric and tugged them down. Her hips writhed for the return of his hand, but instead she was met with a hard length covered by fabric.

"Manny," she moaned.

She felt him fumble with his belt and zipper. In a flash the fabric was gone. When he returned, both hands seized her hips and this time, instead of the pad of his thumb, she was teased with the throbbing heat of his erection.

"Oh, Malika," he sighed.

He pushed their hips closer together, the width of his erection pressing into her folds.

As his fingers continued to dig into her backside, Pumpkin felt a small square of plastic pressed into his hand. He brought the condom wrapper to his teeth and tore.

"So you were planning to get lucky tonight?" she said.

Manny grinned as he took the strip of foil out of his mouth. "I already did."

His eyes focused in that space where the air met her skin, the part of her that glowed in his eyes. Before she could respond, Manny made quick work of fisting the condom on himself.

When he was finished, he looked again into her eyes, searching for any hesitancy, awaiting her permission.

That was Manny. Ever the gentleman, even in the most intimate of situations. Every hesitation, fear of the future, slipped away from Pumpkin as she looked into those smokey eyes. She reached up to rub her fingers over his brow. He kissed her wrist as it passed his mouth. Then with his eyes still locked on hers, he positioned himself at her entrance and pushed.

Pumpkin exhaled a shaky breath, eyes half lidded. Manny continued to watch her, retreating and then pushing in more. She gasped whispering his name.

Again, he retreated and thrust even deeper. This time her eyes closed. She was tight. It felt as though he was invading her, taking over her body. But somehow, still, she wanted, needed, more of him inside her.

She began to move her hips, trying to undulate him deeper inside. He reached behind one of her knees and pushed it towards her chest. When he did, he slid all the way inside, causing him to sigh in utter contentment.

Pumpkin, on the other hand, cried out his name and dug her nails into his back. He set an urgent rhythm, thrusting deeply and then retreating. With the position he had her in, one and now two knees bent into her chest, she couldn't meet his thrusts. She could only receive them.

And thrust he did. When she and Anthony had had sex, it was always more of a pounding, with her left swollen and sore after. With Manny's thrusts, the impacts left her wanting more. And the way he had her positioned, each undulation provided a delicious friction for her clitoris. A deep pressure built within her. She had had a couple of orgasms before... she thought.

She panted, murmuring Manny's name. Begging him not to stop. She had to see how the story of this pressure would end.

Manny stared at her, sweat on his brow as he continued to thrust. His lips hovered above hers, but he wouldn't kiss her. He watched her, seeming to gather a satisfaction every time she murmured his name.

The pressure built. At any moment, Pumpkin knew she would burst. She had never felt like this before. Never this much sensation. The crest was so near. He must've sensed it, too. He thrust deeply into her and the damn broke.

Her breath caught as her body began to tremble. The trembling began from her core. It radiated outwards, crawling up her spine and arching her back. Down to her feet it went, and curled her toes.

No doubt about it now. This was her first orgasm.

Finally, it reached her throat, and she cried out Manny's name in a long, low moan.

He closed his eyes, as she spasmed around his shaft.

It took Pumpkin awhile to come down. And when she did, she noticed two things. First, Manny was still hard and throbbing inside of her.

He hadn't come.

Secondly, he watched her intently. Pumpkin realized that what she thought was intent was a barely held thread.

Slowly, still keeping his eyes on her for any hint of distress, Manny unbent her legs and placed them over his shoulders.

Pumpkin gasped at the change of angle. Manny slowly pulled her closer to him. Her eyes widened in absolute shock. She couldn't believe there was another inch of her to be filled, but there was.

Manny was on his knees now. His head lolled back in ecstasy.

He opened his eyes, again searching for any sign of distress. But Pumpkin's mind had stopped working. If she disagreed with what he was doing to her, she doubted she could form a sentence of protest.

Manny began to thrust, and Pumpkin lost all her faculties. She threw her hands over her head, grabbing onto the bars of the headboard. Her back arched, her head rolled back as he thrust impossibly deeper into her. Her mind told her that she should feel pain with this level of penetration, but her body eagerly received each thrust and waited in anticipation for the next.

And then, that delicious pressure began to build once more.

Manny called her name as his thrusts increased in speed and need. The sound of her name was like a drug. She understood now why he wanted her to say his name.

She could tell he was close. His gray eyes fixed on her. They were at the crossroads of urgency and ecstasy. Pumpkin was once again at the crest of her orgasm. The spasms began radiating once more. This time, if possible, even more powerful. She didn't tremble this time, she shook from the power of this orgasm that came from a deeper place.

Manny, she somehow noticed, had stopped thrusting. His head thrown back, he called out her name in a deep groan.

For a moment, Pumpkin felt she should tell him to be quiet. The noise might prove problematic. But for the life of her, she couldn't remember why? She was lost in the sensations of her body and the reverberations of his.

Finally, with the both of them spent, Manny collapsed onto the bed beside her. They both shivered as he pulled the comforter over their naked bodies, though it wasn't cold. Manny snaked out an arm and pulled her back into him.

He sighed into her ear, "That was beyond my wildest fantasy. You were worth the long wait..."

CHAPTER SIXTEEN

WARMTH SURROUNDED MANNY. IT PULLED him from a peaceful sleep and into wakefulness. His hands met warm flesh that left his fingertips tingling and sped up his heartbeat. He opened his eyes.

Pumpkin.

His gaze was hazy as he looked down at her bare shoulder. The slope of her neck beckoned to be kissed, tasted. He blinked, clearing the haze of sleep, and he saw it. The faint glow coming off her brown skin. The sight knocked the breath out of him.

All these years he'd waited to see this sight. He wanted to take in a lungful of air and shout from the rooftops. Instead, he whispered.

"Good morning." Manny pulled Pumpkin's warm, glowing body to him.

Her eyes blinked open instantly. She inhaled sharply, "Hey."

Was that intake of breath surprise? Regret? Desire? Satisfaction? Manny decided to ask. "How are you feeling?" He placed a light kiss on the shell of her ear.

She let out something between a sigh and a laugh. "My toes are cramped from all the curling."

Satisfied. She was feeling satisfied. Perfect.

Manny ran his hands southward down her body. She let out another sharp intake of breath.

"I didn't hurt you," he asked. "Did I?"

He knew he'd gone a little overboard last night, penetrating her as deeply as he had. After her first orgasm something in him snapped. Every part of him urged him to get closer, deeper. To claim not just her body, but her soul. He'd have crawled under her skin and rested in her heart if he could've. He'd forgotten her warning that it had been a long while for her. He should've taken things slower, shallower at least.

Pumpkin turned in his arms. "No," she shook her head. "You didn't hurt me. You…"

She looked away. Her teeth caught her lower lip. Her fingers worried the covers. Manny did what he'd been wanting to do for days, he tugged her lip from her teeth with his mouth. With her lip free, his tongue sought entry and was immediately granted access. Her hands let go of the cover and snaked around his neck, tugging him in closer. He released her mouth and went to her neck.

"I thought I'd had an orgasm before," she said. "But after last night, I realized that I was wrong."

Manny released her neck and let out a relieved laugh. He flopped back onto the mattress and continued laughing.

Pumpkin rose up on her elbows and narrowed her eyes on him.

"No, I'm not laughing at you, I promise," he ran his hand over her face smoothing away the frown. "I'm relieved. I got a little carried away last night." Manny looked up at her sheepishly, a child caught with his hand in the cookie jar. "I just couldn't get close enough to you."

His face turned serious as he eyed her with a sense of wonder. He ran a hand down her body, stretching along the length of her so that they were touching at every possible place.

It was there. Just like his grandfather, his father, and his aunt said it would be. It was faint, dimming to a shadow when he wasn't trying to see it. But every time he blinked and cleared his vision, there it was. A faint glow around the woman he was destined to spend the rest of his life with.

His face hovered just above hers, a slow smile spreading across his lips as his eyes dipped to her lips. A reverent kiss to his golden girl, The One. It was Pumpkin, a woman he enjoyed spending time with. A woman who understood him in a way no one else had his whole life. A woman he could laugh with, play with. A woman he'd confessed his fears and hopes to before he'd ever kissed her.

Manny gathered her to him, his erection throbbed as it sought her heat. He pulled away to look into her face. This was right. The certainty of it gave him peace. The only problem was in the crinkle on her brow. There he saw her uncertainty.

That had never occurred to him: that his One wouldn't be sure about him.

"Hey," he said touching the space between her brow. "What's that about?"

"I just don't want my baggage to weigh you down," she said.

"What baggage?"

Pumpkin bit her lip again. "I'm not some pristine society miss, Manny. Working on your campaign is the only bit of charity I've ever done."

"So now I'm a charity case?" he grinned.

"I'm serious," she said. "I believe you're the best candidate for this city. But I don't think I'm the best candidate for you."

"Why don't you let me be the judge of that."

"I can't. You're blinded."

Manny grinned, shaking his head. "I think I knew it all along. I denied it because I didn't..." He indicated the air before her body. "I didn't see it. And the last thing I wanted to do was disappoint you; have you hate me and never speak to me again. The thought of not speaking to you... not my favorite idea."

"It's not my favorite idea, either," she said.

"But now you're stuck with me." Manny brushed his hand over her mouth, a mouth he would kiss every day for the rest of his life.

He kissed her again. And then again. But then, he pulled away in concern.

"Should I sneak out of here?" Manny looked towards the door.

"What?" Pumpkin's body, warm and pliable just a moment ago, stiffened as if he'd doused her with cold water.

"Seth. I don't suppose it would be good for him to find me here?"

"Oh," Pumpkin sighed. "Seth."

Manny grinned. "Yeah, him. That cute little kid who freeloads off of you. You guys have the birds and bees talk yet?"

"Neither a bird nor a bee could pull off what you did to me last night. You had me buzzing like a humming bird."

This brought a very male grin to Manny's face. He looked down her body once again, reliving last night's events, planning future ones.

"I would be lying if I said I could make it quick." Manny's erection aimed at her belly button. "I have plans to savor every inch of you." He looked down at the lower half of her body, which was still naked. A pained expression crossed his face. "I could try to be quick..."

"Mama!"

They both froze. Pumpkin raised her eyebrows in question. Manny shrugged, palms up. Being a bachelor, he had no clue what to do in this situation.

"Mama! Can I have some cereal for breakfast?"

"Um... yeah, sure," Pumpkin shouted to the closed door.

They both held their breath for a moment until they heard Seth in the kitchen going through the silverware drawer.

"What do we do?" Pumpkin whispered.

Manny turned a bewildered look to her. "I have not a clue."

Pumpkin frowned. "Surely, you've had to sneak out of some woman's apartment before."

"You're calling me a ho while you're the one trapped with your pants down."

She glanced down and then pulled a pillow over her midsection. Manny burst out laughing and then shoved a hand over his own mouth. They both glanced at the door.

"He probably heard that," Manny said.

"We'll just handle this like adults." Pumpkin feigned confidence and climbed of the bed. She shoved on the sweatpants and t-shirt from the night before. Still braless.

Manny buttoned his own pants, tugged on his dress shirt, and grabbed his suit jacket.

Pumpkin opened the bedroom door. From down the hall, Manny could see that Seth had seated himself at the dining room table with an overflowing bowl of Captain Crunch cereal. Seth looked up and then narrowed his eyes on Manny.

"Good morning, sweetie," Pumpkin said.

"What's Mr. Charming doing here?"

"Um, well... We had a sleep over." Pumpkin glanced over at Manny who had his eyebrows raised in amusement.

"Yes," Manny backed her up. "Your mom lost her shoe at my party, and I came and brought it back. Then we talked... Then we fell asleep."

Manny's pause conveniently left out the most satisfying sexual experience of his life. They both looked at Seth to see if he bought their story. The kid simply shrugged and dug his spoon back into his bowl. They were home free.

"Is Mr. Darrell coming over today?"

So close.

"No... he's not," Pumpkin said. "Seth, I'm going to walk Mr. Charmayne out and I'll be right back, okay?"

Seth mumbled around his spoon.

Pumpkin led Manny to the door. At the threshold, they both paused. Mouths grinning at the hilarity of the morning, nostrils flaring remembering the passion of the night, eyes wide at the possibilities of tomorrow.

Manny trailed a hand down the side of her face looking again at the golden halo resting on her skin. "I have some campaign stuff to do tonight," he said.

"Oh. Okay."

He smiled at her disappointment and stole a quick kiss. "Can I see you tomorrow?"

"Yes," she smiled.

He lingered for a longer kiss. "Can I call you tonight?"

"Hmmm."

He pulled away reluctantly, his lips still on hers as he opened the door.

A clicking sound and flashing light broke the kiss.

A small crowd of reporters stood gathered outside Pumpkin's door.

"A little late night campaigning, Mr. Charmayne?"

"I knew it wouldn't be long before he returned to his old ways."

"Is this your new three-month fling?"

Manny shielded Pumpkin with his body. The flashes kept on snapping. It took his mind a moment to focus. He felt her body shrinking away from him. He reached behind him and grasped her hand. It was a reflexive move. The sharks may go after him, but they wouldn't touch her.

"Despite what my opponent may put out there, my personal life is not a part of this campaign. It's my ideas and my policies that will lead this city forward. However, I will say this regarding my personal life." From behind his back, he gave Pumpkin's hand a firm squeeze. "I am definitively no longer available on the dating market."

Manny released Pumpkin's hand and shut the door. The reporters followed him out, but he ignored the rest of their questions. All they caught in their lenses was his grinning face.

CHAPTER SEVENTEEN

"I CAN'T BELIEVE YOU ACTUALLY got him into bed."

"What did you do? Trip him and then his penis fell into you?"

Pumpkin looked away from LaRon and LaTom as they made rude gestures to illustrate their hypothesis. Pumpkin's eyes were trained on the television set instead. She'd made the evening news.

"Seems Armand Charmayne is up to his old tricks," said the announcer. "After publicly stating just two weeks ago that he was committed to his mayoral campaign and would not be dating, the playboy millionaire is back out on the dating pond."

Millionaire?

Pumpkin knew Manny was wealthy, but she'd never Googled how wealthy.

LaRon and LaTom immediately ceased their mocking and tuned into the television set.

"Charmayne has been spotted getting close to one of his campaign volunteers."

A snapshot of her and Manny in the closet at the charity ball faded over the reporter's face. In the photo, Manny shielded her with his body, but the orange of her dress was unmistakable. A second snapshot showed them kissing just inside her door. Again, you couldn't tell it was Pumpkin unless you knew her—

"The woman has been identified as high school, English teacher, Malika Tavares."

Pumpkin shut her eyes and groaned. She groaned at the mention of her name. She shut her eyes at the horrible faculty photo that flashed across the screen. It had not been a good hair day. Her eyes were wide because the flash had caught her off guard. Her smile was frozen in fake sincerity in an attempt to show that she loved her job.

In the present, Pumpkin opened her eyes and focused on the reporter as he ran down her resume: her years teaching, where she went to college. She held her breath. Her heart pounded to escape her chest. Her head strained to find a way out. She focused so hard that she could see the reporter scanning the teleprompter screen from left to right. At some point, the reporter was going to get to the line in the prompter script about her marriage.

"Charmayne is known to have made his way through the socialite crowd, but now that he's courting the working class vote it appears his dating habits have followed suite. We'll have to see how long Charmayne is hot for teacher."

The reporter gathered up the papers on the desk, papers he'd never glanced at while reading the news in the prompter. He gathered the stack in a neat pile, straightened them with a staccato bounce on the desk, and then turned to face another camera.

"In other news, the waterways cleanup continues to slug along. Tensions are rising between the Fishermen's Union and Charmayne Industries."

Pumpkin released her held breath, her heart slowed, and her brain cleared. They hadn't mentioned Anthony. She only had two weeks left until her divorce was final. Anthony had been in the wind for over three years now, without once contacting her. She knew the paperwork would go through uncontested in light of his long absence. But two weeks was a long time to try and hide such a big secret. And now with the news media snooping around, looking for the juicy bits of her love affair with the city's number one bachelor, she was certain he was going to find out.

The ringing of her phone made Pumpkin jump. She looked down at the caller ID. It showed Manny's number and name. She ducked into the hallway to answer it.

"Hey."

"Pumpkin? Is everything all right?"

Her throat ceased up.

Oh god, he knew something was wrong. He'd found out about Anthony. He'd gone to law school, so maybe one of his buddies happened to look up her file and see that she was a no good adulterer.

Or maybe he'd simply realized that he'd made a mistake about her. He didn't see anything special about her after all, and was returning to dating socialites who were more on his level.

Manny sighed and Pumpkin's heart sank to her toes. "I'm so sorry about this, sweetheart."

Sweetheart? She felt dizzy at the speed her heart rose to her head. She'd never been called an endearment. Well, Gale called her dear, which she just now realized that she really liked. But, aside from her father, no man had ever given her his own pet name.

"Please don't be angry with me," Manny said.

"Why would I be angry with you?"

"The news can get away with saying the most vile things in the name of entertainment."

The laugh bubbled up and out of her unexpectedly. "Oh, them? Please, if you thought that was vile, you haven't met my cousins."

"I'm going to place an injunction on that station. They'll need to retract everything they said about you."

"No, Manny don't. You'll just fuel the fire. I'm not bothered by a little name calling, really."

"Sweetheart, you were bothered when I assumed you'd gone to community college."

"That's different. If they'd attacked my intelligence I'd tell you to pounce."

Manny chuckled. Pumpkin joined him. She belonged with this man.

She'd exchanged vows with Anthony, but neither had looked each other in the eye when they said their vows at the county court house. Pumpkin had stared intently at the Justice of the Peace, trying to make sure she got the words right. She could've been promising the Justice that she'd love, honor and obey him. Anthony had never said he'd loved her. She'd found a ripped thong in his pocket the next week. And he was never around for her to defy. The truth was they'd only gotten married because they both believed it was the right thing to do under the circumstances of her pregnancy. It became crystal clear that they were totally wrong for each other.

But this, between her and Manny, this was good. It was right and easy between them. Pumpkin could stay in this quiet, warm bubble with Manny for the rest of her life and be content. But they didn't live in a bubble. There were too many outside forces pushing up against them.

"I just don't want any of this to hurt you and the campaign,"

Pumpkin said. "We should probably keep this... thing between us quiet for now."

"This thing between us is magic, Pumpkin. There's no way I can pretend or keep quiet about it. And I won't let anyone hurt you."

Pumpkin felt the flimsy material of their bubble strengthen exponentially.

"We clear?" Manny said.

"Crystal." She heard his smile across the phone line.

"I miss your face," he said. "You're tugging your bottom lip into your mouth right now, aren't you."

She was shocked to feel the bite of her teeth on her lower lip. How did he know that? Were there more psychic powers she didn't know about?

"You do that whenever someone pays you a compliment or does something nice for you."

"I do?"

"Hmmm."

The sound he made was what she imagined a lion made, as it played with its food before devouring it whole.

"I get to see you tomorrow tonight," he said. "Gale said she'd take Seth for the night and mix a troll elixir."

"Yeah," Pumpkin tugged at her lip again. "I'll see you then."

Pumpkin hung up her phone with a smile. She entered the dining room where her cousins had moved to, allowing the kids the use of the television.

Spread out on the table was this morning's newspaper with a photo of Manny with some shoeless, unidentified leg wrapped around his waist.

"Did he buy you that dress?" asked LaRon

"He had to," said LaTom. "She can't afford that on a tutor's salary."

Pumpkin didn't bother to correct her cousins' assumption that Manny was buying her clothing nor the misidentification of her job. She went over to the sink and ran herself a cup of cold water. Her throat suddenly felt dry. She spent so much time keeping her mouth shut around her family as they continually insulted her intelligence and assaulted her independence. The cold water did not satisfy the dry spell.

"Look at her," said LaTom. "She thinks she's living in a fairytale."

They were right. One night in Manny's arms and Pumpkin felt like she could reach up and pluck her dreams out of the stars. It was a heady feeling. A scary feeling, having that much power. Like, if it were taken away, she would fall. Fall hard. Maybe not get up again. Not even look up again. Or reach out for anyone, to anyone. She turned back to the faucet and ran another cup of water.

"You're stupid if you think you can keep him," said LaTom.

At the moment, Pumpkin was feeling stupid. Stupid that she kept coming here to this house. She placed the empty cup in the sink and leaned against the counter. She saw cracks in the paint job beneath the cabinets. Beneath the bright yellow was the original dull paint. She heard gunshots from the living room, intermixed with a thumping techno beat. The sound of her adolescent nephews playing a violent video game rated M for mature.

This was her mother's childhood home, but there was nothing left of her mother. Pumpkin's eyes caught at the backdoor where a welcome mat was set before the closed storm door. Pumpkin had never felt comfortable in this house, never felt welcomed. She'd never been supported. She'd hardly been given any attention or supervision.

In the last two weeks, Manny and Gale had stepped up more than her family had in her entire life. Even DaeHo had come to her rescue. And then there was... Darrell.

"If she's as smart as she thinks she is, she'd get pregnant by him."

"That's right. Get that support, and get out."

In other words, use Manny like LaTom and LaRon used men. Like she'd used Darrell.

Pumpkin had never been after Darrell for his money. She'd sought him out because of his qualities. Qualities that she'd planned to use for her benefit. The problem was she'd never offered Darrell anything in return. Certainly not her heart, barely her attention. She'd always been focused on Manny, welcoming his company at every turn. She'd taken Manny's support when she'd had car trouble, never once considering calling on Darrell. Before she'd ever shared her body with Manny, she'd already shared the deepest parts of herself with him.

She owed Darrell an apology. A different apology, for her real transgression.

"Mama, Mr. Charming's on the TV."

Pumpkin didn't immediately turn at the sound of Seth's voice. She turned when she heard her name spoken in Manny's voice.

Entering the living room, Pumpkin saw her nephews perusing their large library of war games. While they battled over what game to play next, Manny stood on the screen in his campaign offices. An annoyed Lorielle stood on one side of him. Heather, continually glancing down at her handheld, stood on the other.

"Malika Tavares is a trusted friend," Manny said into the bouquet of microphones. "A loyal volunteer, a devoted teacher, and a brilliant writer who has been instrumental in the advancement of my campaign. It is true that I'd planned to put my personal life on hold while I ran for office. One thing that I've learned while campaigning in our community is that my initial plan can change as new information presents itself."

Manny smiled into the camera, a twinkle in his gray eyes.

"After spending time and getting to know Ms. Tavares, I've come to see her in a new light."

Pumpkin couldn't see the particular light like he did, but she felt it warm her over. Her heart kicked into high gear. It beat so fast she thought she would faint. Her mind cleared and her mouth opened, ready to tell the television set how she felt. She was uncensored when it came to Manny, unmuted.

"I've seen her in a new light," Manny continued, "and I've changed my relationship status. However..." His easy gaze turned to stone. "Ms. Tavares is a private citizen. She is not running for office. Your time would be better spent grilling me instead of her. This subject is not up for discussion. I will not be taking any questions."

Manny looked pointedly at the camera, then he turned and walked back into his office, shutting the door behind him.

"What the hell?"

"Does she have some type of voodoo vagina?"

Pumpkin frowned as seven little heads turned to look at the adults.

"Voo voo vina," babbled little LaRico.

Pumpkin turned to the tall, twin role models in the room. LaRon and LaTom paused and stared at the baby and then burst into laughter. All of their children followed suite. Between howls of laughter there were shouts of Voo Voo Vina and Voodo Vagina.

Aside from herself and a bewildered Seth, Pumpkin noticed that her aunt wasn't laughing. She regarded Pumpkin with a scrutinizing look, her thumb scratching at the band on her left ring finger. Flicking it up and scratching the underside, then flipping her hand over and doing the same on her knuckle. Shifting the band from this side to that, to get at the places that irritated her most, but never taking it off.

Pumpkin's left hand was bare. She'd taken her ring off the day Anthony left. But though her hand had been bare for years, she'd been living quietly in the shadows, as though the band still choked her hand. Unlike LaVerne, Pumpkin had not scratched at the disturbance. She'd sat still and taken the irritation. Allowed the disturbance to keep her uncomfortable. Had even assisted it by telling its lies; that she was unworthy of more because she had put the wrong band on. She'd rejected any attention as though the band still owned her.

She wasn't going to do that anymore. Pumpkin glanced up again at her aunt. LaVerne had stopped itching the ring and slid it back firmly into place. "What are you going to do, Pumpkin?" she asked.

Pumpkin turned away from her aunt. "Seth, grab your coat. It's time to go."

"Can't you take a joke?" said LaTom.

"We're just trying to help you," said LaRon.

"No, you're not." Pumpkin tried to keep her voice down. Seth was in the hall waiting impatiently. "You've never tried to help me. I bend over backwards whenever you ask me for anything, regardless of how crazy or inconvenient. And when I'm so hard up that I've had to ask you guys for help, none of you have ever come through for me. In the short time that I've known him, Manny has been there even when I haven't asked."

"I took you in," LaVerne's voice was raised. "I didn't have to. I could have let you go into foster care. But I didn't. I took you in."

"You never took me in," said Pumpkin. "You've always pushed me away. You've even taught me to do it. Taught me to never let anyone get close enough to me. Taught me to reject them so that I don't get hurt."

"Men don't stay, Pumpkin" interjected Verne. "They leave. They always leave. There's always someone younger, or thinner. Someone else. You think you're different from the rest of us. You thought you were, but it happened with Anthony. He left you for someone else. It'll happen with Charmayne, too."

Pumpkin grabbed her son, turned and left that house, with no plans to ever return.

CHAPTER EIGHTEEN

CRACK!

THE NEWSPAPER MADE THE sound of a whip as it hit Manny's desk. The picture of him shielding his face from the light with his hand, and using his body to shield Pumpkin, made him wince. He hated that she was being exposed in this.

"You're lucky this didn't blow up in your face," accused Lorielle. "Right now the press is just chalking it up to your old playboy ways."

"You've got a four point rise in the polls with 18-30 year old males," said Heather from behind her tablet. "This could work out in our favor."

Manny wasn't listening. His fingers traced the outline of the unidentified leg on the newsprint. He'd had that leg in his hand in the flesh. The only thing missing from the photograph was the faint golden shimmer that only he could see. But that wasn't the only thing Pumpkin showed that only he could see.

Only he could see the determined set to her chin when she picked a position and decided to stick it out. Only he got her wit and obscure movie references. Only he got her genuine smile, her vulnerability. He got her. He got her. She was his.

Heather continued to go over the numbers and their implications. Lorielle continued sifting through the newsprint and media, trying to spin the facts. Something outside his office caught Manny's eye. Or rather someone. Manny moved to the door.

"Darrell?"

Darrell's back went rigid. He carried a box in his hand. He didn't turn. "They told me you were out at a meeting."

"I'm about to leave for it." Manny slowly walked toward his friend, approaching Darrell as though he were a wary, wild animal. "You got a moment?" Manny said to Darrell's shoulder.

"No," Darrell said without turning around. His jaw was so tense Manny was surprised he got the one word out. Darrell started moving again.

Manny almost let him go. Almost. "She's The One."

Darrell paused, his shoulders even tenser.

"She's golden," Manny clarified. "I tried to stay away from her, but I kept feeling this pull. And then I saw it. I saw the light. She's my golden girl."

Darrell was quiet for a long time. And then, "I didn't notice." Darrell turned around, brown eyes blazing. "I didn't notice you trying to stay away from her because it never occurred to me that you were the type of guy to go after a friend's girl. I didn't notice that she could possibly be the one for you because I was too busy noticing she could have been the one for me. And in case you didn't notice," Darrell indicated the box in his hands. "I quit."

Darrell stormed towards the door, but Gale was there blocking his exit. Darrell drew to a stop.

"I'm sorry, Aunt Gale, but I have to go."

Gale smiled that knowing smile. "Nothing to be sorry about, my dear boy." She cupped the side of his face. "Just be patient. Love will awaken soon. Then you'll see."

Darrell's scowl lessened for a fraction of a second. Then he sighed and gave Aunt Gale a quick peck on the cheek. "Goodbye, Galinda."

"Not for long, dear."

Darrell stepped around Gale and walked out the door.

Gale turned to Manny. "So, now you see?"

Manny nodded, turning away from the door with a sigh. "I just wish it hadn't cost me a friendship."

Gale rubbed his back as she'd done when he was a kid. "Well it wouldn't have if you'd listened to me and gone for her when I told you to."

Manny looked back at the closed door.

"Just give him some time," Gale said. "His story's coming soon."

"You've said that to me all my life."

"And I was right."

"Yeah, but it took years."

"It was always there. It was simply waiting for you."

Manny looked down at his aunt. Her eyes were the same pale gray as his, but they'd always felt brighter than the sun. Gale had loved early and lost. He'd never heard a resentful word from her about her misfortune. She joyed in others' connections.

"I love you, Auntie Gale." He leaned down and kissed her cheek.

"I've known that all your life, dear boy. Now, head off to your meeting before the sun goes down. I fear it's going to be a dark night."

When Manny entered the room, he saw Satterfeld on one side and Mr. Jackson on the other, a wide gulf of a brown table between them. Mr. Jackson rose with his hand extended.

Satterfeld cut him off. "Good to see you, son."

Manny took Satterfeld's hand and then turned his body so that they included Mr. Jackson. "I'm glad you both agreed to meet with me today. I believe the two of you are not as far apart as you think. I hope we can reach an agreement today."

"So do I, my boy," said Mr. Jackson. "My men need to get back to work."

"And mine," said Satterfeld, "need to make sure jobs and money keep flowing in the city."

"Why don't we take a seat, gentlemen?" Manny reached for the seat at the head of the table. He indicated for Mr. Jackson to sit at his right, and Satterfeld at his left.

"We're here because the union feels that the board is running slow on the Coastal Restoration Project." Manny turned and addressed Satterfeld directly. "The board has had the funds from the federal government for over a year now. There hasn't been much progress in the clean-up."

"If speed is what you want," said Satterfeld, "we should consider river diversions."

"That would be a disaster," said Mr. Jackson. "A diversion will destroy the habitat, which will severely damage the coastal community economics. And it will remove future storm surge protection. If you intend to take this long, the fishing community deserves to be compensated for the year of work that was stolen from us. If you continue to take an indefinite amount of time, we should continue to be compensated while we wait."

"This clean-up could take months, years," said Satterfeld. "We can't support you for that long. Isn't that what your union dues are for."

"We've reinvested our money into the business, into our boats. We expected that, in good faith, the clean-up would be complete by now."

"Well, it's hard to clean up when we get protests at every turn."

"You corporate big wigs don't understand the delicate balance of the water system."

Satterfeld's cheeks were red with irritation. Mr. Jackson's nostrils flared with indignation.

Manny decided to jump in before the shouting match turned to include fists.

"You both have valid points. You both have strong positions that are worth fighting for, but it's not as big of a fight as you think. There's middle ground here."

"You can't compromise when the other party has nothing you want, son."

"I'd have to agree, my boy."

Manny wanted to point out that they just agreed on something. Unfortunately, it was the wrong thing. "At the end of the day we all want our community and our families to thrive."

Both of the older men nodded their heads. Before either of them could open their mouths and speak, Manny continued.

"What the two of you are lacking is trust. What we need is transparency."

"We'd suggested federal oversight of the funds," offered Mr. Jackson.

"That's a good idea," Manny grabbed for it. "Except, I think it needs to be local. The Charmayne Foundation could oversee the funds."

Satterfeld thought on that for a moment. "I could agree to that. But I won't agree to a year's compensation."

"What about four months?" Manny offered.

Mr. Jackson opened his mouth to protest, but Manny continued to bridge this fragile gap.

"Four months of retro pay," Manny said. "Then in another four months we come back to this table to check the progress of the Restoration Project. If there has been no movement, then the union gets another payout."

Mr. Jackson thought for a moment. Manny saw the gap lessening each second.

"In addition," Manny turned to Satterfeld, "you commit to hiring the union fishermen to help with the clean-up effort. No one knows the waterways better than they do."

Satterfeld grumbled, but Manny could tell he'd brought the two closer than they'd ever been before.

It turned out that Manny was right. They weren't as far apart as they all thought. And in the end, they each gave a little and received a bit. No one was entirely happy, but they reached an agreement that everyone could live with.

Once the deal was inked, Manny watched the two men sign the contract. He released his held breath, glad that he no longer had anything to worry about with this situation. The two sides had come together, made a commitment and put it in a contract. Nothing could go wrong.

CHAPTER NINETEEN

PUMPKIN'S PHONE RANG. THE NAME on the caller ID gave her butterflies.

"I'm coming to sweep you off your feet."

"Manny!" she laughed. It was a joyous sound. She almost didn't believe the girlish sound came from her. "I have to pick up Seth in twenty minutes." She sat at her desk, filing away poorly written term papers in the English Department's offices.

"All taken care of," Manny said.

"What?"

"Gale is on her way to pick him up. You just have to call his school and tell them it's okay that he leaves with her."

Pumpkin was speechless.

"Are you biting your lip?" His voice was the low register of a lion's once more.

The sharp sting on her lower lip told her she was doing as he predicted. Her first instinct had been to say that she didn't want to inconvenience him or Gale. That she would handle this matter on her own. Always on her own. Everything on her own.

Pumpkin released her hold on her lip. "Thank you. You guys... you guys are great."

"I missed seeing you today." Manny's voice turned serious.

Pumpkin's heart was in her throat; her head believed his words but still she said, "You did?"

"Yeah," he sighed into the receiver. "I've got a plan for tonight. Candles, romance, all the trimmings. Get ready to be wooed. Okay?"

"Manny, you know I'm a sure thing, right?"

His roar was one of laughter. "No, Pumpkin," he said when he sobered. "You're the real thing."

She had no come back for that one. She was somebody's One. Someone had chosen her to fill the role of princess, heroine, star.

"I'll be there in five minutes."

Pumpkin made the call to Seth's school. She packed up her things and headed down the steps to the exit. When she got there a white horse was waiting for her. A silver horse, on a white car. The engine revved in greeting.

Manny hopped out, a grin as large as a horse's on his handsome face. His step faltered as he came closer. His eyes did that glazing thing where he looked at something just beyond her.

Pumpkin skated her hands over her arm wishing she saw what he did.

Manny approached slowly, his eyes roving over every inch of her until they came to rest on her face. "Can I kiss you?"

She smiled, confidence welling inside her. "You have to ask?"

"We're on school grounds. Isn't there a rule about cavorting."

"I think that's between teachers and students."

The kiss began slow, and then quickly turned urgent. Parting for the briefest second, Manny inhaled like he was taking a drag, then dove once more for her lips.

His arms came around her, pulling Pumpkin closer to him, while his body pressed her against the door of the car. They didn't stop until they heard catcalls coming from the vicinity of the football field.

Manny took Pumpkin's arm and walked her to the passenger door. He deposited her inside and then rushed around to jump into the driver's seat. Putting the car in gear, Manny pulled out of the lot.

"I'm sorry about the Press Conference," he said. "I probably should've warned you. I know you didn't sign up for all of this."

Pumpkin took a deep breath. This was the perfect segue into the conversation she needed to have with him tonight. The one where she told him she was his, except for one minor, contractual detail, which was her soon to be ex-husband.

"I've signed up for things I've later regretted..." she began and then faltered.

Her marriage had been a mistake. She'd known that for sure when she caught Anthony checking out the MILF-y clerk who handed them their marriage license. But at the time, her head told her this was the smart thing to do for her child.

She was a smart girl. She would figure out how to make it work. Her heart had protested the lack of love, or connection, or fidelity in her relationship with Anthony.

When she looked over at Manny, it was there. They'd connected on a soul deep level. No one had ever touched her like he did and no one else ever would.

And love?

She felt it from her toenails to her hair roots.

"Listen, Pumpkin. I don't have a storybook past. I've made some mistakes, broken a few hearts." Manny stopped at a light and turned to her. When he smiled he looked directly into her eyes, directly into her soul. "But you probably have a skeleton or two in your own closet?"

It was another perfect segue to her story.

Pumpkin remained mute.

"But, hey, let's not open those doors right now," he said. "We can deal with it in the morning. I just want to curl myself around you tonight."

And finally, she found her voice. "Okay."

Manny leaned in to kiss her, but the blare of a car horn stopped him. "Hold that thought." He hit the gas.

They stopped at her apartment first. She let Gale and Seth in and grabbed a change of clothes for work in the morning. By the time she was ready to leave, Seth and Gale were so engrossed in their troll concoction that Seth barely registered her departure.

Twenty minutes later Pumpkin found herself wandering through ornate white columns, past a uniformed butler, and into the colossus that was Charmayne House.

"What do you think?" Manny asked.

"That I knew you were too good to be true. You still live in your parents' house."

Manny barked out a laugh and steered her towards his wing of the compound. His rooms were masculine in design, with deep browns and blacks, a few accents of color here and there. There were pictures of Manny's family along a mantelpiece. A huge flat screen TV mounted onto the wall. The bathroom was tidy. She poked her head into his bedroom, and grew nervous of the huge four-poster bed that she spied in there.

"That's for later." Manny came up behind her, resting his hand on her hip, his chin on her shoulder. He planted a trail of kisses from her neck to her ear. "You hungry?" He turned her around and aimed them toward the dining area. "I got you pasta. Your favorite right."

Pumpkin looked at him stunned. "It is my favorite. How did you know that?"

"I overheard you tell one of the volunteers."

She blinked and then shook her head. "I'm just not used to anyone paying that much attention to me."

Manny pulled out her chair. "I'm used to being scrutinized, but no one ever really sees me for me. But you do." He leaned down and gave her a soft kiss on her lower lip, tugging it from her teeth. Then he pulled away and took a seat next to her.

What he'd said, about being scrutinized, that had been another good segue. Her past couldn't wait until the morning. Manny had laid himself bare to her, but she was still cloaked in secrets.

Pumpkin took a deep breath. "I wanted to talk to you about that, people scrutinizing you." She pushed the pasta away. "There are things about me that people might use against you."

"Things like what?"

"Well, that I'm a single mother for one—"

"Pumpkin, you know I don't care about—"

"Manny, I know you don't care, but I don't want anyone using my choices against you."

"So, what are you saying?"

"Well," she swallowed a lump in her throat. "That I'd be okay if we kept our relationship to ourselves. I think you should retract what you said earlier today."

Manny sat up, regarded her. "You're saying not only do you want me to look like a flip-flopper, you also want me to become a liar."

Pumpkin sighed. She just needed to spit it out. "Manny—"

No," he said. "You're the woman I want to be with. You're in my life. I'll protect you from the press, but I'm not hiding you. It took me too long to find you." He picked up his fork and aimed it at her. "You're lucky I'm not shouting it from the rooftop."

Pumpkin's heart welled at his impassioned speech. She reached for her own plate, but not before giving it one last shot. "I just don't want to be the cause of you not achieving your dreams."

"Because you stepped away from yours?"

The sterling silver fork clattered to the china plate. Pumpkin jerked back like she'd been slapped. Manny rose from his place. He came within an inch of her, cupping her face, then angling it so that she stared him straight in his gray eyes.

"We're both going to reach for exactly what we want in our lives. No more excuses. No more trying to be other people's image of us. I see you, Malika Tavares. I liked what I saw before you began to glow before my eyes. We don't hide what we want anymore, especially from one another. Deal?"

Pumpkin's breaths trembled when they passed her lips. She wasn't hiding. Anthony wasn't a part of her any longer. He was in her past. Her family couldn't hurt her anymore either. She'd cut them off and they wouldn't be able to hurt Manny if they couldn't touch her. She was free, unencumbered, gathered inside a warm protective bubble, fortified by the strength of this man who held her so dearly.

Pumpkin took in a deep steady breath. "Deal," she said.

Manny took her lips then, nibbling on her lower lip. But he pulled away too soon.

"Now," he returned to his seat. "Tell me about your day," he said, digging into his food.

"My day?"

"Hmmm."

"I... Manny are we going to make love —I mean have sex?" Pumpkin didn't mean to sound so eager, but she was.

Manny grinned lazily as he chewed. He took his time swallowing. "I fully intend to bury myself deeply inside of you, so that you will curl yourself all around me." He paused and took a sip from his glass, his eyes never leaving hers. "But I haven't seen you for nearly two days. And I actually like talking to you. After I make love to you," he made sure to emphasize those two words, "you won't be able to stand, much less hold a conversation. So, Pumpkin, my sweetheart, tell me about your day."

Words began to spill out of Pumpkin's mouth. They had to be mundane words, completely uninteresting words, but Manny watched her, listened to her. He made comments, asked questions, but mostly he just watched her, a slight smile on his face. His eyes constantly dipping to her lips.

Before long, his plate was clear and hers, too. He led them to the couch, no room between them. He continued to ask her questions about her lessons, about her students. And then at some point he began to slowly undress her. If she stopped talking, he stopped the undressing. Soon, Pumpkin was completely naked and in his lap. Manny was no longer watching her lips move, he was more interested in her breasts.

Without warning, his mouth ensnared one of her nipples. He began to suckle, to make wet circles with his tongue. He rubbed a light touch over the other breast. The polar sensations of wetness and air drove Pumpkin out of her mind. She tried to arch into his touch, but as she did, he would pull away. It was sweet torture. She began to whimper.

"Tell me what you want," he said. His deep voice rumbled like a beast in the fields. His light eyes went dark.

"You. I want you."

His lips met hers in an urgent kiss. "You have me, sweetheart," he said against her lips. "Tell me what you want me to do to you."

Pumpkin's mind went blank. She really had no clue as to what she liked. She was just so proud to have worn lace underwear instead of her usual cotton.

Her silence caught Manny's attention. He pulled away, and looked down at her. She swallowed and took a breath before saying anything.

"I've only had one partner, and he was more interested in his own pleasure than mine." She paused looking up into his gray eyes. "I don't know what I like."

"Well," Manny smiled. "We'll just have to try a little of everything and figure it out together."

CHAPTER TWENTY

MANNY CARRIED PUMPKIN TO HIS bedroom. Of course, it was amidst protests of being too heavy, being too silly, being too much. He wanted to wipe that inner dialogue from her brain and replace it. Replace it with expectations of being held, and supported.

He laid Pumpkin down on his bed. Her brown skin shimmered gold on the black sheets.

The sight caught him. He looked at her eyes. Those eyes that had ducked away from his as she proclaimed herself a lesser character in the story of their lives. He leaned down and kissed each one, wishing that she saw this Sight. That she felt the certainty that he did.

He ran his fingers over the mouth that cast forth words that stumped him, that challenged him. He leaned down and laid light kisses at each corner.

Manny undressed quickly. He grabbed a condom and slid onto the mattress. Lying beside Pumpkin, he caught both of her hands in his own. He kissed each one in reverence, watching the slight flecks of gold play across her skin. She writhed beneath him, waiting to follow his command.

Manny rolled himself under Pumpkin so that she was on top
of him. He let go of her hands and wrapped his fingers around the
headboard.

"I'm yours," he told her.

Pumpkin's eyes widened. Not in passion. She was anxious, sitting
over top of him in a position of power.

"There's nothing you could do that would displease me. Just do
what feels good to you," he encouraged. Then he rose up and laid a
light kiss on her lips. "I'm yours," he repeated. "Go on, sweetheart.
Have your way with me."

Manny grinned, but there was an open challenge in his voice. He
returned to his prone position, once again gripping the headboard,
completely at her mercy. Giving her free reign of his body.

Pumpkin licked her lips and he read her thoughts in real time. She
was more concerned that she make him feel good.

"Do what feels good to you," he said. "I promise you it'll feel the
same to me."

Finally, she reached out her hand and grabbed hold of his cock.
Manny sucked in a breath and gripped the headboard. She rose up
and slid down onto him. He fought to keep his eyes open as her
tight heat molded around him. They stayed that way for a moment,
connected. And then she began to move.

She began slowly, her hips making a circular movement that was
absolute heaven. It wasn't long before she became lost in it. Her
movements came faster and more accentuated. Manny had to dig his
nails into the wooden headboard as he strained to hold on and not
interrupt her with his touch.

Then the little vixen grinned down at him, realizing with glee that
he was in fact enjoying this. Enjoying her. His eyes were glued on her,

desire clearly written over his features. Tiny beads of sweat on his forehead and chest. He panted. Pumpkin sucked in her lower lip and Manny lost it.

He released the headboard and grabbed the nape of her neck, pulling her into him. His thrusts quick and urgent; his kisses slow and gentle. The polarity of the two sensations threatened to split them in two. Pumpkin whimpered against his lips. And that's when he began to whisper in her ear.

"Aw, Pumpkin, you fit me so perfectly."

"Oh, Pumpkin, I can't get close enough to you."

"God, Pumpkin, you're the most precious thing in my life."

That one completely shattered her and her body exploded from the inside out. Manny felt the contractions of her inner muscles as they gripped his cock from the root to the tip. Manny held her tightly. She continued to shiver and shake. He rained kisses down her neck, across her forehead. He'd never felt so whole in all his life as he did holding the woman he loved while she came apart in his arms.

The woman he loved? It was true. He'd been falling for her before his eyes told him to do so.

"Catch your breath, Pumpkin," he said. "Because I'm not finished with you yet."

With lightning-quick speed, he flipped her on her back. Tossing her legs over his shoulders. He pumped into her deeply, needing to get to the heart of her, the core of her.

Desperate to touch the source of the light he saw. It didn't take many thrusts. He felt her swelling around him. In a matter of seconds, something burst from both of them.

They came together, calling out each other's names. If Manny hadn't known before, he knew now that his world had changed.

Manny awoke the next morning with his body wrapped around warm, supple woman. One arm thrown over his head, a second held the warm flesh securely tucked into his side. He opened one eyelid to find Pumpkin staring at him. When she realized he was awake, she blinked and looked away.

"What's going through your head this morning?" he asked.

"I..." She tried to duck her head, but he wouldn't let her.

"Don't hide from me," he urged.

"I dreamed of you."

"Last night?"

She shook her head. "Kinda my whole life. I just always wrote someone else into the role. Some imaginary, faceless man."

"I don't want anyone else for this role, Pumpkin."

"Neither do I." She put her hand on his cheek, testing its realness. Then her hand slipped to his heart. "I want to be your fairytale princess. I want it so bad. But..."

She paused and took a deep breath. Manny wanted to lend her his certainty. To let her know that there was nothing she could do or say that would dissuade him. Golden light or not, he was all in.

"Forget the fairytale," he said. "I'm not interested in having a damsel in distress at my side. I want a strong, grown woman. We write our own story from this moment on. You and me. And I think it's time for another love scene right about now."

Pumpkin reached up and captured his lips. Manny felt her smiling against his lips before teasing his tongue into her mouth. Her hands clutched at his back as she tried to launch deeper into his mouth, pressing herself closer and closer to him. She wrapped one, then another leg around his waist.

He reached his hand toward his bedside table and came up with air. Manny looked up at the box of condoms. "Damn it. We're out."

Pumpkin frowned. She raised her head to peer into the box, which was indeed empty. Pumpkin's head collapsed onto the pillow. She ran a toe up his thigh. Undulated her hips into his own. Manny was ready to attack when she trapped her bottom lip into her mouth before meeting his eyes.

"If you come over to my place tonight," she said, "I'll be sure and have a super pack ready and waiting for you."

"Deal," he grinned and kissed her languidly.

It took an eternity for them to get dressed. There was much kissing and tasting with each article of clothing as it went on each of their bodies. Especially on Manny's part, because Pumpkin tasted as good as she looked, and the fact that she liked this indulgence of his only spurred him on.

Finally, they were in his car and heading to the high school. Pumpkin lounged back in the seat, looking utterly content. At some point, he entwined his hand with hers and had her work the gearshift with him. They didn't speak, but they both sported small smiles in the silence of the car.

Pulling up at the school, Manny got out and opened the door for her. When Pumpkin got out, he pressed her against the passenger door.

"Mr. Charmayne! I'm supposed to be setting an example for my students," she laughed.

"We'll show them how it's done properly then." He captured her lips in a deep and probing kiss which left her breathless and grinning stupidly.

"Take your hands off my wife!"

Pumpkin froze in his arms.

Manny looked around in confusion. He'd heard the words, but they didn't make sense.

A dark man in a leather jacket with a close-shaved head stepped out from the shadows of the building, his eyes intent on Pumpkin.

"That's," the man pointed to Pumpkin, "my wife."

Manny shook his head. They were only three words, but he could not comprehend them.

Manny looked down at Pumpkin. Her eyes were huge, the top half of her body clung to him. The hand he had on her lower back pulled her into his side, protectively, possessively. His gray eyes searched hers; waiting for the denial that only she could give.

"Pumpkin? Do you know this man?"

"This is Seth's dad."

"I'm her husband," the man said.

Manny released his hand from Pumpkin's lower back, but she refused to let him go.

"You're married," Manny accused quietly.

"Yes, but—"

Manny turned away from her, scrubbing a hand over his face.

"I filed for divorce weeks ago," she said.

"Weeks," Manny turned back to Pumpkin. His face a mix of torment and betrayal. He opened his mouth to speak, but in the end just let out a breath, shaking his head. This could not be. She was his. He saw it as clearly as day.

"I was going to tell you last night," she insisted.

"Tell me what? That you were getting divorced? Or that you were married to begin with?"

He blinked at her, his eyesight going blurry, his Sight failing. He reached out a hand to steady himself on his car.

"Manny?" Pumpkin reached for him, her palm landing on his heart.

Manny jerked away from her.

Pumpkin cradled her hand to her own heart. Her teeth captured her lower lip, biting hard. Her brow wrinkled, frowning deeply. A tear sparkled at the corner of each eyelid.

Manny's every instinct urged him to kiss the pain away from her lips and brow, to enfold her in his arms and wipe away the hurt. His eyes flicked once more to the man behind her. The man, her husband, made no move to comfort her, no move to claim her.

"I'm sorry," Pumpkin said. She stepped aside, out of the way of both males.

Manny couldn't look at her. The sight of her hurt his eyes. He dipped inside his car, kicked the Mustang into gear, and reared the car out of there.

CHAPTER TWENTY-ONE

PUMPKIN WATCHED MANNY PULL AWAY. The cloud of exhaust left her cold. Her fingers trembled. Her hands skated up her arms in an attempt to find warmth. Her eyes struggled to keep Manny's silhouette in the driver's side in focus, but his shape blurred as he sped away. The man beside her came into sharp focus.

"Three years." Pumpkin was surprised at the lack of emotion in her voice.

She should be angry, hysterical, but she was calm, clear, and collected. This turn of events was not unexpected. She'd snuck into this fairytale land on a lie. It had to strike midnight at some point in time. She just wished it had been under the cover of night instead of the light of dawn. At least that way she'd be able to crawl under her covers and hide. Instead, she addressed the frog who'd crawled back from out of the swamp.

"Three years and nothing from you." Pumpkin's eyes stayed on the growing distance between the Mustang and her.

From the corner of her eye, she saw Anthony reached out his

hand, think better of it, and shove his hand in his pocket. "That was wrong of me," he said.

"Wrong?" Pumpkin turned to him.

"I came back to try and make things better." His voice didn't sound as she remembered it. And there was a grimace on his face where there had always been a smirk.

"Make things better?" she repeated.

"Look, I'm sorry, Pumpkin."

"Sorry?" Pumpkin parroted.

Anthony looked down at his feet, as though he were actually sad about that. The Anthony she knew wouldn't care less. The Anthony she knew never once apologized for anything.

"I'm here to make things better," he said. "Man up and handle my responsibilities."

"Man up? You just destroyed my life in sixty seconds."

Anthony looked down the road, down to where Manny's car had long since disappeared. "I thought maybe we could give it—us— another chance." The words didn't flow smoothly from his mouth. He shoved his hands in his pockets. His shoulders hunched.

"You think I've been sitting around waiting for you to come back and make things better." It wasn't a question. She saw it clearly on his face. The residual shock at seeing her with another man. "I've filed for divorce," she continued. "It's nearly finalized."

Anthony frowned. No, actually he pouted. "You can't do that without my consent." There was the Anthony she knew.

"You abandoned us. Technically, you stopped being my husband after the first year."

"Look, would you just give me another chance?" His tone reminded her of Seth arguing about bedtime. Anthony reached for her hand.

Pumpkin jerked away and out of his reach. "You're not the man I want."

Something flashed across his face. The emotion was nothing like the anguish she'd witnessed moments before on Manny's face. "I want to see my son."

God, Manny. What was she going to do about Manny?

The distance between them crushed her. She had to talk to him, try to explain. Why hadn't she done this last night as she'd planned?

"Are you listening to me?"

She knew why. She was a coward. At the first sign of trouble, she'd shrunk into the shadows like a sidekick. She'd stepped off the uphill main road and back down to easy street.

"Pumpkin!"

The sound of her name on Anthony's tongue grated her nerves. Pumpkin turned and headed into the school building. She couldn't deal with this now. She had to get through the school day so that she could get to Manny.

"Pumpkin," Anthony called after her, but he didn't follow.

The school day went by in a blur. If it hadn't been for DaeHo handling her TA duties, Pumpkin wouldn't have made it through. The moment the bell rang, she shot out of the school and headed towards the campaign offices. Seth had Chess Club, which bought her an hour of time to try to talk to Manny.

She had no idea what she would say to him. Movie monologues played in her head all day long. But none seemed appropriate. This had to be done face-to-face, straight from the heart.

Climbing the stairs to the campaign offices, she knew something was wrong. When she opened the door, the office was in an uproar.

Pumpkin caught a hold of someone she'd manned booths with. "What's going on?"

The girl raised her eyebrows at Pumpkin. You don't know, they said. "The news got hold of court papers." She looked Pumpkin up and down, accusation and judgment clearly written on her brow. She moved away from Pumpkin in a harried fashion.

Pumpkin looked up to catch the whole office looking at her with a mixture of pity and scorn. Pumpkin ducked her chin to her chest as she made her way to Manny's office. She stepped carefully. Each step felt like a rough patch. Her legs felt like jelly.

The door was open. Manny sat at his desk. His brows drawn as he rubbed his chin. Pumpkin caught glimpses of him in snatches. Lorielle and Heather circled him, pacing back and forward.

"You could've at least kept it under the sheets, Armand." Lorielle said.

"You've lost ground with married women," said Heather.

"I told you she was bad for your numbers." Lorielle's heels tapped out a harsh tune.

"But you've gained ground with men 18 to 45." Heather tapped on her tablet, cycling through more numbers.

"You need to end it," Lorielle said.

Armand tugged at his lip, then his hand went down to his heart. As though he sensed her, his eyes rose and landed on Pumpkin. Surprise passed through his smokey eyes, followed by the briefest flare of desire, or that may have been her imagination. Then his eyes shuttered and he looked everywhere but at her.

"You? Haven't you done enough?"

"Lorielle," Manny's admonishment was quietly dealt.

The silence that followed was awkward.

Pumpkin gathered her courage and took a step forward. "Can we talk?"

Manny took his time pushing away from his desk. She could see he was stalling, thinking through his answer. When it came, it was not what she hoped for. "Now's not a good time, Malika."

Malika?

"I know," Pumpkin said. "And I know it's my fault. Not telling you, the poll numbers—"

Lorielle huffed at that.

"But I want to help." Pumpkin's voice faltered and she took a step back. "The campaign, I mean. I'll just tell them it wasn't me — the woman you're dating. That we are just friends." God, did he hear the hope in her voice that she could salvage at least that.

Manny's gray eyes flashed on hers and locked. He stared at her. Not looking in front of her or through her. At her, like he would a normal person. Pumpkin felt her knees about to give out. The soles of her feet ached.

"That could work." Lorielle picked up her pacing. "You never did confirm that you two were actually dating. I could spin this."

Manny's jaw tensed. Pumpkin saw it moving, grinding down as though chewing on words. She rested her hand against the doorframe for support. She held her breath, unsure which words she wanted to hear: the ones that would potentially save his campaign, or the ones that would deny what they had had been real.

Manny's eyes flickered over her shoulder and narrowed. Pumpkin turned around. DaeHo came through the door. Her face flushed and she was out of breath.

"DaeHo? What is it?" Pumpkin touched her shoulder. "What's wrong?"

"It's Tyler," Dae said between breaths. "He's been arrested."

"Arrested," said Manny. "For what?"

"They caught him trying to hack into your opponent's website. He put up some vulgar picture last night before they caught it and took it down. They were able to trace it back to him somehow."

"Dae, sweetie, calm down," Pumpkin told her.

"Where is he now?" asked Manny.

"He was taken into custody," DaeHo said. "I was his one phone call. I don't know his mom's phone number."

"Malika?" Manny looked at her expectantly. "You have his mother's contact information at the school, right?"

"Yeah." But what did that have to do with anything?

"You call her and let her know what's going on. I'll go down to the precinct and see if I can get him out."

"What!"

Lorielle and Pumpkin said it together at the same time. Manny's surprised eyes landed on Pumpkin though.

"Manny," Lorielle started. "We have a serious situation to handle. Let his teacher handle at least one of the messes she's brought to our door."

"This isn't her mess," Manny said. "It's mine. The kid did this because of me."

"No," said Pumpkin crossing the threshold. "He did it because he thought he could get away with it."

"Malika," Manny's tone was an admonishment. "However misguided, he's our responsibility. Call his mother. I'll go get him out."

"But—" Pumpkin didn't get a chance to get her words out as Manny and DaeHo marched past her and out the door.

CHAPTER TWENTY-TWO

"THANKS FOR GETTING ME OUT, Mr. Charmayne." Tyler looked at the floor as he spoke. His hands jammed into his jean pockets. His body caved in on itself, protectively. Ready to shield itself from the oncoming storm of admonishment.

They sat in a holding room. Tiled walls and plastic chairs. The cold air blew in through a vent and sank under Manny's skin. Manny looked at Tyler. The kid wore a jacket, but Manny spied a tremor run down his shoulders.

Manny didn't ask the kid why he did it. He knew why. He'd done it himself years earlier. Only, tampering with a poster wasn't a crime. Hacking into a website was.

"I got you out," Manny said, "because I don't think you'll make a habit of this type of behavior. Getting arrested, I mean. Am I wrong? You are the type of man who learns from his mistakes?"

"Yeah?" Tyler said the one word as a question, as though he was unsure of what type of man he was and he was waiting to be told the answer. He looked for Manny to continue, to write on the parchment of who he would become.

"What you did was stupid, Tyler."

Like an iron gate, Tyler's entire being shuttered. His eyes dimmed to half-mast. His fists clenched. His back went rigid.

"Just like I was when I was a kid," Manny continued. "When I pulled that stupid prank."

When Manny had rearranged those letters on his opponent's poster, he'd told himself that it wasn't a lie. The facts were still in there in the mixed up letters. The poster just led people away from the truth.

"People still got hurt," Manny admitted. "I've made a lot of mistakes in my life. I hurt a lot of people because I thought I knew something that they didn't."

Manny had his three-month dating rule in place to try and protect the women he dated. Or so he'd always told himself. He knew in an instant that it wouldn't last. And so he put a time limit on their feelings. They always wound up hurt at the end of their time together, expecting things to turn down one road while he headed in the opposite direction. It didn't protect them. It protected him.

"I stole a good friend's girl."

"No offense, Mr. Charmayne, but I really don't want to hear about you and Ms. Tavares."

Mrs. Tavares, Manny almost corrected him.

Or was it Mrs. Something Else? Maybe Tavares was her maiden name? He didn't know. How could he not know that about The One?

"No, this has nothing to do with Miss Tavares." Manny got out of his own head and turned to face the young man who had been released into his charge. "It's about you. You looked shocked when I came in here to get you. Probably thought nobody was coming for you. Probably think nobody believes in you. But you're wrong. You've got at least two people who believe in you, two people who've got your back. The other one's on the other side of that door."

Tyler looked to the door as though he could see DaeHo on the other side. A tentative smile lit his face. He took a step towards the door, but Manny's hand stopped him.

"Here's the deal though. If we're gonna fight for you, you have to fight for you, too. Okay?"

Tyler's eyes went wide, and then grim. "Yes. I will... Thank you."

Manny stuck out his hand. Tyler grasped it and shook. The kid walked quickly to the door, but once he got to it, he hesitated. He turned the knob slowly and pulled the door a crack open. Tyler peered out through the few inches he allowed open.

The door was wrenched open by a flurry of black hair. Small arms enveloped Tyler's body, a face burrowed into his chest.

Tyler's arms came around DaeHo slowly, as though fearful she was a mirage, the wishful thinking of a man dying of thirst. And then, once he seemed convinced that she was real, he held on so tightly she let out a squeak of protest. No, actually, it was a small laugh.

Manny left the precinct, got in his car, and drove. The picture of Tyler being embraced in the security of DaeHo's arms played over and over in his head. The young girl had been steady in her pursuit of getting him free. She never asserted his innocence. She made no excuses for what he'd done. But she'd been adamant that she was standing by him through the consequences.

At first, Manny's direction was aimless. The Mustang caught in the slow lanes of rush hour, he watched others zooming by in the fast lanes. The double occupancy cars enjoyed the luxury of speed. His Mustang grunted as he down shifted to an even slower speed in the gridlock on the highway.

Before he knew it, he was on the road that led to Pumpkin's place. Manny pulled up to the curb outside her complex and put the car in park at the building next to hers. It had to be his imagination, but he felt that she was nearby. The urge to go to her, embrace her, was so strong. He sat in his car and he waited.

He'd waited all his life for her. Imagined what she would be like. What she would look like, sound like.

The door to her complex opened and she stepped out. Manny's heart beat out of his chest at the Sight of her and the brilliant halo of gold that surrounded her person. He'd thought that he might not see it any longer, now that he knew of her husband. But it was still there. There was no denying it.

She'd changed her clothing. She stood in jeans that molded to her hips. Hips he wanted to feel in his hands, under his body. She wore a plain t-shirt, but it did not hamper Manny's imagination. He'd had her breasts in his mouth. Pumpkin looked out at the horizon, hugging her shoulders, frowning. It was the frown that made Manny open the driver's side door.

When he got out, his anger and hurt all but dissipated. With each step closer to her, the light blinded him. She hadn't told him she was married, but she'd said she'd filed for divorce. She'd said that her husband abandoned them years ago. Was that an outright lie? She'd rearranged the truth. Hadn't he been guilty of that nearly all his life? Showing the women he dated that he was interested in them. Behaving like a model boyfriend until the three-month mark, and then leaving them with the vague explanation that they weren't The One; something he'd known all along. But he'd rearranged the truth to suit his needs.

He used his hand to shield the sun from his eyes as he headed towards her. She must've seen him coming. A smile spread across her face. A beatific smile full of amusement and relief. Her lips began moving, but he couldn't quite make out her words. She held out her arms and a little body smashed into hers. It was Seth and he was not alone.

Manny's feet stopped moving. He watched Pumpkin straighten and stand before her husband. Her eyes surveyed the man as he spoke. The man beamed down at their son, who in turn beamed up at him. Seth laughed at something and it created a domino effect. First the dad-husband laughed. Then Pumpkin began to laugh. Her shoulders shook, her eyes crinkled in that way. Seth said something else and the three of them laughed even harder. The sun chose that moment to shine its rays directly on the family, casting them in a warm glow.

Seeing the three of them together, in that light, was a slap to Manny's very being. He'd known all along that he wasn't The One for the women he'd dated. They all thought they could convince him otherwise and when they couldn't, they lashed out. Manny had accepted each lashing as his due course. But this time was different.

Pumpkin was The One. Even when the sun moved behind a cloud, there was no doubt in Manny's mind. He hadn't known at the moment he'd met her, but he'd started to hope after he'd grown to know her, and care for her, and feel a connection to her. He'd hoped that there was some way he could keep her in his life for all time. The moment he saw her, he'd felt a tremendous amount of relief. Not because he finally had his Sight, but because it was her. Pumpkin was the woman he would've chosen if he had a choice. He didn't imagine that she might belong to another.

Never once had he thought it possible that she might not choose him.

Manny retreated to his car, quickly, so as not to be seen. He dove into the Mustang, turned the ignition, cringing at the engine's roar. He peeled off as quickly as he could, without looking back.

CHAPTER TWENTY-THREE

PUMPKIN LOOKED BETWEEN HER SON and his father. In addition to the uni-brow, she'd never realized that Seth had Anthony's smile. Probably because it looked angelic on her kid, but devilish on his dad.

"Thanks, Dad. I've been wanting to see that movie.""

Seth hadn't seen his dad since he was five. Even during that time, Anthony hadn't been around much. When the two of them spent time together back then it was usually in front of the television watching cartoons.

"I'll see you this weekend?" Seth looked up at his dad, hope in his hazel eyes.

Anthony looked at Pumpkin, the same hazel eyes, reflecting the same hopeful expression.

They hadn't talked about another visit beyond this one. Anthony had gotten her number from her aunt. He'd called as she left Manny's campaign offices, asking to see Seth. They'd met at the Rec Center, and to her surprise, Seth jumped at the chance to hang out with his father. Pumpkin had watched her son's small hand slip easily into his father's large ones as the two went off.

"We'll have to see, buddy," Pumpkin said.

Both of their faces fell. Seth ducked inside the door, leaving her alone with Anthony.

"Look, Pumpkin, I know I haven't been the best husband—"

"You haven't been a husband at all."

"I want to try and be a better father if—"

"You never were an actual father to begin with."

"Well, you were no prize, either."

Pumpkin's hands itched to slam the door in his face, but Anthony's hand rested on the doorjamb.

"You never let me in," he said. "You were so busy pretending you were Cinderella with your wicked aunts and cousins, thinking you deserved some guy to come and sweep you off your feet. And that's what you got; a horny dude who swept you up and onto your back."

Pumpkin tried to slam the door against Anthony's vile words, but he caught it, forcing it to stay open.

Anthony sighed, looking defeated. He took a step back, but didn't relinquish his hold on the door. "I'm trying to be real with you now. I thought maybe you could get to know the real me and..." He shook his head. "But I doubt you'd like the real me. I'm still a horny guy who'd likely sweep you onto your back. And you? You're still chasing after princes."

Anthony let go of the door. So did she.

"I'm a better man than I was," he said. "But I still have my warts. I want Seth to get to know me, the real me, and make his own decisions. Just give me an actual chance this time."

Pumpkin stared up at this man. His uni-brow was furrowed, his shoulders hunched, his head hung low waiting for her verdict. He chanced a glance at her, his hazel eyes, eyes she did not remember ever looking directly at her, held the tiniest spark of hope. His lips, which she'd only known to spout lies, compressed in a grim line. She couldn't remember how she'd fallen for this guy. She didn't know a true thing about him.

"Look," Anthony said, "I'll sign the divorce papers. I know you've got someone new."

"Had someone new," Pumpkin corrected. "You messed that up."

"I'm not the one who lied to him, Pumpkin. You're the one who misrepresented yourself."

Pumpkin jerked back as though he'd thrown cold water on her face.

Anthony closed his eyes and pressed his lips together, as though wishing he could take the words back. "I'm sorry." He opened his eyes. "But it is the truth. Look, I just want to spend some time with my son. It can be supervised, if that's what you need."

Pumpkin felt movement behind her. She turned. "Seth?"

"I wanted to give my dad something." Seth held out the vial of dragon's elixir he'd made with Gale. "For when you leave again. It's supposed to help keep the bad guys away."

Anthony reached out his hand. He turned the vial this way and then that way. "Thanks, buddy, but I'm sticking around." Anthony handed the elixir back to Seth.

Seth shoved his hands in his pockets, a move, Pumpkin realized now, came from his dad. "It's yours. I made it for you."

Pumpkin looked between the two.

"Why don't you come over after school tomorrow," she said. "You can take him to the library and help him with his homework. And then... whatever you guys want to do. Just have him home by dinner."

Anthony turned to her. His grin lit up his features, separating his uni-brow and showcasing his strong chin. "I'll do that. Thank you, Pumpkin."

Seth stepped forward and wrapped his arms around his father's waist. "Good night, dad. Love you."

Pumpkin heard Anthony gasp. She saw a light come on in his eyes as he looked down at Seth's head. Anthony's hand went to cradle the back of his son's neck. Seth looked up and smiled.

"I love you, too, son." Anthony's words were whispered, shaky.

Seth turned and went back inside.

Anthony stood still, watching the empty space for a moment before pulling himself together. He made as though to hug Pumpkin, but stopped himself. He stuck out his hand as though to shake hers. In the end, he rubbed her shoulder awkwardly.

When Seth was born, Pumpkin fell in love with him at first sight. Anthony had not been present. In the days, months, years following Seth's birth, Anthony had barely been present with his son. Never held him or held a conversation with him. Yet in the matter of a few hours, the two had clicked and bonded.

In the five years that she and Anthony were together, they'd never exchanged those three little words. She'd hoped for them, even tried to initiate them once, but the attempt failed. It failed because it wasn't true. Hearing it now between Seth and Anthony, it was evident that it was true.

"You've reached the voicemail of Armand Charmayne. I'm sorry I wasn't available to take your call. Please leave a message and I will return your call at my earliest convenience."

Beep!

That beep grated on Pumpkin's nerves. Their relationship had been reduced to an irritating tone. An impersonal, standardized voice message. She clicked off the phone instead of talking to the beep for the tenth? eleventh? time. It had been three days since she'd seen or heard from Manny. She needed to face facts. It was over. Over before it had even begun. No happy ever after for her. That's what she got for venturing out of her lane.

The beetle puttered along the oneway street. The motor mirroring Pumpkin's mood. She arrived at the recreation center to pick up Seth. Stepping into the building, another failure awaited her.

"Mama, look who's here!"

The man turned slowly, apprehension written on his face.

"Hello, Darrell."

"Malika," Darrell nodded. "I'm just filling in for Brigit. She had her baby last week and they called to see if I'd help out for a couple of weeks while she's on maternity leave."

"Oh, right. I forgot you used to be a part of chess club."

There was an awkward silence, in which Seth looked back and forth between the two of them. Darrell wouldn't look directly at Pumpkin.

"Seth, go get your things." The little man scrambled off to the coatroom. "Darrell—"

"Don't."

Pumpkin sighed. "I just need you to know that it was nothing you did, or didn't do."

Darrell laughed. "That's not true. I obviously didn't do something right. Otherwise you wouldn't have let my friend put his tongue down your throat."

He began to walk away. But stopped and turned back.

"Tell me the truth, Malika."

Pumpkin took a breath. "The truth is I made a mistake. I was attracted to Manny before I met you, but I was scared. And you were..."

"I was what?"

Pumpkin took another breath and tried to pull the bandage off slowly. "You were a good guy. I wanted to be with a good guy, who would be a good role model for my son. Who would really care about me. And you were all those things. I thought you were the smarter choice. And so I chose you."

Darrell turned her words over in his head.

"You're a great guy, Darrell."

"Which is why girls are constantly flocking all over me."

Pumpkin grinned. "That was kind of funny."

Darrell glared.

"If you meant it to be a joke, that is. Which you didn't. I'm sorry. I'll... I'll go." She turned to walk away.

"Did you ever feel anything for me?"

Pumpkin turned back, ready to affirm his question. But then she paused. He deserved the truth. "I liked you."

His face fell.

"A lot," she emphasized. "We made sense together. You and me. I thought that was enough."

"And you and him?"

"I felt a connection to Manny the first time I met him. But I didn't want to date someone like him. I didn't think..."

"Didn't think what?"

With this breath, Pumpkin pulled up her big girl panties. "I didn't think I was good enough."

Darrell's jaw tightened as though chomping down on words he didn't want to escape. "Which translates, you didn't think I was good enough, either."

"No, that's not it." She reached for his arm and he allowed the brief touch. "I didn't think either of us were A-type characters. I thought we were B-story characters."

"What?"

"B-story, supporting characters. The sidekicks."

Darrell looked at her as though she were crazy.

"It's not a bad thing. I thought you were a Ducky. Everybody loves Ducky."

Darrell blinked. "Did you just call me a duck?"

"God, this sounds crazy now, but it's a compliment. You remember the movie, Pretty in Pink? The Jon Cryer character?"

"Jon Cryer? The brother on Two and a Half Men?"

Pumpkin sighed internally instead of lamenting the crumbling state of today's entertainment. "Yeah."

"He's a chiropractor."

"Exactly."

"So, you're likening me to an 80's supporting character, who doesn't get the hot girl in high school, and grows up to mooch off his more successful, womanizing brother?"

"Um... yeah."

"That's supposed to be a compliment how?" Darrell looked at her with his jaw set, eyebrows raised, and shoulders tense.

"It sounds so stupid now."

"Yeah," he said. "It does. I didn't ask you out because I thought you were a lesser character. I thought you were amazing. I really liked you."

"I really liked you, too."

"Just not enough."

"No, not enough," she agreed. "Every girl wants to date the

Charlie, but every girl wants to marry the Ducky and... Okay, maybe
not the Alan. But I think you get my point. Nice guys don't finish
last. Nice guys last."

"But you chose Armand."

"I dated Armand. It didn't last."

"Then he's a fool," Darrell said.

Pumpkin studied Darrell for a second. He was still the smart
choice. Maybe... but she knew she couldn't. Regardless of whether
she and Manny would ever be together again, she still felt that
connection that drew them together in the first place. It was alive and
kicking, whether Manny would pay attention to it or not.

She smiled up at Darrell and shook her head. "It's my fault. I
screwed it up. And I don't know if he can get over it."

"If it's meant to be, it'll work out." Darrell reached out and
rubbed her shoulder.

Pumpkin grasped his hand and smiled. "You sound like Gale."

Darrell looked at her. He wasn't smiling at her, but he wasn't
exactly throwing daggers at her with his eyes any longer. Maybe
they'd be okay.

"Ready, mama?"

Pumpkin turned and smiled down at Seth.

"Mr. Darrell, I'll see you at the chess tournament next weekend?"

"Of course," Darrell said to Seth. As the kid headed for the exit,
Darrell turned to face a wide-eyed Pumpkin. He shrugged. "I broke
up with you, not Seth."

Pumpkin looked between the two of them. Even if she and
Darrell couldn't be friends, she knew that he and Seth had something
special and she wouldn't stand in the way of that.

"Thank you, Darrell."

He shrugged and turned to go, but then looked back. "You know,

Malika, maybe you should stop living in the story world of what people should be like, and give the two of you an actual chance in reality."

Pumpkin's mouth fell open at his proclamation. When she was ready to respond, Darrell turned and walked back into the rec room.

When Pumpkin walked into class the next morning, Tyler was back in school. But before she could get to him to admonish him for nearly costing Manny his campaign, DaeHo stepped in her path.

"Don't worry, Ms. T. I already ripped him a new one."

Pumpkin stared down at the tiny girl who had her hands on her nonexistent hips and a stern look on her face. She glanced over in Tyler's direction. Upon seeing her look, he sobered up from the conversation he was having with another classmate. His spine actually straightened and an uncertain smile played at his lips. Pumpkin looked between the two.

Finally, DaeHo broke into a soft smile and Tyler relaxed a little. "I really don't think he knew any better, Ms. T," she said. "I'm not saying that as an excuse. He really respects Mr. Charmayne and he wanted to help him. In a messed up way, though."

Of course, he did. Tyler didn't have any home training. But then again, neither did Pumpkin. Her family's training was anything but good. But she, at least, knew better. Didn't she?

"It's not your responsibility to try and teach him right from wrong, Dae."

"There I disagree with you, Ms. T." Wise eyes smiled back at Pumpkin. "How can someone learn calculus, if they don't first know arithmetic?"

"But if someone's not willing to learn arithmetic?"

"But he is," DaeHo insisted. "It's just that no one ever paid him enough attention to see that."

Meaning that no one believed in Tyler until DaeHo. And then Manny.

"I'm smarter than you think, Ms. T. In subjects other than Math and English. I like him a lot. And I believe in him. He knows I'm not going to put up with foolishness. He's going to make amends for this. I've forgiven him. Mr. Charmayne has forgiven him. You should consider doing the same. Just consider giving him an actual chance, Ms. T."

An actual chance. It was the third time someone used those exact words with her. Pumpkin had handed out tons of chances in her lifetime. But who had ever given her one? Manny had given Tyler another chance. But he hadn't answered any of her calls.

At the end of class, Tyler came up to her desk.

"Thank you," he said.

Pumpkin did a theatrical double-take, only no acting was involved.

Tyler rolled his eyes at her dubious expression and almost turned to walk away. But then, "I know you don't like me. I know you think I'm gonna hurt her. About a month ago, you'd have been right. But now..."

He shrugged and stared at his shoes. When he looked back up, Pumpkin could have sworn there was earnestness in his demonic eyes.

"She stuck by me," he said. "No one's ever done that. My mom didn't even come to bail me out... this time."

Tyler looked away, and for a moment, Pumpkin actually felt sorry for the little devil.

"Mr. Charmayne stuck his neck out for me," Tyler continued.

"He said it was because of you."

"Me?" Manny had talked about her?

"Well, he said it wasn't about you, but I got the impression that it was."

"What did he say?" Pumpkin hedged.

"He told me that if he was gonna fight for me, that I would have to fight for me, too."

But Manny wasn't even fighting for them. He'd given up on their relationship by evidence of not returning any of her calls.

"Anyway, I just wanted to tell you all that. And," Tyler reached in his backpack. "And hand in this. It's all my makeup work from…" He shrugged. "From before. And here's a draft of this week's assignment. Might have some grammatical errors because Dae hasn't looked at it yet."

Pumpkin took the papers, utterly speechless. All this rhetoric sounded great, but…

"Look, whatever, Ms. Tavares. We don't have to go all after-school special now, okay."

"Good," she nodded relieved.

"Good."

"Tyler?" DaeHo was in the door. "You ready?"

Tyler nodded and turned to join her. Dae cast her teacher a look, hoping for approval. Pumpkin sighed and mentally threw up her hands. She gave her TA a weak smile as the two walked out the door together.

Pumpkin stared at the door long after it closed. One of the fluorescent lights buzzing over her head caught her ear. The sound mimicked Manny's voice mail beep.

She'd thought Tyler had swept DaeHo off her feet, when in fact it was the other way around. The buzzing overhead faded out as the light blinked fully on. It struck Pumpkin that she had made a mistake. She had miscast DaeHo and Tyler.

Sure, she and Dae were alike in that they both were the smart outcasts. Other than that, DaeHo had led a charmed life full of love and privilege in her family, like a little princess. She'd even saved Tyler from danger, like a real live heroine straight out of a main plot, A-story line.

Tyler may not have wanted for much in the money department, but he was void when it came to family. He didn't have anyone who loved and believed in him. He'd never learned to believe in himself. He'd played the role others pushed him into with that lack of belief.

No loved one had pushed Pumpkin into her role of B-story support. She'd stepped willingly into that lane. She'd never fought to get into any other place. Maybe now it was time to switch to a fast lane and take on a big story.

CHAPTER TWENTY-FOUR

THE MESSAGE LIGHT ON HIS phone flashed in tune to the beat of his heart. Manny ran his thumb over Pumpkin's name. He'd taken a picture of her orange beetle one day and used it as a screen saver. At the time, he'd thought it was safer than taking a picture of her face. He'd caught himself one too many times sneaking glances, and even all-out staring, at her while she worked his voter registration booths. Even now, the picture of the round vehicle brought to mind the curve of her ass, her breasts.

Manny turned the phone over so that he would not see the message indicator or the car any longer. But still, images of her flashed through his mind. He saw her smiling, but it wasn't at him. It was at her son and his father. Every time he saw Pumpkin's face now it was with the two of them standing in the sun, looking like a picture perfect family.

Manny shoved away from his desk and stalked over to the picture window that overlooked the city. The sun was a golden disk in the sky; he felt its warmth on his face. He yanked the blinds shut.

"It's a shame to hide such a lovely view, on such a bright and sunny day."

"Did you know she was married?" Manny asked.

"I knew there had to be some other man in her life at some point. My clue was the kid."

Manny turned and looked at his aunt. Gale stood in his doorway.

"I could see that she tried to love someone, forced herself really. When I met her, her head and heart chakras were out of tune. That changed in a matter of days of being around you."

"She belongs to someone else."

"People haven't belonged to other people in hundreds of years, Armand."

"Tell that to the courts. She's still married. It's a binding, legal contract."

"Armand—"

"I thought that when I finally saw her, that my Sight would be a guarantee." He thought he and The One would be riding off into the sunset, instead of him standing by on her front stoop, while she laughed with her son and husband.

"Love is not a guarantee." Gale came and placed her hands on his shoulders, steady hands. "Love is a gift."

Manny turned back towards the window. The blinds hid the sunlight from his view.

"Have you talked to her?" asked Gale.

No, he hadn't. The thought made his heart beat hard. He'd lived in a kind of limbo his whole life, waiting for her. And now that she was here, and there existed the possibility of not having her, of her choosing someone else over him, Manny felt paralyzed.

"It doesn't work that way, Armand. The Sight is all the magic we get. It tells us who our best match is, but after that hint, we're just like everyone else in the world. We have to work at love, work to make it strong, work to make it last. It's not magic, it's give and take."

Manny turned to address his aunt, but Heather poked her head into the door.

"We have a problem," she said looking at him instead of her tablet.

Manny picked up the phone and pressed the button to the line Heather indicated.

"Mr. Satterfeld," Manny said into the phone, "is there a problem?"

"No, no problem son. Just a new arrangement."

Ice ran down Manny's back before the man began to outline his new arrangement.

"Four months of back pay is just too steep for us."

"It's what everyone agreed to," Manny said.

"True, but I've had my people look at it and we've seen that the cost will be too much to bear. However, if we went ahead with the river diversion—"

"The Union is entirely against any diversion," Manny said.

"Only a partial diversion," said Satterfeld. "The oil and energy companies are willing to invest heavily in such a project."

"Mr. Satterfeld, this is not the original plan. You're changing the terms of the agreement."

"If you're going to be mayor of this town, son, you can't give in to every demand the people want. I'm simply rearranging some of the terms..."

Manny stopped listening. His head throbbed as the deal he'd cultivated began falling apart. It was all falling apart. Everything he had worked for was falling apart. Everything in his life was falling apart.

Manny looked down at the contract that both sides had signed. He'd spent so much time on this contract. He'd spent so much time with each side, hearing their grievances, working toward a common goal. He couldn't let it go.

"You all signed a contract," Manny insisted.

"Just because you sign a contract doesn't mean things will go smoothly, son." Satterfeld's voice was dismissive on the other end of the line.

Manny opened his mouth to say more, but his rebuttal stuck in his throat. He'd signed a contract with Pumpkin. Not a written one, but one that wrote on the soul of his being.

With his words and his being, he had promised her his heart, his fidelity, his soul.

A contract.

They'd made promises, but things hadn't gone smoothly.

"What the board wants and what the union wants are two different things," Satterfeld went on. "There's not enough to go around for everyone, son."

But there was enough. There were millions of dollars in that fund. There were literally enough fish in the sea for all parties involved. But Satterfeld was so used to hoarding, that he couldn't see it.

"Mr. Satterfeld, if you take this to the Union, the whole deal will fall apart. Everyone will lose. Is that what you want?"

Manny wondered if that's what she thought? If Pumpkin had come to him and told him the real deal, that she was still legally married to a man who'd abandoned her, would he have even given her a chance?

"I want what's best for this company," Satterfeld was saying. "For your family's company."

"When you sign a contract it's the best case scenario," Manny said.

"That was the best case, a few days ago. But now new information has come to light."

When Manny found out about Pumpkin's marriage, he'd left. Left because he'd gotten scared. Scared that she wouldn't choose him, but he knew he'd choose her. He knew that she was The One for him, even with his eyes closed. He couldn't imagine anyone he wanted to spend his days with more. Anyone he'd happily sit quietly with or watch a movie with. Anyone whose hand he wanted to hold, or to stand by him for support. He wanted to pull her into the light with him and watch her shine. Instead, he'd turned his back on her and left.

Love is not a guarantee, it's a gift.

"I was wrong," Manny said to no one in particular.

"So you agree with me, son?"

Manny looked down at the phone he cradled in his hand. "Agree with you? God, no. If you bring this to the Union, everything will fall apart and you'll be right back where you started. And do you know why?"

Satterfeld's answer was an unintelligible grunt.

"You're going to fail because you think the Union, the community, can't succeed without your help. The plan we came up with together is not a hand out. It allows people the opportunity to stand on their own two feet, while giving the Company the opportunity to prove its word to a community that lost faith in it. But if you go back on this deal, you'll not only cause the whole of the community to lose, you'll perpetuate a vicious cycle of resentment between the community and the company."

Manny looked up and saw his aunt smiling at him as she walked out of his door. She left the door wide open as she departed.

"Well, what if we—" Satterfeld began, but Manny cut him off.

"You can't fumble your way through this. If you make a mistake, a second chance will be extremely hard to come by in this scenario. No one will be there to save you."

Manny hung up the phone and left the room, closing his door behind him.

CHAPTER TWENTY-FIVE

PUMPKIN EXITED THROUGH THE TEACHER exit that led to the school's parking lot. She was glad to leave. She hadn't been able to concentrate much after her chat with DaeHo and Tyler.

Speak of the devil. As she pulled into the queue of cars to make the left-hand turn out of the school, she spied Tyler and DaeHo leaving together, holding hands. A few girls sniggered behind DaeHo's back. Before Dae's smile could falter, Tyler turned a death glare onto the girls; girls he'd had his arms around just weeks ago. The girls' laughter stopped immediately. Tyler turned back to DaeHo. He kissed her forehead before handing her into his car.

Pumpkin sat dumbfounded as she watched the two drive in the opposite direction of her, towards the bright horizon. How did that just happen? Tyler made so many mistakes. But there he was, behind the wheel, steering his own destiny, with the girl he purported to care for sitting beside him. And they were driving off into the freaking sunset.

Pumpkin eyed her phone, which rested in the center cup holder. It sat there silently. A horn sounded behind Pumpkin, telling her to move forward. She moved the few inches forward until she was at the crossroads. The red stoplight flashed in her face. It seemed to take a long time to turn to green. She continued to sit there and wait, her silent phone lazing in the cup holder.

Pumpkin reached for her phone tapped the unlock code. But then the light changed. She hesitated for another second, causing the horn to blare behind her again. She put her phone back into the cup holder and pulled into traffic. This had to be done face to face, anyway.

The wheels in her head turned. This was not the end of the story between her and Manny, it couldn't be. It had been a plot-perfect Cinderella trope thus far. Commoner yearns for a royal life —check. When the door to that world opens, crucial information about herself is withheld from the prince —double check. Manny should be gallivanting around the city trying to find her, with her missing shoe in hand. But her shoe was in her closet, meaning the ball was back in her court. It was up to Pumpkin to fix this and get the HEA back on track.

She needed to get past this turn in the road. She knew the next part of this story. It was the Grand Gesture. The place where it appeared that all hope was lost and the lovers couldn't see a path back towards each other. Unless and until the one who screwed up came up with some crazy idea to get them back.

That was it. She just had to think of something big, something bold, to get her man back. Something that would show him that she was a changed woman.

Pumpkin wracked her brain, scrolling through her mental rolodex of movie plots for a clue of how to handle this situation.

She could go with old faithful and lift a boom box over her head. But Manny lived in a mansion. She doubted anyone but the maids would hear her overture.

She could pretend to be a reporter and make a coded statement at a press junket, like Hugh Grant did for Julia Roberts in Notting Hill. That one sounded like a winner, only she'd have to arrange a press conference.

Then she caught herself. She was doing it again. Living in her fantasy world instead of reality. In the real world people went and had conversations with each other when they had problems. They didn't pull off crazy stunts. She needed to give them an actual chance.

Pumpkin pulled up to the campaign offices, parked, and dashed up the stairs to Manny's office. When she got there, most people were packing up for the day to go home. She peered inside his office to find it empty.

"He left hours ago." Lorielle came up behind her. Her steely eyes surveyed Pumpkin.

"I don't suppose you'll tell me where he went?"

"No," Lorielle said.

"Why? Because you don't think I'm good enough for him?"

"That sounds like your issue, Melissa—"

"It's Malika. My name is Malika."

"I don't really care, Malika. Or Pumpkin. Or whatever fairytale princess you've made up for yourself. While you've been playing house in Lala land, I've been dealing in the reality of this campaign. Armand is the real thing. He could impact real environmental change in this state, maybe in the country, and in time, globally."

Pumpkin looked Lorielle up and down. Lorielle was dressed to the nine's, as always, in a leather skirt. "I didn't know you cared so much about the environment."

"The skirt's faux-leather," Lorielle said catching Pumpkin's eye gaze. "Even though I don't wear animal skin I still care about how I look. And no, I don't think you're good enough for him. Not because you're a single mother. Wait, scratch that —a married woman."

Lorielle held up a newspaper. The headline read "Charmayne Girlfriend Married. Polls plummet." Pumpkin felt her heart sink.

"You're not good enough for him because you're not strong enough to handle what would come your way if you two stayed together. Whomever Armand chooses to have in his life will be scrutinized, regardless if they're a high society virgin, or a streetwalker with ten kids. I don't think for a second that you can handle the glare of that spotlight."

Lorielle slapped the paper down and walked away. Pumpkin scanned the article. The spotlight was well and truly on her and, standing alone in Manny's office, she squirmed.

Lorielle was right. Pumpkin couldn't fight this. She couldn't make some big overture when her past kept weighing her down. And now it threatened to drag down the man she loved.

Her instincts were to go and crawl under her covers and wait until everyone forgot about her. Luckily, that was possible since Seth and Anthony were having their first sleepover tonight.

Pumpkin left the office and got on the highway. It was rush hour, bumper-to-bumper traffic. When she finally pulled up to her complex, there were news trucks and reporters in the parking lot. The scene called to her mind a battlefield where warriors, armed to the teeth with digital cameras, lights, pens and paper, laid in wait for her.

Pumpkin put the car in reverse. But it was too late. They'd spotted her. She couldn't run. Her only escape lay inside her apartment, but she'd have to make her way through these obstacles first. She parked and stepped out of the car.

For a second, she thought she saw Manny's face, but a flash nearly blinded her. When she looked again, there was no one there who resembled him. She kept her head down and made slow and steady progress towards her building. The reporters surrounded her.

"Ms. Tavares, care to comment on the drop in Mr. Charmayne's polls?"

"If he loses the race, will it be your fault?"

"Is it true that Mr. Charmayne and your husband got into a fist fight?"

Pumpkin's head shot up at that. "What? No, that never happened."

"But your husband did show up at your place of work?"

"Yes," she said. "But they didn't get into a fight."

"So you admit, you are still married."

"I..."Pumpkin faltered on the step. "I was married. My divorce was finalized as of yesterday when my ex-husband amicably signed the papers. Before that, he and I were living separate lives for three years."

Pumpkin climbed the stairs, reaching higher ground. She was nearly in the clear when—

"You know what? There's no story here. Just a grasping single mother trying to hit the jackpot with a new baby daddy."

Pumpkin should have let it go. But her internal filter was bursting from the inside out. Pumpkin turned and faced the reporter. "Is that a question?"

The reporter turned back around. A smile on his face that said she was completely out of her depth.

"Is that what you think of all single mothers?" Pumpkin asked. "That we're all uneducated, welfare queens with a string of baby daddies just looking for the next check?"

That had been Pumpkin's example growing up. That had been the constant feed through the media. All of the reporters, all of them men, looked around at each other like they believed it, too. That, in fact, there was no story here. They all packed up their cameras, preparing to leave.

Pumpkin should shut up. That's exactly what she wanted; for them all to leave so that she could go and suffer in silence. Instead, she stood on the top step of her stoop, opened her mouth, and spoke loudly.

"Well, we're not. Most single mothers have at least two jobs. Their day job, or their night shift, and then they come home to perform the most important of the two: the job of raising our children."

Now, nearly all of the reporters were done packing up their gear and turning to go. Pumpkin knew she should do the same. Shut her mouth and go into her apartment. But she couldn't. Something bubbled inside of her, demanding to make it to the surface, and break free.

All her life she'd been waiting for someone to save her. To rescue her from her wicked aunt and cousins. To sweep her from obscurity and onto life's stage. But each time she'd waited and reached out her hand, she'd been disappointed by her savior for not handing her, her dreams.

"Society sets single mothers up for impossible expectations," Pumpkin continued. "Better yourself through education, they say. Work two jobs, make a nutritious dinner from scratch, get your kids into enrichment activities after school and after your long day of work. Work harder, do better, even though we're already maxed out. And then we're told to keep it tight and sexy so that we'll find a daddy for our kid. Is it any wonder we start to think that love is a fairytale? And no fairytale involves mothers, definitely not single mothers."

"Go tell it to a feminist."

"You don't get it," Pumpkin shook her head.

Even when she proclaimed to have given up on the fantasy, she still clung to it in the recesses of her mind. She'd been burned by love so many times, by her aunt and cousins, by Anthony, by Affinity Films even. But each time, she'd brushed herself off, gotten up and tried again. Some would call that insanity, but Pumpkin chose to call it courage. Out on her own, even when she was given very little to work with, she made due. All by herself, without any supporting characters or sidekicks.

"You want to know what a single mother is? She's a hero. All mothers are. We never give up. We face insurmountable odds every day. All this time I've been looking for someone to rescue me when the only person who could save me, was me."

Pumpkin looked out at the group of men before her. In the silence, all she heard was the zipping of camera bags.

"So, I'm too late then?"

Pumpkin turned at the sound of that deep voice. Manny stood behind all of the reporters, arms crossed over his chest, smile on his lips, amusement, instead of wariness, in his light eyes.

The reporters turned, saw him, and then scrambled for their cameras.

"Manny," Pumpkin said. "What are you doing here?"

"I came for you." He made his way through the sea of cameras and mics, ignoring all questions as he made a beeline for her. "I had planned this whole grand gesture, but it looks like you beat me to it."

"You shouldn't be here. The polls, the voters..."

Manny reached her and reached out for her. Pumpkin came into his arms as though drawn there; like magnets.

"The voters will need to get to know the amazingly brilliant, and loyal woman that I choose to have by my side. The woman who has been my support, my sidekick, and now, my hero. They'll need to know that we're a package deal, warts and all."

Pumpkin placed a hand on Manny's chest to test his realness.

"You look shocked that I came here for you," he said.

"I didn't think you were going to give me a second chance."

"I'm sorry," he whispered.

"You're sorry?" she said. "What did you do wrong?"

"I should have given you a chance to explain that day. When he showed up, and he called you his wife," Manny shook his head at the memory. "It just caught me off guard, Pumpkin."

She sighed at the sound of her nickname on his lips.

Manny took her hands in his, looking into her once more. "That night, when I saw you and you literally lit up my life..." he grinned at the cliché. Then he shook his head again, becoming serious. "Just the thought of not being able to have you, it hurt so much that I just shut down rather than feel the full effects of losing you."

Manny tilted her head up. "I thought this was going to be a guarantee. But it's not. What's between us is a gift and we have to take care of it, not take it for granted or fumble our way through it."

"I don't have any more secrets, I swear."

His lips came down to hers, then. He nibbled hungrily at her lower lip before teasing his tongue inside and stroking the tip. Pumpkin in turn pressed her body into his. Before she closed her eyes, she felt certain she saw a golden light emanating off Manny. She opened them to find cameras surrounding them, bulbs flashing.

Manny maneuvered her body in front of his so that she was at her door. Pumpkin took out her key.

"And now if you'll excuse us," he said as the door clicked open, "I need some time to convince Ms. Tavares to spend the rest of her life with me."

Pumpkin's hand faltered as she turned the knob. Manny wrapped an arm around Pumpkin's waist and escorted her inside.

Once inside, he shut the door and scooped her up into his arms. "Do you mind if we take this to the bedroom?" He never broke his stride in that direction as he spoke. "Or are we starting completely over from the beginning?"

"Well, I did let you into my bed before the first date."

"That's right. I forgot. You're easy."

"Only for you, Manny."

"And it's going to stay that way."

He closed her bedroom door with his foot and then laid her down on the bed like she was a prize. When he had her completely naked, he paused and admired his work.

Pumpkin began to squirm, not because she was embarrassed or uncomfortable. In the bedroom, Manny had always made her feel beautiful and desirable. She writhed because she was impatient to have him next to her, on top of her, inside of her.

She reached her hands out to him. Manny smiled as he stood before her and slowly undressed himself. He grabbed a condom from his back pocket. Then he knelt on the bed and prowled up her body. Anticipation lit each of Pumpkin's limbs.

Manny placed a kiss on the inside of her thigh. She fought to keep her head from falling back so that she could keep watching him.

He used his other hand to curl her other knee up and open. Pumpkin's core was completely bare to him now. She saw the desire light on his face. He looked up and caught her eye once again. A devilish look was on his face. He lowered himself to the bed and then his face disappeared between her thighs.

At the first brush of his tongue, Pumpkin cried out. The wet velvet of his tongue against her core sent a wave of pleasure like she'd never known through her body. His tongue teasingly flicked a few more times and she felt the tension building at the base of her spine. Her hands tangled and gripped the bed sheets. When he encircled her clitoris in the most intimate kiss of her life, Pumpkin could no longer hold herself up.

She collapsed onto the sheets and whimpered, waiting for the orgasm she knew was soon to come. But Manny played her like a practiced instrument. Nipping at the folds of her outer lips, kissing her thighs when she arched off the bed, and then Frenching the bud at her core the instant she relaxed onto the pillows. It was maddening. And when Pumpkin finally did explode, tears sprang to her eyes and she cried in earnest.

She watched as the world came apart and then fit itself back together. Her heart ceased its beating, and then slowly came up to speed again. She trembled at every juncture of her being, until Manny was holding her to him. Her head tucked under his chin. His arms wrapped tightly around her. His voice whispering in her ear. And his solid length throbbing patiently against her belly.

"You're as delicious as you are beautiful," he said. "I can't wait to do that again."

Pumpkin looked up at this man who had changed her world. This man who helped her see herself for who she truly was. This man whom she loved so deeply. She reached up and tugged his head down, taking his lips. She could taste herself on his lips and it turned her on. Yeah, they would be doing that again, and soon she would be returning the favor.

Pumpkin parted her thighs, wiggling, urging his length closer to her still trembling core. Manny chuckled against her lips.

"Please," she urged him. "I need to feel you inside me."

She felt his hand between them, fisting his length. He aimed at her entrance but did not push in.

"Please, Manny." She arched her hips until it caused him to breach the lips of her core.

Pumpkin sighed in contentment, but Manny retreated. Another mischievous smile playing at his lips. He put those lips against her, nibbling at her lower lip.

"Move in with me," he said.

"What?" She was going out of her mind. Her hips chasing his as he rubbed his length's width against her core.

"I don't think I can ask you to marry me until we have at least one proper date." He undulated his hips and they both hissed. "But moving in seems reasonable, don't you think?"

"Are you using sex to strong-arm me?"

"What's between us may be a gift, but I'm grasping for any legal contract I can place between us. A lease, a marriage contract, both carry a level of guarantee." He dipped inside her and she shuddered. But then he pulled out again.

"Please, please," Pumpkin whimpered.

"Are you agreeing to my terms?"

"I'll agree to anything to get you inside of me."

"God, you're going to be a pushover in this marriage."

Pumpkin opened her mouth to speak but Manny shoved into her.

She gasped, closing her eyes at the sheer deliciousness of him. "Yes..." she sighed.

"Yes, what?"

Pumpkin opened her eyes to find smokey gray ones staring at her. Behind the desire, she saw hope. Behind the hope, she saw an emotion she only knew because she felt it, too.

"Yes, to all of it. I love you," she said.

Manny withdrew and pushed back into her. All the way into her. Pumpkin closed her eyes and groaned.

"Say it, again," he demanded.

Pumpkin opened her eyes and stared into gray eyes that were unrelenting. "I love you, Manny." It came out as a whisper.

In response, he pulled out and then pushed back in. Her toes curled and her fingers dug into his back.

"Say it again."

"I love—"

His lips crashed into hers as he continued moving in and out of her.

"Say it again," he said when he came up for air, still plunging deeply into her.

"I love you, Manny."

The words seemed to fuel him. So, she kept repeating them. He plunged into her body as though it were his last meal. And he savored every morsel. He threw her knees over his shoulders and buried himself deep inside of her.

By then Pumpkin could only pant, forming one word of the phrase every so often. Soon, she felt another orgasm building.

Manny grabbed hold of her face, angling it so that she couldn't throw her head back with her release. He stared right into her eyes as he continued pumping into her. She could tell that he was close, too.

Pumpkin reached her hand up to his face. They stayed locked on each other, neither looking away. They came almost in unison, barely blinking as they watched one another in the throes of passion.

When Manny finally came down, he released her legs and pulled her tightly to him. He whispered something in her ear that sent her head into the clouds and made her fragile heart skip yet another beat.

"I love you, Pumpkin."

EPILOGUE

"THEY SAY NICE GUYS FINISH LAST."

Pumpkin smiled up at DaeHo who stood on the podium in her cap and gown. The sun was shining on the late spring day as the high school graduation kicked into gear.

"They say good girls go after the bad boys."

DaeHo had insisted on working on her valedictorian speech on her own. Pumpkin wasn't sure where the speech was headed. At least there were no Dr. Seuss references.

"But you can't live your life as a cliché. Sometimes the guy you thought was so bad, is actually a real charmer and the good girl isn't as smart as she thinks."

Pumpkin saw the young woman's eyes connect with someone in the audience. Tyler's blonde hair stuck out. His blue eyes burned into Dae's, a smile on his face. A few girls around him tried to capture his attention, but he had eyes only for the girl on the stage.

DaeHo had been accepted early into LSU on a full scholarship. Many other kids were wait-listed. Tyler, who applied only a month ago with a 2.5 average, had somehow gained an acceptance.

"As we move forward," DaeHo said to a rapt audience of her graduating classmates, "we have to remember that we write our own stories. Don't let someone else do that for you, because they may get your storyline and your casting all wrong."

The crowd erupted in applause. Pumpkin stood and applauded, too. DaeHo was a smart girl. A good, smart girl with her feet firmly on the ground and her head on straight. Pumpkin couldn't wait to see how her story turned out.

"Oh, my dear, you nearly blinded me with that rock." Mrs. Beard stood beside Pumpkin. The elderly woman referred to the engagement ring on Pumpkin's finger. "I'm so glad you finally decided to get your boy a proper role model."

Pumpkin had tried to escape her long time sub for the past few days, but it had been nearly impossible. Mrs. Beard was now a full time faculty member in the English Department.

"My son always had a proper role model in me, Mrs. Beard." Pumpkin took one last look at the stage as DaeHo accepted her diploma. She realized that her favorite student was no longer a child anymore, but a woman grown and capable of having a great life. Even if she decided to include a wolf in sheep's clothing in her story.

"Excuse me, Mrs. Beard." Pumpkin made moves to step into the aisle.

"But you'll miss the end."

Pumpkin chose to ignore the woman, who was wrong again. This wasn't the end for her students; it was their beginning. But it was an end for her. It was her last day as a teacher.

Pumpkin made her way to the exit. Her ride was already waiting for her. She walked over to the white Mustang. The car roared to life as she approached. Manny got out and opened the passenger side door. Before she climbed in, he captured her lips in a kiss.

"Ready?" he asked.

Pumpkin nodded and ducked into the passenger seat.

"You excited?" he asked.

"About what?" There was a lot going on in her life at the moment. She'd quit her teaching job. Graduation was the last of her duties. Next week she was starting anew in her old career. Gulf and Foster's Media Group had made good on their threat to hire her away from Manny after his campaign ended. She would be heading up the new young adult division of the media firm.

"Are you excited about seeing the dress?" Manny asked.

And she was getting married. "Oh, that. I know it'll be stunning. Midori Miller is the same designer who made my ball gown."

"The gold one?"

Pumpkin turned to her fiancé. "It was orange, and you know it."

Manny shrugged, a grin on his face. "We see what we want to see."

He took her hand in his, shifting the gears into a faster speed as they moved into the fast lane. In no time at all, Manny pulled up to the dressmaker's shop. Midori Miller's boutique sat on a busy street in the market district. Pumpkin had happened by it one day while on a break from the voter registration table. Pumpkin never claimed to be a fashionista, but the color combinations in the windows caught her eyes. She'd gone in that day and come out with a killer ball gown, and a burgeoning friendship.

"I'll be back in an hour," said Manny. "I just have to grab some files and have a quick chat with Lorielle."

"An hour should be fine. Seth's having dinner with his dad tonight." Pumpkin leaned over for a quick peck. She should've known better. Manny was never quick.

The kiss went on and on. When she tried to pull away, Manny caught her lower lip with his teeth.

"I hab boo go," she mumbled into his mouth.

Manny chuckled releasing her lip. "I'm coming after that top lip when I get back."

"When you come back..." Pumpkin ducked out of the car before he could catch another part of her anatomy. "...I'll let you catch it."

She waved him off, watching the Mustang retreat down the street. She turned into the shop, her feet barely feeling as though they touched the ground.

"Looks like somebody's getting some, and getting it good." Midori leaned against the shoulder of a mannequin. Pink measuring tape around her neck, a pair of scissors in her hand. "You need to take that smile down by about a thousand so the rest of us who still live here on Earth don't get blinded."

Midori was a stunning woman. Her exotic features were arresting. Her father was African-American and her mother Japanese. Pumpkin had always thought her cousins were Amazons, but Midori's height and curves put both LaTom and LaRon to shame. To top her height off, Midori always wore stilettos. Today her modelesque body was wrapped in a silk wrap dress that cinched just under her ample breasts.

"I'm sure there's a line of guys waiting to sweep you off your feet, Midori."

Midori looked out the window at the bright sun. A shadow passed across her cat-like eyes. "Not everybody gets a happy ending, Pumpkin."

Before Pumpkin could respond, the bell over the door sounded. Gale swept inside in a flurry of skirts and color. "So this is the famous Midori Miller." Gale glanced around the shop, eyebrows rising in approval. "My dear, I can see you have a golden touch."

From above, a beautiful melody rang out in a lovely soprano voice. All the adults' heads turned heavenward.

"That's my daughter," Midori said.

"Your daughter has the voice of an angel," said Gale.

Maternal pride shone brightly in Midori's eyes. "She's won a few talent shows, but it's hard to get her any real recognition. This isn't exactly the big city."

"Maybe you should bring the big city here, my dear." Gale reached in her bag and pulled out business card. The card was gold embossed. "I happen to know a music producer. He's been known to spin records into golden hits. His name is Rumpel, Guy Rumpel."

Midori pocketed the card and then turned back to Pumpkin. "You ready to try on your wedding dress?"

Midori went into a closet and pulled out a voluminous, white gown on a hanger. She guided Pumpkin over to a mirror and placed the gown in front of her reflection.

"It's perfect," Pumpkin sighed.

"That it is, my dear," Gale winked. "Like something out of a fairytale."

ACKNOWLEDGEMENTS

This manuscript was my first attempt at NANO and my second attempt at novel writing. My fairy book sistahs waved their lead-based wands to help turn it into what you just read. So, if you enjoyed it, you should be thanking Leslye, Kara, Angela, and Michelle.

This story is based on actual events. Shortly after my divorce, I was out with my two children at a community farmer's market. A really handsome politician waved me over and began chatting with me about his platform. I was more interested in his light-colored eyes. But my burgeoning fantasy was dashed when my son sauntered over and embarrassing words spewed from his mouth. I ushered myself and my kids away, chiding my silly imagination. What man would be interested in a single mother of two school-aged kids? There are no fairytales featuring mothers as the heroines.

That night, I rewrote the events of the day to my liking. In my imagination, the light-eyed politician asked me out, after winning over my guard dog of a son. We got married and I moved out of my apartment and into some big mansion with a closet stocked full of name brand clothes. Oh, that closet...

Anyway, it was October, and so I plotted the book for the next month of NANO. The completed manuscript sat in a drawer for years because I didn't think anyone would want to read a story where a single mother was the hero. Thankfully, I was wrong. Every woman deserves an HEA.

Enter a world where single mothers get a second chance at happily ever after with Book Two in the Cindermama Series.

In this new spin on an old fairytale, Guy Rumpel's golden touch could put a wrinkle in Midori Miller's designs.

ON SALE NOW!

Former model, Midori Miller, left the fashion world in disgrace and now lives quietly as a small town dressmaker and single mom. When her talented daughter catches the ear of a New York record producer, the last thing Midori wants is to return to the harsh glare of the spotlight. Caught between the producer's charms, her daughter's dreams, and her own new chance at success, Midori isn't sure she can design the right path for herself or her family, especially when the producer makes a play for her heart.

After a string of flops, producer Guy Rumpel believes he's lost his golden touch. He needs to turn his career around with a hit record, and the young songbird from his hometown just may be the key. But when his family's gift for finding their one true love shines its light on Midori, he'll have to convince her to make the deal of a lifetime.

Rumpeled is the second book in Ines Johnson's bestselling *Cindermama Series*. If you love contemporary romance with a touch of magic then this series is for you.

Buy *Rumpeled: a Cindermama Story* and bring this modern fairytale into your world today!

Ines Johnson
Erotica, Paranormal, and Fairytales -Oh my!

Join Ines' newsletter
and be among the first to learn about
upcoming releases, special promotions,
giveaways and sneak peeks!

Sign up at
http://bit.ly/CindermamaNews
or
visit **www.ineswrites.com**
to learn more!

www.ingramcontent.com/pod-product-compliance
Lightning Source LLC
Chambersburg PA
CBHW072211170626
46813CB00003B/884